SPIN

A NOVEL

JIM LINDHEIM

Spin

Published by Wheatmark®
2030 East Speedway Boulevard, Suite 106
Tucson, Arizona 85719 USA
www.wheatmark.com

ISBN: 978-1-62787-642-1 (paperback)
ISBN: 978-1-62787-643-8 (ebook)
LCCN: 2018954949

To all the clients and colleagues
who had the patience to teach me

There is no fire like passion, there is no shark like hatred,
there is no snare like folly, there is no torrent like greed.
—Gautama Buddha

Shall we their fond pageant see?
Lord, what fools these mortals be!
—William Shakespeare, *A Midsummer Night's Dream*

CONTENTS

1

THURSDAY–FRIDAY

It was the corporate jet that convinced me. I'm a sucker for a Gulfstream.

I had sworn that I'd never work for Bradford Sisley again. But here I was winging my way back into his insane world.

Both times that I had helped Sisley manage a crisis the relationship ended with him screaming at me and then stiffing me for part of the final bill. That was the kind of sweetheart guy he was—a Silicon Valley thug, and everybody knew it. But then they would line up to kiss his butt. After all, his company, BeeLine, one of the world leaders in the vast and ever-expanding world of consumer electronics, had changed the universe. And it still continued to astound the marketplace with new digital gadgets that raked in mind-bending gobs of money.

Having been a crisis guy—a spin doctor—for decades, I'd had a lot of experience with people caught up in a mess, usually of their own making or the idiocy or venality of someone they trusted. So half my job often consisted of being a shrink for someone in a panic. The other half was helping them find their better instinct. Assuming they had one. Typically, I'd ask them to think about how they would explain themselves to their kids. Or to their mother. That would usually get them to the right place.

But nothing, I learned, worked with Bradford Sisley. That core of humanity that is supposed to lie hidden somewhere in the vulnerable heart of every human being simply did not exist in this man. His ex-wives knew that. Folks who worked for him sure did. BeeLine was a revolving door of talent going in and broken people limping out.

So why did I agree to enter his lion's den again? Mostly, I was bored with the earnest Swedes I was dealing with.

They had a crisis with their hugely popular floorboards, which they proudly sold as recycled material. The problem was the little miasma of formaldehyde that wafted from the boards. Nothing to worry about, I had helped them argue. Sure, formaldehyde is a poison and a carcinogen, but this was only a little exposure. A tiny exposure, really—really nothing harmful for your little Swedish tots crawling innocently around the living room.

But my client was up against Ingrid, a poster child dragged out by a Swedish activist group with a name I could never learn to pronounce. Ingrid had asthma. Without question, the activist group insisted, the floorboards had attacked her little pink lungs.

Not surprisingly, we failed at the "a small dose of a big toxin is fine" defense. It always fails, but lawyers and scientists always insist on trying. In this case, one of the company scientists took it upon himself to mock up a print ad that made the claim that the formaldehyde exposure from the floorboards created less cancer risk than milk served with two cookies. Apparently, the data backed him up on the claim. I had to spend three days arguing the unbelievably stupid idea down. Finally, I got them to run a focus group on the ad. I didn't need to speak Swedish to understand what was happening in the room on the other side of the one-way glass. They didn't run the ad, thanks Gott.

So now the company lawyers and accountants were developing some sort of settlement scheme. They'd pay some modest amount to everyone who had purchased the floorboards. And if the homeowner absolutely insisted on replacing the floor, the company would provide new, less toxic boards for *free*. All the homeowner had to do was rip up his house, remove the old boards, and install the new ones at his own expense. What a deal!

So I was just hanging around Stockholm while people with spreadsheets argued in Swedish, and the sweet old guy who owned the business watched the value of his kid's inheritance shrink. They didn't need me for the announcement of whatever settlement scheme they finally designed. I would never understand the numbers anyway, and not just because they were denominated in krona. Math is not my thing.

The worst part was that they were making me stay in this horrible Ikea-decorated hotel on the outskirts of Stockholm with tiny rooms and hideously blond paneling. I'd look down at my feet, knowing full well that the floorboards were slowly poisoning me.

So I needed an excuse to flee the scene, particularly

since the dark Swedish winter was creeping in. Sisley offered me the Gulfstream. All the way to San Jose. Plus use of a plush corporate apartment.

And undoubtedly he was in some unbelievably complicated mess. His specialty and mine.

When I landed, a corporate car—a deep-blue Tesla with a cream interior—was waiting at the bottom of the airplane steps, as was a very attractive girl from the PR Department. She had a kind of Betty Boop quality. Betty Boop with a nose ring.

I lumbered down the steps slowly. My enormous girth, long a part of my "oversized" personality as well as a personification of my "gravitas" and my "weighty" judgment, had become, in my advancing years, a real pain in the rear and in other parts of my anatomy. My feet were failing me, and the knees were not far behind. So a cane had become part of the shtick.

I used to wear wild ties to attract attention. Now no one was wearing ties. But canes, it turns out, have all kinds of possibilities. My favorite was my flag cane—looking like it was wrapped in an American flag. But I had not taken that one to Sweden; they wouldn't see the irony. Instead, I had in my possession my crow cane: a surrealistic depiction, in black and red, of a bird. The handle was an angry-looking crow's head with red-and-green glass eyes.

Memorable is never a bad thing to be.

The blinding California setting sun—and the lateness of the hour in my body's time clock—made me slightly dizzy, so I halted unsteadily on the stairs of the Gulfstream. I could see the bright smile on the young lady become hesitant and worried. The legendary crisis manager was going to become his own medical crisis. Well, if so, I wasn't worried. I'd be in the capable hands of BeeLine, which had to have endowed every medical facility within an ambulance's easy reach.

Once I was in the car, my nausea lifted, and the young lady, with the distrustful name of Tiffany, relaxed. She handed over a large sealed envelope for my review and explained the schedule: a drink with the senior VP for public relations at six o'clock and a breakfast meeting with Bradford Sisley in the morning. Other than that, I was expected to enjoy my jet lag in the corporate apartment.

As Tiffany blithered on about how renowned I was and how excited she was to meet me, I kept sullenly quiet. There was a time when I would have responded eagerly to fawning flattery, reveled in it, and fished for more. I would have asked polite questions about the fawner and told hilarious tales about my many adventures as a young PR person having to stuff five hundred press kits or replace all the slides in the carousel because some idiot put them in backwards.

But all these stories—mostly cribbed from other people's experiences—had long ago lost their meaning. A young person today doesn't know what a press kit is or that a slide carousel was needed to show pictures on a screen. And I don't know how Facebook or Instagram works. I knew I had nothing for Tiffany. My reputation, bless its little soul, was based on ancient history. Best to remain a silent sphinx. Let Tiffany fill in the blanks.

I wondered how often a person has to clean a nose ring to keep it from turning grossly infectious.

The senior VP for public relations had known to send a car to take me the several blocks to the bar. Otherwise it would have taken me thirty minutes for the journey on foot, and I would have arrived sweat covered and cranky.

The sealed envelope Tiffany had given me contained nothing of import, just corporate crap like the annual report and some speeches. So I was still in the dark as to why I had been flown halfway across the world on "an urgent matter." A shower and brief nap had revived my brain a bit for this critical meeting at what was, for me, three o'clock in the morning.

A very attractive middle-aged woman waved at me as I surveyed the upscale bar, a posh cocktail lounge really, decorated to resemble a dark, wood-shrouded men's club. I'm always surprised when Californians imitate a traditional East Coast milieu. It seems somewhat desperate, as if they're longing for something missing from their lives.

As I limped slowly over to her, I strategized how to let her know that I don't sit in booths. I can't get in, and I can't get out. The only thing I can do is to sit on the outside, creating a huge blockade for everyone else.

No dummy she, however. As I approached, she slid out of the booth to shake my hand in greeting. And then she pointed to a nearby corner table as probably better for our chat.

"Mr. Keaton, it is such a pleasure to meet you at last," she purred as we settled in. "Bradford is not the first person who has mentioned you to me over the years."

"Please call me Jonathan."

"And I'm Wanda."

And I was wanda-ing where I might have met this person before. I'm good with faces, particularly of pretty women, and this long-faced beauty with thick brownish red hair pulled back in a bun was somehow familiar. It was the eyes—her eyes were deeply brown, softly inviting. They were sweet brown pools that drew me in. Her carefully tailored dark pantsuit, unassuming flats, and modest jewelry suggested that she had come directly from work.

I had Googled her earlier and found no obvious overlaps in our histories. So I asked.

"Have we met before? You look familiar."

"No, not that I recall. And I suspect I would, given your reputation."

And my outlandish appearance and personality. There are lots of reasons to remember me.

Drinks and snacks were ordered. Mini-bios exchanged. Praise of Bradford served up. All the usual preliminaries that constitute the early stages of sizing up another person.

Experience had taught me the dangers of the particular relationship that Wanda Fletcher and I were about to have. When the boss tells the PR person that he needs an outside expert, that's an implicit put-down. There's a failure of confidence. As a hired gun, I'd seen all the possible reactions that Wanda Fletchers around the world might have: anger, suspicion, a determination to undermine, an opposite determination to co-opt and, occasionally, relief that a nasty job was now someone else's problem.

But what was Wanda thinking? She wasn't showing me her hand. She was a shrewd player. Everything was seemingly open and accepting. She'd provide me everything: a security pass and anything else I needed. She'd pay my bills; she'd be a sounding board, a helping partner if I wanted. But the offers of assistance lacked sincerity. If there was a knife, it still was sheathed. And my instincts were telling me to keep my guard up.

"So what is this about?" I asked my new best buddy.

"Bradford hasn't told you?" she responded with seeming wonder.

"No, he only told me he needed me here ASAP and that he'd send the plane."

Disappointment passed over her pretty features. "Well, Jonathan, then we're in the same boat. All he has said to me is that a firestorm is coming and that I'll know more when I need to."

I pondered her obvious frustration, and several things fit in place. This wasn't really a welcoming drink or a get-to-know-you chat. We weren't here in our cozy corner at three o'clock in the morning to talk about a budding partnership between us. This disruption of the rhythm of my jet lag had been arranged so that I would bring Wanda into the loop.

Sorry, girlfriend. No can do. And, I was thinking, I should avoid making any promises of future information sharing. At least until I talked to Sisley.

"Well," I said, "I guess we'll both be informed in good time."

"Jonathan, you and I both know all the things that we communications people have to do to be able to survive a firestorm," she said, leaning in. I was glad I'd showered and had rinsed my mouth. We were now within smelling distance, and she smelled expensive. "Bradford doesn't understand that. So at any point in this process, if you can clue me in to what we're dealing with—a heads-up—that would be very, very appreciated."

Her smile was void of sexual content, definitely not seductive. Which was not surprising to me. Only a prostitute—or a fetishist—would be seductive with an old, ugly porker like me. But both Wanda and I knew what had just happened. The person who would make all my work possible or excruciatingly painful and would be paying my bills had just told me what she wanted: I should share my client's secrets with her even if he wanted to keep her in the dark.

I decided to order a bacon burger with fries. It was too early for breakfast.

The next morning, Bradford Sisley greeted me elaborately, like an old friend. As he bro-hugged me, I recalled some of his words from our last conversation: "You are a total piece of shit, fat man. You're a complete fraud and a cheat. I'm going to hang you out to dry."

Now held tight in his arms, I thought about goosing him just for the satisfaction of throwing a wrench in whatever game he was playing on this painfully bright morning.

Did I say morning? In Stockholm it was midafternoon. I'd gotten only three hours' sleep before waking with a start in the darkness of early November. Thank God for Turner Classic Movies and Joan Crawford. And the Harvey Weinstein sex scandal, which was raging that November.

I could tell that Sisley had had some face work done, probably body work as well. When he was younger, he looked vaguely reptilian, with eyes too close and nose and chin too pointy. In those days he spent thousands of dollars on his clothes, his hair, and his acne-scarred skin to try to redo what the good Lord had handed him. A short, skinny guy, he had spent a lot of time at the gym and at the shoemaker, trying to look bigger.

Now he had moved from an alteration strategy to one of preservation. He looked slightly embalmed, his skin like a resident in Madame Tussaud's. The clothes were meticulously chosen to look casual. The glasses were gone.

He proudly toured me around his art collection, which was hung from floor to ceiling on the one real wall in his glass-wrapped office. Painting stacked on painting, like a museum collection that had overgrown its space. He told me there was $100 million on the wall and that that figure was going up by the hour. I actually know something about art. He had mostly second-rate pieces from big-name twentieth-century artists. It's not hard to find a bad Warhol or an uninspired Motherwell.

On the credenza behind his desk were the requisite pictures of his teenage kids but no happy family scenes. I had read that wife number three had taken up with another Silicon Valley tycoon. He was currently wifeless and, presumably, on the prowl. The other items on display were framed magazine covers that featured him. He probably didn't remember that I had made one of those covers happen in a mad scramble to restore his reputation after a settlement with the SEC.

"Have a seat," he offered, gesturing to a conference table transformed for dining purposes. He had thoughtfully replaced the usual modern conference room chairs with two fine old dining chairs, mine without arms so that my girth could happily spread.

"What's with the cane, Jonathan?" he asked as I hobbled across the room.

"Just a phase. I'm thinking about moving on to the next level: a motorized wheelchair. I'm going to cover it in decals commemorating all the Indian logos that the sports teams have to give up. Just so they don't get lost," I responded.

I actually had started to make such a collection. The problem was where to put it for maximum offensiveness. And longevity. This was the first time I had considered a motorized wheelchair.

"My mom has a motorized chair," he said, ignoring my decal indelicacy. "I've put a team to work on new digitized control systems, sort of like driverless cars."

"Great. Send me the beta for testing."

An absolutely stunning woman suddenly appeared—perhaps summoned by a hidden digital command—and asked me what I wanted for breakfast. She didn't appear to be an android, but she was awfully close to perfect, and there was something odd about her flawless skin. I could imagine Sisley thinking a gorgeous robot waitress was an awesome concept.

I ordered a big breakfast of eggs, pancakes, and bacon, not having eaten since Wanda left me devouring my very tasty burger in the fancy bar. Sisley ordered up something distressingly healthy.

We started with a chatty reminiscence of our past adventures together. Apparently, he had made a war story out of a routine I had used in my middle years to intimidate reporters if I thought the questions were getting too hostile and I needed to close down a session.

I would pull out a gun and place it on the table. Not say a word about it. Not threaten anything. Just a gun on the table.

According to Sisley, I had done it with a kid from *Businessweek* who thought he was a tough investigative reporter. As Sisley told it, it made a good story.

"What's that?" the kid had asked. Sisley delivered the line in a slightly choked voice.

"A gun," I had supposedly answered in a bass tone that was way below my actual range.

"Is it loaded?" (*High voice.*)

"Why would anyone carry an unloaded gun?" (*My supposedly deep voice.*)

"Why did you put it there?"

"It was uncomfortable in my pocket. Don't worry about it. No big deal. So we just about done here?"

Sisley said the kid packed in his notebook and was out the door in less than a minute.

"How was the article in the end?" I asked. I honestly remembered none of this.

"Never ran," he said. "Kid ran. The story never did."

I knew this was a well-worn line he had used. I could have stolen it, but I had stopped telling the gun-on-the-table stories. It now made people nervous. Times had changed. Just like telling "I got so damned drunk" stories. No longer fashionable and not yet retro.

The robot woman reappeared with our food and set it on the table. I tried to smell her arm as it went by my face. Nothing.

I was about to dig in when my host decided it was time to get down to business.

"So they're trying to get rid of me," he said. "Since the company is flying high, they can't find any justification. So they're playing dirty. They've found some woman to say I sexually harassed her. It's the scandal du jour, you know. Harassing women."

It certainly was. For the past month, the media had been bursting with stories of famous, powerful men who had behaved crudely or worse with women. And down they were falling from their high perches. Politicians, journalists, actors, businessmen, fashion designers, musicians, and even heads of important nonprofits were drowning in sexual scandal. Apparently, the Catholic Church, for once, had been in the forefront of a social trend.

I held my fork in midair and pondered my next move. There was so much bullshit potential in what Bradford Sisley had just said. People were out to get him. Somebody had trumped up an accusation, which I noticed he wasn't directly denying. Sisley was being victimized. He was a lamb surrounded by wolves who had seized on the momentum of the #MeToo movement to entrap him.

"Who's the woman?" I asked.

"I don't know."

"Well, tell me what you do know."

"I got a call from that LA attorney woman who handles this kind of crap."

"Sandra Farber?" I put down my fork and took a sip of coffee.

"Yeah, her. She told me there'd be a press conference this coming Monday, and I wouldn't be at all happy about it. She had a client who says I attacked her in an elevator."

"That would be sexual assault, not sexual harassment."

"Whatever. It's all bullshit."

"But what is Farber asking you to do?"

"I'm supposed to send my attorney to LA to talk to her about a settlement."

"A settlement with an unknown, unidentified woman?"

"I know who it is."

"You just told me you didn't know . . ." I stopped myself. Why waste time getting him to admit to a lie so fresh it was still hanging in the air? Contradiction was standard fare with Sisley. The truth was always elusive, both in reality and in his head.

"So who is it?" I asked.

"She's a hooker. A high-class hooker who hangs out at the Peninsula in New York. They probably hired her to entrap me."

"And did she?"

Now he got little-boy churlish. "Well, the way she came on to me, I thought we were on the clock."

Time to take a big bite out of my stack of delicious buttermilk pancakes dripping with warm maple syrup. The one thing I knew for certain was that Sandra Farber would not take on a hooker for an assault case against a big-league guy like Sisley. Whoever the woman was, she was not a hooker. So maybe it was an honest mistake made in the fog of some drinks: he thought one thing, she thought another, mistakes were made.

"So have you told your attorney to go down there and talk to Farber?"

"No fucking way. No fucking way I'm going to make a settlement with that lying bitch. I'm going to bring her down—and Farber too. That's why you're here. That's why I brought you halfway around the fucking world. You and me, we're going to save mankind—*man*-kind—from all this sexual harassment bullshit. I'm the one being sexually harassed. I'm the victim here."

And I was Alice down the rabbit hole. The man actually thought he was making sense. He thought he could take this on and win. Not only win but miraculously become a champion. A hero to misogynists everywhere.

I circled the conversation back to his theory that there was a grand conspiracy against him. I tried to convince him that a big battle with Sandra Farber and a weeping woman who said she had been attacked in an elevator would be exactly what the conspirators would want. To let a lawsuit go forward would play to their advantage (whoever "they" were). If he took the issue on publicly, he would be playing right into their strategy.

"Wrong. Wrong," he said, shaking his head at my ignorance. "A settlement is what they want. Then I'm guilty. You make a settlement, you're guilty. I make a settlement, they leak it, and I'm dead meat. No, the way to survive this is to win it. Out in the open. You and me—we're going to bring her down. Show that she's a liar."

"But did you or did you not make a move on her in the elevator?"

"A move. A move. It was a little kiss and a squeeze where she's soft. She asked for it. She's a whore. That's why I win. She's a call girl. I can prove that!"

By then I had stopped eating. I was wishing I could just give back the food, give back the plane ride and the corporate apartment. I was old and crippled and far too world-weary to take on this situation. In earlier days, I would have been naïve enough to take Bradford Sisley at his word and just plow on ahead. But his surrealistic take on his situation, heaped on top of the pancakes and the jet lag, was making me sick. I wanted to rewind all the tapes and not find myself where I now was. Even a Master of Disaster like me can't stop a train wreck that the conductor wants to occur.

But boredom and greed had led me here to this breakfast under a $100 million art wall. I had made my bed.

At least the floorboards looked nonthreatening.

"So you're not going to tell me?"

She was really pissed, and I didn't blame her. I had argued with him about it, but he said he wanted to keep her in the dark. I pointed out that she would learn everything next Monday when the press conference happened, so it wasn't a secret he could keep from her. All he was doing by not telling her in advance was making it harder for her. She would be on her back foot rather than ready to go. He said that was where he wanted her. I got the feeling that he thought maybe she was part of "them."

I didn't tell her that I had argued with him about it. My client was my client. So I told her that we thought it best to keep things close over the weekend.

She tapped her well-manicured fingernails on her desk, staring at me with bitter fury. It wasn't like we were old friends or something and I had betrayed our long-standing relationship. But I had let her down twice—last night when I didn't know anything and now when I did. She was probably keeping score: one more strike and I'd be out.

I didn't want to annoy her, because I needed her. Specifically, I needed a secure internet connection and a corporate landline phone. I needed secure ways to talk to my media contacts.

The dumb thing about Sisley's decision to leave her out was that she should have been spending her weekend calling all her people to give them a heads-up: press, company managers, board directors, friendly government officials, investment analysts, etcetera. The best strategy for when you see the boat headed for the rocks is to tell your friends that you're going to need their help. Three message points: our boy is about to be accused, it's all a fabrication, and he needs you to stand with him.

My weekend job was different from hers; I needed to position myself as Sisley's ambassador to the media. I needed to reach out to all the reporters I knew at every major outlet, let them know that a big one was bearing down on Sisley and that I was their guy. I would give them what they needed. I would make each and every one a journalistic hero.

And, of course, I had to write his response statement—an angry denial that was somehow tinged with sadness that he would be tarred in such a way, since he's really a respectful guy with women. And then I had to get him to approve the statement. From experience, I knew that would be a battle.

But first I had to get Wanda to get me secure phone and internet lines. So I asked for an office.

"I'll get the IT people over to the corporate apartment and wire you up over there," she said coldly, and she started to tap on her computer. Her body language was telling me she wanted me to leave her office as fast as my crow cane and my aching knees and feet would permit.

"It probably would be better for me to set up somewhere closer to you," I said.

"I don't intend to be here this weekend, since apparently I have nothing pressing to do," she responded in a sarcastic tone. "If I let you be here in the building, you'd be all alone, or worse yet, you'd cause my staff to speculate." She was saying all this to her computer screen, tapping away. Eye contact between us had been aborted.

"Very soon we'll be working together, and we'll need physical proximity," I pointed out from my apparently invisible chair across her desk.

"Well, do let me know when that's required," she said in the direction of the computer. "Right now I have to go to a staff meeting. You'll want to get back to the apartment. I've told IT to get there before noon." Tap, tap, *tap* with a finishing flourish.

I was thinking, It's not me, Wanda. Don't hate me. It's him. It's that maniac you work for. For a brief second, I considered telling her that. But that would be giving in and would betray my client's wishes. So I heaved myself out of my seat, and, as often happened, I slipped onto one knee as a step along the way to rising to my feet.

She leapt out of her chair and hurried around the desk. "Are you okay? Are you hurt?" she asked with what seemed like sincere concern. Her face had changed entirely from the frigid anger of our meeting. Once again I had the odd sensation of seeing a face that I had seen before. Now that her countenance was soft and concerned, she again looked familiar.

"I'm fine, I'm fine," I said. She took my free hand, and I smiled up at her from my kneeling position. "Since I'm already down on one knee, perhaps I should propose to you now."

"How terribly flattering," she retorted. "It's been a long time."

We laughed together as I used the cane and her hand to lift my bulk to a vertical position.

"I'm sorry," I said, referring to the whole situation.

"You might have said that before," she responded softly.

She was right, of course. I had become a bit of a shit. Most likely, Wanda was a good person who was only trying to do a good job, a professional job. Me, I was a professional, but I was not a good person; I had given up on that possibility years ago with one moral compromise too many. But probably Wanda had struggled up a miserably difficult ladder, having to prove herself so many times over. Now in a plum job at one of the hottest companies in America, she knew that, once again, she was going to have to go more than an extra mile to prove herself. And I wasn't helping.

What she didn't know was that this wasn't going to be the usual corporate mess. She would be called to defend a very creepy guy from a tawdry accusation that was probably true. She deserved better than that. Hell, even I deserved better than that.

2

MONDAY

Before California even woke up on Monday morning, Sandra Farber's PR machinery went into gear. She sent out an advisory of a press conference at ten thirty about a sexual assault by a "major Silicon Valley executive."

I had done my work over the weekend, letting my crowd of contacts know I was involved with Sisley and something was about to happen. When Farber's advisory came out, it didn't take much for them to put two and two together. They now could impress their colleagues and buddies with inside knowledge of who was going to be on Sandra Farber's chopping block. Do a favor, hopefully get a favor.

One East Coast reporter filed a story right away saying that "sources indicated" that Bradford Sisley was Sandra Farber's Silicon Valley target. That was enough for me to finally let Wanda know what was going on. Since I was still holed up in the corporate apartment, I gave her a call. I was sorry not to see her face when she got the news. But the tone of her voice conveyed disgust. She urged me to come to her office for a powwow.

Sisley had been out of town over the weekend, so I had dealt with him by phone and e-mail. I had drafted a statement of firm denial with a second sentence about his deep respect for women. Given two hugely publicized marital breakups complete with accusations in one case of abuse and in the other of infidelity, he was hardly credible as a respecter of women. But what else could I write as a second sentence to relieve the aggressiveness of the first?

Well, he had an idea.

"I told you, Jonathan," he said from his cell phone, oblivious to its vulnerabilities (remember Prince Charles wanting to be Camilla's tampon?), "I want this to be a crusade against all these women bringing down the men they don't like. It's time to put a stop to this assault against anyone who just fucking flirts with a woman. Write that in the statement. That this is where the bullshit stops!"

"Bradford," I replied, "I'll talk to the reporters about that—the ones who I know won't turn it on us. I promise you. I'll get that out. But if we put it in the statement, it'll be attacked. There's just no fertile ground for that kind of message right now. Anyone who goes down that road will be shot at from all sides. You'll be dead meat within a day."

"Of course it will be attacked. I'm not afraid of being attacked. That's what this is about—they're already attacking me."

"I know, I know, I know," I insisted. "And I swear, I promise, we will get that out. But not in the statement."

"I want it in there."

"Fine, I'll draft it, and we'll look at it after Sandra Farber holds her press conference. Okay?"

Back off now. Kill it later.

The draft statement I showed to Wanda early Monday had a third sentence presented in a set of parentheses way down the page. It was Sisley's message of finally standing up against a massive witch hunt where every man was considered guilty and wasn't given a chance to defend himself. I put it in parentheses because I didn't want her to think—not even for one second—that I was supporting a declaration of war against the #MeToo movement.

One of her staff members, a guy named Charlie Franklin, had joined us. Charlie was a big, well-built guy who looked like a football player. His skin was a deep ebony, so when he smiled, his very white teeth (looking reconstructed) filled the room. I guessed him to be in his early thirties. Wanda said he was her external relations guy. He looked like he could have been her bodyguard as well.

Wanda read the draft in silence and then handed it across her desk to Charlie.

"What's with that third sentence?" she asked me. I heard Charlie, seated on my right, grunt.

"That's Bradford," I said. "Haven't been able to talk him out of it yet."

"Do you think you can?" she asked.

"I'll take care of it, I promise you," I said. "It won't see the light of day. Leave it in for now, and I promise I'll kill it."

She paused to think about my promise. Her life—both short term and long term—would be easier if she didn't have to go to battle about this sentence and could just trust me to take care of it. I wasn't going to tell her about my promise to Bradford to carry his "to the barricades" message to select reporters. I wasn't even sure whether I was going to do that. But I knew that telling her of that possibility would not create a bridge-building moment between us.

"Fine," she said. "You can leave it in for now. But don't show it to anyone else besides the three of us, Charlie."

"Got it," he said. He held on to the piece of paper. Apparently, he was the one who would ultimately issue the statement. That meant that Wanda, not I, was going to push the button on the release.

"Meanwhile," Wanda continued, "Charlie, you need to get someone in LA to livestream the press conference back to us here."

"Got it," he said. "I'll get it all set up in Conference Room A."

"No," she said. "I want it here in my office. I don't want a bunch of people watching that press conference. Just the three of us."

"Got it," he said.

"And let's both pull up the crisis contacts list and divvy it up between you, me, and Miley. Once that press conference is over and we release the statement, we need to be calling folks inside and out."

"Got it," he said.

"And, Charlie, you and Jonathan need to compare lists of media contacts. Whoever Jonathan wants, he gets. Understood?"

"Got it."

I could hear Charlie tapping away on a phone or tablet

next to me. I was watching Wanda, generalissimo of the communications army. She knew what she was doing, was obviously very prepared, and didn't need a hell of a lot from me.

For decades, my livelihood had depended on idiots who sat where Wanda was sitting now. People—overwhelmingly men—who never would think of writing a draft statement in advance, monitoring the press conference, or having a ready list of stakeholders to reach out to. Apparently, I was going to have a partner here who probably didn't need me. On the one hand, that was good—less effort on my part. On the other, I wanted to prove my worth, bring some value, to Wanda.

Hell, I wanted to win her respect.

"Just so you know," I said, "I begged him to settle this thing before it went public like this."

She looked at me, her brown eyes trying to pierce my skull. "And you failed because?"

"It's mostly about that third sentence. Well, also the first. He claims he's innocent."

She smiled ruefully. One of her eyebrows went up in cynical disbelief.

"I'm going to keep trying," I declared. "I think he absolutely needs to settle."

"Good luck with that," she said.

"I think a couple of days of bad press may work to soften him up," I said.

"Or get both of us fired," she said without a smile. "Okay, Charlie, get cracking!"

Poor Wanda. She thought she would contain the viewing of Sandra Farber's press conference to just her own private connection between Charlie's buddy with a cell phone down in Los Angeles and her office computer. She didn't realize that fun stuff like a Sandra Farber press conference gets livestreamed on Facebook as a matter of course. Throughout all of BeeLine—in offices and homes all over the world—employees, business customers, average consumers, and the media were watching the Sandra Show. And she definitely knew how to produce one.

She started with a speech about sexual misbehavior and all the powerful men in the world who somehow think they are entitled to physically touch and fondle women. There was a difference, she said, between flirtatiousness and assault, and too many men—particularly powerful men—didn't know the difference. Or chose to ignore it because they thought they had the right, or the opportunity. It was time for them to finally learn: Time's Up!

She then set up her client, a woman named Katherine Davis. Davis sat at the table next to where Farber's podium and mike were perched. She was the model of demure middle age, dressed in a quiet blue business blazer and a frilly blouse. Her frizzy blond hair was pulled back, creating a kind of angelic halo around her face. I could mentally undo her hair clip and imagine how long hair would make the roundness of her face less prominent. Her makeup was so simple that she looked washed out in the television lights. She kept her eyes down, seeming to be embarrassed at finding herself in public view.

She was the perfect victim.

"My client works at a high-end hotel in New York,

where she serves as an events manager. Three weeks ago—on October 10—her job required her to show some hotel meeting room options to Bradford Sisley, the CEO of BeeLine Inc., who alleged that he was going to be hosting a worldwide management meeting."

"Alleged?" asked Charlie, who presumably wanted to stand up for the boss. "That's just bullshit. We set up that meeting for him at the Peninsula to look the place over."

"'Alleged' is just a word that lawyers like to use," I said. "It's their way of saying that someone said something without necessarily offering proof."

"Shh!" said Wanda. Charlie gestured frustration, presumably at lawyers, not at Wanda.

"Ms. Davis entered an express elevator at approximately ten fifteen a.m. with Mr. Sisley to take him to see the roof-deck lounge."

Well, that timing pretty much eliminated any chance that the two people had been drunk and had misunderstood one another's intention.

"Soon after the doors closed, Mr. Sisley forced himself upon my client. He grabbed her into an intimate embrace with one arm and put his other hand on her breast. He then tried to kiss her. She tried pushing him away, but he had her in a strong grip. He told her that if she wanted BeeLine's business, she had better be cooperative. They struggled, and she ultimately freed herself with a classic knee maneuver known to most women."

The crowded press conference room was filled with chortles and one "You go girl." I glanced over at Wanda; she didn't seem amused. Charlie was grimacing in sympathy with his boss.

Sandra Faber waited for the twittering to die down.

"Mr. Sisley then threatened Ms. Davis by telling her that she would regret what she had done. At that point, the doors opened, and Ms. Davis quickly exited and went straight to the ladies' room, where she locked herself in a stall. After several minutes, she left the stall and exited the ladies' room. Mr. Sisley was nowhere to be found."

Farber went on to describe why Davis was pursuing civil damages rather than criminal charges. It was a pretty convoluted lecture on the higher burden of proof in a criminal case, particularly in a he said/she said situation. But it was all bullshit. This was about money. Winning criminal charges against Sisley did nothing for Katherine Davis's bank account. But a civil judgment—or a settlement—sure would.

I made a mental note to remind reporters about that.

Reporters probed Farber about the usual stuff—whether Katherine Davis had told anyone, whether there had been any witnesses, whether she had bruises or other physical evidence—but Farber was giving no more than what she had given. She said that other details would come out in the courtroom. When asked about a possible settlement, she said that she never discussed such things in public. As far as she and her client were concerned, this was going to court.

The whole thing took only about fifteen minutes. Katherine Davis never said a word, never lifted her eyes, and never changed her perfectly stolid abused-person expression. Farber had apparently made a decision that a silent client would be a more sympathetic client. Who knows, maybe she talked like a streetwalker. Maybe that's why Bradford had gotten confused.

Just kidding.

As soon as the press conference ended, Charlie handed me two versions of the response statement. He had taken my original draft and surrounded it with all the other stuff, like the date, the fact that it was a statement from Bradford Sisley, the explanation that no further comments were to be made at this point because of pending litigation, etcetera.

The short version had the denial ("I absolutely deny these allegations and will vigorously defend myself in court from these lies") and the sadness ("I am not the kind of person who would do anything like this, and it hurts me deeply that someone would even think to make such an accusation").

The longer version had the call to arms ("In taking on my defense, I hope to change the tide of current events, which seems to encourage so many baseless attacks and exaggerations against men who don't deserve such condemnation. It's time to stop the witch hunt").

"So?" Charlie asked. "Which is it?"

I waited a moment to give Wanda the opportunity to intervene in this decision, even though I had told her I'd take care of it.

She was simply staring at me. Her face said it all: Okay, hotshot, you promised you'd take care of it and take the heat with the man upstairs. Show me.

"Short version," I responded, handing that one back to Charlie.

"Have you told him?" Wanda asked.

"No, but I will," I responded. And, I thought, I'll once again promise him that I'll personally carry his battle cry in background chats with reporters. That way, it would be more from me than seeming to come from him. Assuming, of course, that I did it at all.

"He'll be furious," she said.

"He's going to be furious for the next two days anyway," I responded. "This will just be the warm-up session."

Suddenly, a device on Wanda's desk buzzed, and she jumped. She looked at the screen of what must have been the internal paging system. I had noticed one of these devices on Charlie's belt as well as on the belts of other men I had seen at BeeLine. Women had to figure out another way to keep them accessible, I guess. I always referred to these devices as corporate tethers. No one is ever out of reach. I had always been successful at convincing my clients that they would be risking corporate confidentiality if they ever tried to hang one on me.

"Oh shit," Wanda said. "Miley says that employees all over the company watched the press conference and are buzzing about it. I have to go help her with this."

"Just send out Sisley's statement internally," I suggested as Wanda rose from her seat, stuffing her tethering device into her purse.

"Do they really pay you money for giving such sage advice?" she asked. "Charlie, set Socrates here up in Renata's office. We need him close by so we can bask in the light of his wisdom."

This was a new side of Wanda. The other day when she was mad at me for keeping her in the dark, the anger was cold and controlled. This was more on edge. It was snippy and annoyed. She was clearly pissed at me. But why?

Charlie ushered me to an office three down from Wanda's. Since he walked at a normal pace, he got to the doorway ahead of me and used the time to poke at his tablet, which, of course, was a BeePad, the company's fairly unsuccessful entry into that particular tech product segment.

I turned into the office, which was covered—walls, windowsills, desk, cabinet tops—with photos. It was like a photo museum. And in every shot there was the same woman, a short, squat, husky woman with curly black hair who apparently skied, hiked, whitewater rafted, biked, played tennis, and won golf tournaments. Not very pretty, but she definitely had a very strong body. And an active lifestyle. And a very engaging smile.

This was Renata. And I would be living with her face for the next several days. Renata in the mountains, Renata on the water, Renata in the woods, Renata on the golf course. I appreciated her leaving this album of her adventurous life behind for me. As I made all my calls, struggling to sell the world on the idea that my guy had been unjustly accused, she would always be there smiling at me, having a really good time. I would watch her conquering Kilimanjaro while I sat on my ass hawking my story. She would be accomplishing things, constantly reminding me that I was not.

I quickly figured out that I would not be sitting in Renata's seat. She used one of those big balls to perch on. Not happening.

Normally, I would have asked my host to move the furniture around, but he was too busy with his BeePad. Besides, he was black and might think that was the reason

I asked him to move furniture. So I put my cane down on the desk and started to drag a chair around to the other side. I decided the safest thing would be to turn all the framed photos on the credenza down flat so that I wouldn't knock them over with my stomach as I lumbered past. Once I finally got both the chair and myself safely to the other side of the desk, I picked up my cane to poke the big ball away. It took three pokes to keep it at bay in the corner, next to the dumbbells. Dumbbells at the office? Jesus, Renata. Give it a break!

"Hey, let me help you," Charlie offered, now that I was done.

"That's okay. You have a statement to issue. Go do it."

"Just did it," he said, waving the BeePad in the air.

So easy. Tap, tap, tap, and your words have flown out into the world. When I started in this game, you needed a team of messengers and then some secretary slowly faxing a document to a long list of phone numbers, one by one. No wonder the world was on information overload. It was just too damn easy to state your piece.

With lightning speed, Charlie hooked me up at Renata's desk. With one phone call, he transferred the corporate apartment's phone line to Renata's instrument. And then, tap, tap, tap, he gave me a guest account on her computer. I was now ready to start dealing with all my contacts.

But I was hungry.

"Hey, Charlie," I said. "Wanna grab a bite?"

He glanced at his watch, which looked like one of those things that counted his steps, measured his pulse, and gave regular readings of his body mass index.

"It's just eleven thirty, dude," he said.

I am not a dude, I thought. I am anything but a dude.

"Well, I'm still on Sweden time, where they're probably stuffing pickled herring down their throats," I said. "Anyway, we need to give the world an hour or so to take in the statement, laugh at it, and think about what questions they can throw at us to break down our refusal to comment further. You ever been through one of these before?"

"One of what? A sex scandal?"

"No, a stonewalling. Where you stand behind a statement and don't give them anything else."

"Sure—that's half of what we do around here," he said. "Half the time we bury them in information, trying to get them to cover us, and then the other half we want them to just go away. But why did you say they'll laugh at the statement?"

"Let's get some food and talk about it," I said. I was really, really hungry.

Forty-five minutes later Charlie and I were finishing our cafeteria meal. As cafeterias go, BeeLine's was attractive—kind of a massive food court with multiple stations offering both healthy and unhealthy alternatives. For semiambulatory folks like me, they had nice little electric carts—just stick your cane in the back and load up food on the front, which was like a double-sized tray. Perfect!

I was tempted to steal the cart for the long journey back across the corporate campus. It had taken Charlie and me fifteen painful minutes to get to the cafeteria. It was like trying to cross a freeway of joggers and power walkers. They were all perfectly pleasant about having to detour around us, but I definitely felt like a clot in a blood flow—I was preventing the normal thing from happening.

I just don't get the spacious campus thing with the big lawns and gardens and benches. Give me a high-rise any day. Elevators to whisk me wherever I need to go. No squirrels. No birds. No joggers.

Charlie was a salad bar guy. I was a hamburger, mac and cheese, potato leek soup, chocolate pudding, apple pie à la mode guy. I had to settle for a nonalcoholic beer.

By asking a few questions, I got the gist of Charlie's story. Son of a successful car dealer in LA, he had grown up in largely white well-to-do neighborhoods and gone to largely white excellent public schools. Given his size, he had played football, mostly in line positions, but he was indifferent to the game.

"When you're big and black, everyone expects you to play football and be a tough guy," he said. "Coach said I lacked heart. Which was true. I really didn't give a shit about football. Inside of me I was actually a skinny kid with glasses. I was just dressed up as a big black guy. I liked reading. I liked to write. I liked to go to movies. Probably the same kind of stuff you liked being a kid."

It was true that my growing up had revolved around those same things, but unlike Charlie, this wasn't really a choice I had made. I had ached to be doing the other things that boys did. I was desperate to be on the football line of scrimmage, but no team would have me after seeing how hopelessly uncoordinated I was. Everything I did—reading endless amounts of history, going to as many adventure films as Hollywood would make for me—I did in solitude and isolation. Hugely fat people find themselves alone a lot. Maybe big black guys do too. But somehow I expected that Charlie had not been unpopular like me. His minority status—and what seemed to be an affable, winning personality—probably got him a lot of dates.

Putting it another way, all things considered, I'd rather have been a big black guy in high school in the nineties than a pimply obese white guy in high school in the seventies.

"So how did you end up here at BeeLine doing communications work?" I asked as I dug into my apple pie. The crust was tough; it was a perfect specimen of cafeteria pie.

"Well, when I started, it was like a placeholder thing," Charlie said. "My wife was doing her residency at the hospital here, and I needed a job. My dad knew someone who knew someone at BeeLine, and I got an interview with Wanda."

"Did you have any grounding at all in communications?"

He looked annoyed. "I wasn't an affirmative action hire."

"I didn't say that," I said.

"You thought it."

I had thought it. Once again, one of the nasty remnants of my racist childhood had come to the surface. I often fooled myself that I had exorcised all that. That I had overcome my family's and my own hateful prejudices. But here I was in my sixth decade of living, and these little souvenirs would emerge from some dusty storage box inside me.

I could only hope that that deplorable box was lodged nowhere near my heart.

I plowed ahead with Charlie, using pathetic humor to try to pick up the pieces of the mess I had just made.

"What am I supposed to say at this point?" I asked. "Some of my best friends are black?"

He smiled just a little bit.

"Well, they aren't," I said.

"Well, I don't have any obese friends either," he replied.

"So our relationship could be groundbreaking for both of us," I said.

This was one of those guy-guy moments where men don't know what to say next. I had stepped across a macho line by suggesting that we might become friends. I didn't really mean it—it was just something that came tumbling out of my mouth, meant as a light joke but sounding more like an actual proposition. We sat it out in awkward silence while I picked at apple pie crumbs and spun my spoon one more time around the chocolate pudding bowl.

"So what was your communications experience?" I asked.

"I studied journalism at the University of Arizona, and then I worked at the city desk of the *Sacramento Bee* for three years," he said. "Wanda did take a bit of a flier on me, not knowing if I could cross the line from reporter to corporate flack."

"Well, it seems to be working well," I said. "You seem to know what you're doing."

"She's a good teacher," he said.

"You like her?" I wondered if I might get anything out of him. I was still smarting from her snap at me.

He hesitated for a moment. "There's not much to like," he said. "She's like the fifth-grade teacher you had. She pops up at her desk at the beginning of the day and disappears behind it at night. There isn't a person there. There's just a professional person doing a job. A damn good job. If you saw her in the grocery store, you'd faint at the idea that she ate food."

So, closed-off Wanda was not just a persona she had invented for me. Charlie clearly knew that person as well. Dead end in my search for another Wanda. A secret Wanda.

Since I didn't steal the nifty cafeteria electric cart, Charlie and I had a long, slow walk back to our offices. Our conversation in the cafeteria had confirmed what I had already sensed about Charlie: he was direct and honest to a fault. He would tell it like he saw it, irrespective of consideration of nuance or appropriateness. In a strange, old-fashioned kind of way, he was earnest.

He wanted to go back to the unanswered question he had asked in Renata's office.

At that point I had claimed I was too hungry to answer. But now that excuse was gone.

"So you wrote Bradford's denial, right?" he asked. "But you said you think people are going to laugh at it," he said. "Why did you say that?"

"For all the usual reasons," I answered. "He's a man, and she's a woman. I don't need to tell you there was a very long, long time when it worked the other way. People would lean in for the guy and find excuses to dismiss the woman. But now it's flipped. Now we tend to assume that, of course, the guy's guilty. Why would she make something like that up? And on top of all that, in Bradford's case, he has a big reputation for womanizing."

"He has a reputation for having cheated on his wives and dated beautiful women. None of that is the same as attacking someone in an elevator," Charlie said.

"In matters of the groin, people often don't make careful distinctions," I said.

"I think the guy should at least be given the benefit of the doubt," he said. "No one at the company has ever talked about him as a serial harasser or anything."

I was thinking that someone like Charlie was probably the last person to know whether Bradford Sisley had been misbehaving at BeeLine. I had learned that women—long before there was social media—knew how to let each other know about the creeps that lurked in the workplace. They kept each other informed and warned. But rarely would they let their male colleagues in on the news. Particularly someone as earnest as Charlie. He might go up and challenge the guy to a duel.

So here was Charlie offering a defense of Bradford Sisley. Benefit of the doubt. He actually believed it possible that Katherine Davis had made the whole thing up.

I stopped and grabbed Charlie's arm, feigning an amused astonishment.

"Oh my God!" I said. "Charlie! Do you actually believe that Bradford Sisley may be innocent?"

Charlie was looking at me. But he had put on his ultra-cool, wraparound shades with the mirror lenses. Not seeing someone's eyes makes it hard to judge what's happening with a person. The rest of his face was stern, definitely not responding in kind to my effort to be light-hearted.

"Of course I do," he said. "And you don't?"

Not for one San Jose minute! Unlike Charlie, I knew what Sisley had already admitted to me: that he had made a move on her, a physical move on "where she was soft." And while I didn't know the details of what had gone on before or after he had made his move, I definitely was going to favor Katherine Davis's version rather than his.

But that wasn't the question at hand. The question was whether it was *possible* that he was innocent. Of course it was possible. It was also definitely possible that a smart trial attorney could worm a clever pathway around an accusation of sexual assault.

"I think it is *possible* that he's innocent, yes," I said. "But I don't think it's likely. But whatever the truth is, I don't think he should take it to court. I think he should settle."

Charlie had stopped moving. I could see my reflection in his sunglasses. He was shaking his head back and forth in disagreement. I sensed that behind the mirrors of his glasses, his eyes were expressing disappointment in me.

"Let's go," he said, ending our brief pause.

We walked on in silence. A skinny woman dressed in running shorts circled around us onto the lawn, muttering that we should get into single file, presumably because our collective bulk filled the whole broad walkway. I was pleased to see that she had to jump a flower bed to get back on the path.

A little farther on, Charlie broke the silence. "I was accused of sexual assault in college," he said quietly. "You asked me earlier if I had been involved in something like this before. I have been."

I was embarrassed. I had been pretty nonchalant about the issue of innocence and guilt and very definitive about settling the case irrespective. Who knew that Charlie had once been on the razor's edge of exactly those questions?

"What happened?" I asked, keeping my eyes on the ground ahead of me. It would be easier for him to tell his story and for me to hear it if we just walked side by side.

"It was classic, almost textbook," he said. "We met at a frat party, got into a back-and-forth flirting business that only meant one thing, and ended up in my bedroom. We were drunk, and it was a pretty wild encounter—wilder than I was used to. She had a kind of porno side to her. I got into it.

"But I wasn't into her. She was nervous and high-strung, endlessly blithering and kind of, well, superficial. So it was one of those 'in the light of day, I go my separate way' deals.

"Next thing I know, I'm accused of rape. Me, accused of rape! I mean, I should have accused her of rape, given what went down that night!"

He was angry, reliving this accusation. I could hear the younger man inside him, saying those words—"she's the one who should be accused of rape"—to his parents, to his lawyer in his frustration, his anger, his fear. Hopefully they told him never to say those words publicly.

He paused again, and I knew I needed to prompt him forward, out of the memory abyss he had fallen into.

"What happened then?" I asked. I could hear him take a deep sigh.

"It was a fucking yearlong nightmare," he said. "That's what it was. My parents were completely destroyed by the whole thing. It was really awful for them. They totally believed me, but they knew that the cards were so stacked against me—big black dude, skinny little white girl, drinking, sex. They paid for a very expensive LA lawyer and then another lawyer in Arizona who knew how the process worked at the university."

"Did the police get involved?" I asked.

"No, thank God," he said. "In those days, everything stayed on campus. Nowadays, I don't know what they do. But in those days, it was handled by a special disciplinary committee of different people from the administration and the faculty and some students. The crack university police did the investigation."

He paused again. Maybe he was running the story back through his head. Or considering just how much he wanted to tell me.

"And?" I asked.

"And it went on and on. No one but me was in a rush to settle the matter, to get to the truth. I think that was their secret method: drag it on and on until one side or the other leaves the school. But I wasn't leaving, and neither was she. But, man, she was talking. Talking, talking, talking. And no one wanted to hear my side. I became more and more isolated on campus—the invisible six-foot-three black guy. I became untouchable, invisible, totally toxic."

Now he stopped and turned to me. I looked up at him, again seeing only myself in the mirror lenses.

"That's why I was asking you about Mr. Sisley," he said. "Whether you are willing to be fair to him, to give him just a little benefit of the doubt, to consider that maybe, just maybe, he was in an elevator with a fucking nutcase, like the girl I got involved with. It's possible, you know. I know how fucking possible it is."

"Charlie, I know it's possible," I said, mostly to assuage him, not because I necessarily believed what I was saying.

"Damn right it is," he said angrily and then restarted our walk. But he forgot for a moment whom he was walking with. He was fully ten steps ahead of me before he thought to stop and turn around.

"I'm sorry," he said as I limped up to him. He stuck a finger up under his sunglasses. Was it possible he was wiping away a tear?

We started walking again.

"So, how did it finally end?" I asked in order to interrupt the silence that once again had slid between us.

"She nullified the accusation," he said. "By then, most people knew what a mess case she was, probably including her parents and their lawyer. Or maybe my lawyer finally out-lawyered hers. But one day, poof, the whole thing was gone.

"Only it wasn't gone. Not at all. Because under the whole hypocrisy of the so-called *confidential* process, the rape charge had never been publicly communicated. So neither was the nullification. The rumor mill had lost interest months before, so I was left with my reputation shattered and no possibility of vindication. I finished my time and got out of Tucson."

We were almost to the headquarters building before we spoke again. I said something inane about appreciating his sharing such a personal thing with me. That got him stirred up again.

"I'm not looking for sympathy from you, Mr. Keaton," he said. "I told you because I wanted to make you understand that you've got a responsibility here." He was shaking his finger at me, his voice trembling with passion. "This whole place is filled with people who want to assume his guilt, people who are ready to jump on him and tear him to pieces, not necessarily for this but for some other thing he's done or said. And they can't wait to use this, not caring—not for one fucking minute—whether it's true or false.

"You can't let that happen, Mr. Keaton. You've got to keep this thing fair—give the guy the breathing room to make his case. After everything he's done for this company, for this whole fucking world, and despite his many, many faults, he deserves a fair shake here."

"Charlie," I said. "He needs to settle the case. He needs to get it behind him."

Charlie pulled off his sunglasses, and I could see the distress in his eyes.

"A settlement won't put it behind him. A settlement will be with him forever."

"I'm on his side," I said. "You can trust me on that."

"I hope so," he said. "He needs to have some people who are really, sincerely on his team. Not just pretending to be with him. He's already got a lot of those kinds of pretenders."

Charlie's admonitions were a good reminder for me as I headed into my phone marathon with my media contacts. He was right to remind me that I was supposed to be Bradford Sisley's advocate, his defender. And even though I didn't like the guy and I didn't really believe him, I couldn't let my feelings keep me from doing a good job on his behalf.

It wasn't loyalty in the classic sense, and it wasn't really what Charlie was urging me to do—give Sisley a chance to make his case. It was my professional responsibility to stick to the story, the story that I had crafted, and to sell that story with every ounce of my ability.

It was one of the truly miserable sides to the miserable profession I had stumbled into. And over the years, I had had to do what I had to do now: ignore what my head was telling me, swallow any revulsion, and turn my back on any thought of integrity. There had been the drug maker who had ignored the reports of unexpected strokes and deaths. The oil company that had shortchanged the building of the pipeline. The environmentalist who had fired the guy who told him that the calculations they were touting were falsified. Or the banker who had just done what she was told while millions of dollars were laundered under her nose.

And age had not made it easier. It had made it harder. At Charlie's age, I could find the excuse, like his legitimate reasons for wanting to give Bradford Sisley the chance to defend himself, to be considered innocent until proven guilty. Like when I worked for the tobacco company and convinced myself—as I was puffing my nightly illegal marijuana—that people should have the right to choose their own poison and that everyone knew the dangers of smoking. Or when I helped the plastic-bottle people make their case that the bottle's lighter weight did so much for the environment that it didn't matter that it couldn't be recycled. Or believed that the actress's death couldn't possibly be the result of nearly criminal incompetence in a hospital of such a sterling reputation.

But as I had grown older and had gotten better at pulling the wool over other people's eyes, it had become harder to pull the wool over my own. Maybe I had grown too wise to be able to fool myself anymore. My bullshit meter had grown too sensitive for my own good.

So as I stood up in Renata's office and carefully eased my way around her desk, I looked down at the myriad mementos of her personal triumphs. I made a promise to myself. I would promote Bradford Sisley's innocence and trash Katherine Davis's story to the very best of my ability. But I would also fight like hell to make sure that my client settled with her. And if, after several days, my client had failed to honorably end this tawdry mess, I would quit on him. I would fire the son of a bitch.

One more promise to myself that I would fail to keep.

Man at work:

"I'm telling you, Gerald. I'm with the guy, and I'm looking in his eyes. He says he's innocent, and he's really sincere. He says he didn't do anything wrong to that woman."

"You're picking your words carefully, Jonathan. He didn't do anything wrong to that woman. Was he in the elevator with her? Did he touch her?"

"You know I can't talk about a pending case, Gerald. I'm telling you that that woman's story isn't true. It just doesn't add up. I mean, she's an attractive woman for her age. But a guy like Sisley has dated some of the most glamorous women in the world. He is not gonna attack a woman like that at ten in the morning in an elevator. Why would he do that?"

"Because he thought he could get away with it."

"Get away with what? Are they going to have sex in the elevator? On the floor of a hotel meeting room? Head for a broom closet? C'mon, Gerald."

"Listen, I just talked to the hotel folks thirty minutes ago. They're standing by their lady. They say she's a respected person—longtime employee, blah, blah, blah. They say there's never been anything like this before with her."

"Right—she's a saint. Did you ask them if she told anybody about this supposed attack?"

"They refused to answer—pending case, blah, blah. They did tell—"

"It's not their pending goddamned case. You noticed that Sandra Farber didn't mention anything—not one word—about her client telling anyone about this terrible, terrible thing that happened to her. That's usually standard fare in this kind of shit. How come it's not in this one?"

"They did tell me that there probably is an elevator video in the security system."

Oy.

"I'll tell Bradford that. He'll be glad to hear that."

"You really think so?"

"I know so. I'm telling you. What she said happened in that elevator did not happen. You'll see. Sandra Farber will not try to get her hands on that video. It'll blow her case out of the water."

"Well, I'm writing it."

"The video?"

"Yep. So you want to give me a comment on that?"

"Nope. We're just standing behind the statement right now. No other on-the-record comments. But you heard what I said off the record a minute ago. Sandra Farber won't try to get that video."

"Okay, Jonathan, but here's the other thing. Your guy doesn't have a lot of friends. Everyone I'm talking to has bad shit to say about him: he's a liar, he's a thief, he's a sexist, he's a narcissist on steroids. No one has anything nice to say."

"He's no angel. We know that. But you don't seem to be telling me about other claims of assault. No one's talking to you about other women, right? You know, like all those other guys where the women come out of the woodwork. Like Weinstein."

"Not yet."

"Yeah, that's the thing. You gonna write that? The non-news? That no one is popping up with other stories."

"Jonathan, for God's sake. We're only a couple of hours into this."

"Okay, okay. But when it's a couple of days and no one else pops up, write it up that way, okay? I'm telling you, Gerald. This is not one more of those stories about a powerful man with a zipper problem. Sisley's a difficult guy and a pain in the ass. But keep your eye on it. I don't think you're going to find a pattern here. Not with him. The only pattern here is Sandra Farber and her clients trying to make a buck."

"Jonathan, you're not giving me anything."

"Not yet, but I will. Just keep an open mind, Gerald. It's just possible that this one is different. Not just

another Harvey Weinstein. This might be where the tipping point comes: where the woman is lying and the man is unjustly accused. The whole narrative that is dominating everything right now, suddenly it changes. Suddenly, there is another side to the story."

"I'd love to write it. But you've given me nothing."

"I will. I promise I will."

You just climb out on a limb and figure, if it breaks later, you'll improvise.

The stories that started to emerge in midafternoon all contained our statement.

The cable news coverage would flash up the words of Bradford's denial and, in a subtle way, roll their eyes at it. Then they would show old footage of his highly publicized second divorce, when he was caught cheating. They also had clips from his somewhat notorious appearance on *Dancing with the Stars* when he did a sexy tango with a very young, very attractive partner.

It was obvious from my dozen or so calls that, like my Associated Press guy Gerald Berger, journalists found Sisley's denial no more believable than those of any of the other powerful Hollywood, political, media, and business abusers who were caught up in that fall's hunting season. Why would they believe him any more than the others?

And if Bradford Sisley had any friends, they were lying low. As reporters were fishing around for "reactions" (mainly in hope of uncovering additional scandalous behavior), they were getting an earful of off-the-record bad-mouthing. Friends, employees, others in the industry, even people who worked for charities blessed with his donations had bad things to say about Bradford Sisley. Someone from Sisley's tennis club said no one wanted to play with him because he was such a sore loser. A big venture capitalist said he'd decided years ago never to get involved in any deal where Sisley was also an investor—he only created chaos. A woman who had cut his hair called him a creep who wouldn't even know what to do with a woman if she was stupid enough to let him near her.

It was Morris Feldstein all over again.

Morris Feldstein had been at the heart of one of the biggest financial scandals of the eighties. For most of the decade, he had run one of the most successful trading firms on Wall Street. Ever eager for fame and respect, he also became a philanthropist, giving big bucks to Jewish causes, ballet companies, social welfare services, and his alma mater, Brown University. He was honored at charity events, was given humanitarian awards, had facilities named after him at Brown, and had an impressive stack of favorable profile articles lauding the Wall Street wizard with a big heart.

The Feds, thanks to a whistleblower in Feldstein's shop, closed in on him. Turned out that he was part of a vast insider trading network. His trading brilliance was based, not on hours of hard research and analysis (his mantra in speeches to business school classes), but on inside information provided by informants who got kickbacks from his profitable trades.

I was brought in to help announce the plea deal he had negotiated with the Feds. I knew it would be a tough assignment because no one likes a cheater. Particularly one who had so flaunted his successes. But his brilliant lawyer gave him and me the right approach: be contrite. Be so ashamed, so obviously mindful of the gravity of your deception, that the sentencing judge will be satisfied that the defendant before him really understands and deeply regrets the crime.

So I went into crisis mode for Morris. And everything went reasonably well. We issued a very contrite statement, preemptively withdrew from all boards and organizations before they had a chance to make that choice for themselves, wrote scores of letters of apology. We encouraged a kind of Greek drama narrative: the otherwise great man had a tragic flaw, and now he had fallen into shame and deep remorse. He accepted that his life was forever changed, that he was a ruined man and deserved to be.

And the general media coverage over the first couple of days segued from shock to a small modicum of respect for the sinner who, at least, seemed remorseful for his sin.

Then the shit hit the fan. His brilliant lawyer decided to leak the fact that, as part of the negotiated deal, Morris had been wearing a wire for weeks, enticing all his buddies to incriminate themselves on tape. The lawyer thought that leaking this information would add to Morris's image as repentant—not only was the man sorry, but he was trying to help the authorities fix the problem. He was working to make things right and bring a halt to all the illegal behavior. It was the kind of thing the brilliant lawyer might want to say to the judge. But it was no public relations strategy.

There was enormous outrage. The cheater had cheated again. The rat had turned ratfink. This wasn't self-reproach; it was betrayal. What had happened to honor among thieves? Everyone who had expressed a modicum of sadness or sympathy for Morris and his family or who just had stayed neutral now wanted to distance themselves—quickly and adamantly—from Morris Feldstein. He was a villain; he was disgraceful; he was the worst kind of human being. No one, absolutely no one, would say anything remotely nice about him.

I learned many things from my experience with Morris Feldstein. Since he was every bit as sweet tempered as Bradford Sisley, I learned how to take horrible verbal abuse. But mostly Morris taught me that brilliantly manipulative people can use those same misleading skills on themselves to avoid any degree of self-awareness. All the remorse and shame that I had written into the statement was totally false—Morris clearly did not understand the depth of his own depravity. He really thought that by paying his $150 million settlement, he'd done his bit. Paid for his sin. He couldn't understand why others didn't get that.

And I also learned from my time with Morris how a simmering pot of antipathy and dislike towards a person can, in an instant, heat up and boil over. Those who have left behind a trail of resentment and offense are wiring themselves with explosives. And one spark can blow everything to bits.

Late in the day, I got in to see Bradford. I'd e-mailed him the print coverage and promised to bring him copies of the TV coverage that Wanda's team had captured.

He was surprisingly sanguine about what he saw. I had thought he would be furious.

"I think it's working," he said as we wrapped up looking at the TV coverage. I had asked Charlie to excise the one really negative piece that had appeared on MSNBC, in which a female commentator on one of their interchangeable, repetitive talk shows had compared him to Bill Cosby. It wasn't a fair comparison, I thought. Cosby was accused of serial rape, not making a pass in an elevator.

Now I was sorry that I hadn't kept the segment in. My client was too happy. If I was ever going to get him to the settlement table, I had to somehow show him how badly things were going, how the PR strategy was doomed to failure. I had to get him mad at me for failing.

"I think it's a little early to know how we're doing," I said.

"I'm going to win this thing," he said. "I've been getting support all day from all kinds of people." He leaned back in his handsome desk chair and put his hands behind his head.

"Really?" I said with genuine surprise.

He leaned forward across the desk from me. I was shoehorned into one of his uncomfortable, small visitor chairs. I had my yellow notebook pressed against my belly. I've never understood how anyone could take notes on any kind of electronic device. Yellow pads for me. Besides, I like to doodle when bored.

"Yeah, like when I pulled into the garage after lunch, Manuel, the garage guy, gave me a big thumbs-up and said, 'We're with you, boss!' And one of the bankers I had lunch with told me he was glad I was standing up and defending myself. It was about time some man did that."

"Really?" I said again.

"Yeah, all day I've been getting calls and e-mails from people."

"Well, this is great," I said. "I've actually been a little worried because some of the reporters have been telling me that the off-the-record comments have not been positive."

He frowned. "What do you mean?"

"People saying they don't necessarily believe you or talking about some other problem they have with you."

"Like what kind of problem?"

"I don't know. Maybe it's just some folks who don't like you."

"What folks? Who are they talking to? I mean, if they're calling my ex-wives or people I've fired or something—"

"They don't name names for me, Bradford," I said. "But maybe you can. If you've got a bunch of people who will say positive things and say they believe you, we could use that. We could use that right now. Give me some names, and I'll direct reporters to those people."

I lifted my pad. Unfortunately, my pen was in my pocket, crushed into that nasty designer chair. I couldn't possibly reach it unless I stood. A normal person would just have leaned sideways in the chair to get the pen. If I had done that, I undoubtedly would have tipped over. So I just waited, figuring that there would be nothing to write down.

He hesitated.

"Well, what kind of names do you want?" he asked.

"I don't want my friends to be bothered by a bunch of reporters."

"Important people," I said. "Or people who are close to you or even were formerly close to you, like years ago or in college or something. Just to say that you're a stand-up guy and if you say you're innocent, you must be. You said a bunch of people have contacted you today—think about all of them. Give me a couple of them. They don't have to go on the record if they don't want. Just give background stuff to reporters."

He hesitated again. "Let me think on it," he said. "How about Congressman Henkel? I talked to him today. He was very positive."

And very much in your pocket, thanks to years of donations, I thought. And very, very unlikely to put his ass on the line in a situation like this. He probably had hung up the phone and told someone to check into how much money he might have to give back if it came to that.

"Good enough," I said. "I'll get in touch with his press guy."

"Gal. He's got a woman. Very attractive woman."

His eyes rolled up on the word "attractive," and I knew there had to be a story there. Some sort of contact between her and him—hopefully innocent, even if it was not innocent in his libidinous imagination.

"I'll call her."

"Judith Henry," he muttered. "That's her name." His demeanor had become vaguely guilty, like that of a little boy caught doing something naughty.

"I'll call her."

"Say hi for me."

I stared at him for a second, not believing how oblivious he was to his own absurd—and, in this instance, pathetic—behavior. I lowered my pad back to the front of my belly.

"Bradford," I said in a soft, serious voice. "I have to ask you something important."

He looked scared. I think he was afraid I was going to push for details on whatever had transpired with Judith Henry.

"What?" he asked.

"Are we going to get more women coming forward with stories, like this Katherine Davis? I'm not asking about your dating life. I'm asking about women who might have found you to be overly aggressive."

His face darkened. "Who the fuck do you think you're talking to?" he snarled at me.

My question had infuriated him. The mood of our conversation was veering off into the black hole of his anger and, I realized, his fear. "Who the hell do you think I am? Some serial rapist? Some Bill Cosby?"

Odd that he would choose that comparison. Too bad I had taken it out of the segments to show him.

"No," I tried to respond. "I'm just trying to do my job. I really—"

"Well, then fucking do your job!" he bellowed. He leapt from his chair and came around the desk to stand over me. In his anger and his haste, he knocked over a vase of flowers on his desk, and it rolled to the edge and fell off. "You need to get your fat ass out of that chair and get those fucking reporter buddies of yours to tell the real story here. The

real story. That one guy—one very innocent guy—is not going to be run over by this feminist army of bulldozers that has been destroying man after man. He's going to stand his ground and stop this bullshit that says that someone is guilty just because some bitch in a skirt says he is!

"Have you been selling that story, fuckhead? Or are you holding back because you're just so fucking worried that one more allegation is going to come up? And so what if it does? It'll be as phony as the last one. It's all just *bullshit! Bullshit! Bullshit!* A bunch of hysterical women trying to get their hand in some guy's wallet or get even 'cause some guy dumped them."

With that, he took a kick at the vase lying half-broken on the floor. He must have played soccer at some point, because it was a clean kick: the main part of the vase ended up smashing against one of his plate-glass walls.

Well, I had succeeded in getting him to think that things were not going well and in getting him mad at me. But I decided it was probably not the right time to again raise the issue of settling the lawsuit with Katherine Davis. Which also meant I was holding back on letting him know about the possibility of the elevator tape. I knew I wanted to save that ammunition for a calmer moment.

3

TUESDAY

Wanda and I had coffee in her office on Tuesday morning to assess the situation. Good thing I had had a full breakfast catered into the apartment by the concierge, since Wanda was not exactly generous in doling out calories. She offered me a grapefruit, granola, and low-fat yogurt. I couldn't eat the grapefruit on account of my meds, I hate granola with raisins, and low-fat yogurt is like decaf coffee—what's the point?

So when Wanda offered her meager fare, I was able to turn her down, playing my "I'm on a diet" charade.

All the coverage we looked at on Tuesday morning was pretty much the same stuff from the evening before. The Sandra Farber news conference, our denial, a little bit on Bradford's past shenanigans breaking up his marriage and dating starlets, and then blah, blah, blah about the #MeToo movement.

The late-night comedy show hosts had apparently had fun with it. Everyone included it in their monologues. One pulled together a skit where Sisley, known for hustling his products, climbed all over a woman in an elevator, trying to get her to buy some of his new BeeLine products: a health-monitoring G-string and a digitized chastity belt that would shut your legs if your heartbeat got too high. The audience didn't seem to find it very funny.

The morning talk shows put the story fairly far down in their daily news coverage. Only the *Today* show decided to put a focus on it. They had on a former BeeLine employee, a thirty-something woman of Asian descent. When the woman appeared, Wanda grunted and gave me an uh-oh look. Her name was Mary Chan, and she told how she had been repeatedly passed over by men at BeeLine. She described the place as a "boy's club on steroids." When Matt Lauer (before he himself was outed as a sexual predator) leaned in sympathetically to ask if she had had any experiences with Bradford Sisley, she laughed.

"I don't know him at all," she said. "He was miles and miles above me. But I've heard about him. I've heard that he's got a potty mouth about women, even when women are in the room."

"Have you heard about instances of actual sexual harassment at BeeLine?" asked Matt, using his deeply concerned, intimate voice.

She laughed again. "Are you kidding? Of course! Everything you can think of, from stupid adolescent comments to some really serious stuff."

"Including Bradford Sisley?"

"I'm sure if there was such a thing, it would have been hushed up. Someone like me would never hear about it."

It was a strange interview. The woman obviously had her beef with BeeLine the company. But she had zero connection to Bradford Sisley, and he was the news hook. The closing questions focused on Silicon Valley tech companies more broadly and on how hard it was for the Mary Chans of the world to make a career. I wondered what the producer had thought he was getting when he scheduled Mary Chan for an interview. He had to have known that she had nothing on Sisley except hearsay about his sexist language.

"So who is she?" I asked Wanda.

"I think we can safely call her a disgruntled employee," Wanda said. "She quit about two months ago and got herself a lawyer. I figure there's some negotiating going on, and this is part of creating leverage for Mary."

"But why would the *Today* show go for that?" I asked.

"Fill a slot, I guess," she said with a shrug and took a swig of coffee. We were seated at a small conference table in Wanda's office, side by side with our computers. We were facing a wall-mounted flat screen that she used to project both print stories and video segments. She was adept with the technology at her fingertips, toggling among various inputs, putting them up on the screen, highlighting things, rewinding and fast-forwarding with perfect precision. These are not my skills.

Having reviewed the coverage, she pushed her computer away and turned to face me. I figured I'd better do the same. We were getting down to business.

"So what do we do now?" she asked. "It's no better or worse than expected. Unless Farber has another shoe to drop, the story about Bradford doesn't have a lot of legs, does it?"

"Well, Farber is out fishing for more women," I answered. "That's what she does. Will she find them?"

"How would I know? I only work for the guy."

"You would know if there was company stuff, right?"

"Well, ask Mary Chan. There is plenty of company stuff."

"No, I meant company stuff about Bradford. Bad behavior on his part with women employees."

"Probably. I've heard rumors. But they've got a highly developed system here to clean up messes pretty fast and bury them very deeply. They screwed up on Mary Chan, which is pretty unusual."

I found her nonchalance a little disconcerting. Maybe it was sexist of me to assume that she would be sympathetic towards Mary Chan. Women for women and all that. But she seemed awfully cool and removed in the way she was talking. Maybe after all those years of playing tough guy, being one of the boys, it was just habit. But I would have thought that as a woman she would care more about working at a place that, if Mary Chan was right, was a cesspool for women. Moreover, according to Wanda, the company also had a well-developed process for getting rid of nasty situations but not getting rid of the overall problem. Happy to be working here, Wanda?

"Well, as you say, we just have to wait for the next shoe to drop," I said.

"And maybe it doesn't," she said. "Then what?"

"It goes quiet until there's a settlement," I answered.

She raised her eyebrows. "Oh, you think there's going to be a settlement? Is that what he is saying to you?"

I couldn't lie to Wanda. "No. And that's the problem. He still thinks he's going to save America's manhood and take Katherine Davis to trial. Prove that he's innocent and that she's a liar. Problem is, and he doesn't know it yet, there could be a security tape. The hotel has a monitoring system in that elevator."

Wanda nodded her head gently as she pondered this.

"How do you know that?" she asked.

"A reporter told me. He got it from the hotel, which is very supportive of their employee."

"Are you going to tell Bradford that there may be a tape?" she asked.

"I will," I said. "At the right time. Or I may just let the reporter tell him in the media tomorrow."

"And you assume that will make him want to settle?" she asked.

"I don't know. Sort of depends on what actually happened in there, doesn't it?"

"Tapes can be ambiguous," she said.

"Tapes aren't ambiguous. Lawyerly interpretations of them are."

She smiled in agreement.

"Either way," I said, "I assume you agree that Bradford Sisley should not put himself on a witness stand and claim to be victimized. He doesn't seem to understand that in the run-up to a Farber trial, her publicity machinery will start cranking away. He will be raked through more mud than sits in the Mississippi Delta. I don't know who his lawyer is, but that person will have to pull the plug on a trial. Otherwise, they risk destroying their own reputation and ending up with their client in jail for perjury or worse. Who is his lawyer, anyway?" I asked.

She shrugged. "I don't know. Who gave you legal clearance on his statement yesterday?"

Oops. I had never thought about that.

"I assumed you guys—you and Charlie—were taking care of that," I said, trying to shift any blame that might be headed my way.

"Why would you assume that?" she asked sternly. "You handed us a statement like a done deal—except for that third-sentence nonsense. It never had been cleared by his lawyer?"

"I don't know who his lawyer is."

She stared at me for a second. "Can't help you there," she said. "Maybe he's assuming that the corporate Legal Department is his lawyer."

"Well, I need to find out, don't I? Without his lawyer on my side, I'll never get Bradford into a settlement."

"So that's your grand strategy," she said. "Make a settlement, publicity goes away, all is good."

"You got a better one?" I asked. I admit I probably said this in a snotty tone, but her tone had been a little snotty as well. Like I was simpleminded.

"Well, I guess we'll see if you're right," she said. She pushed back her chair, grabbed up her computer. Apparently, our meeting was done.

"Call me if you need anything," she said. "I'll tell Charlie to use our usual deflection statement if anyone calls about the Mary Chan stuff. Actually, that's where I suspect the story is going to go today. But that's not your problem, is it, Jonathan? You're just here for Bradford, not the company. Right?"

Her tone was slightly hostile. But her point wasn't inaccurate. If the story really did drift to larger questions about BeeLine's culture and treatment of women, that had nothing to do with my current assignment. Unless Wanda wanted me to help. And it was obvious that she did not.

I returned to Renata's office and checked my messages and all the usual media. Nothing new seemed to be happening. Gerald Berger had a story out there, but there was nothing in it about elevator tapes. I checked with Charlie. He said no calls had come into his shop either.

With a little luck, this wouldn't be the calm before the storm. It would be the calm before the calm.

So I did what I usually do in such situations: played video solitaire. And each time I won, I'd check all the media again, so I could always claim to be working.

At about nine I got a text on my screen from Wanda saying that she had to see me ASAP.

Charlie was sitting across from Wanda when I arrived. He was finishing whatever he was saying, and she waved me to go sit on her couch.

"C'mon, Charlie," she said. "Let's move over to where Jonathan is. Tell him what just happened."

"I just got a call from *Good Morning America* to discuss logistics for Mr. Sisley's appearance tomorrow morning," Charlie said as he sat down beside me on the couch. It groaned under our combined weight. I imagined that we made quite a sight together, stuck knee to knee, on a couch that was never meant for so much combined human flesh.

"What the fuck?" I said to him.

"No idea," he responded.

I turned to Wanda, who was staring at me with her eyebrows raised in expectation of an explanation. "You can't think I would—" I stammered.

"Well, then, who did?" she asked, standing with her arms crossed like a schoolteacher dealing with a spitball that had suddenly landed on her desk.

"Well, what did you say to the guy?" I asked Charlie.

"I told her it was the first I'd heard about it and I needed to get back to her," Charlie said, allowing my sexist assumption to just slide away.

"You didn't ask her anything about who made the arrangement?" I asked.

"No. I figured one of the two of you did," he said. "I don't always know what's happening around here." It was an accusation made in Charlie's frank way—without guile, without anger. Just laying a fact out there, just in case Wanda didn't know it.

"I can call Frank Liebowitz, the executive producer of the show," Wanda said to me. "Unless you know someone else?"

"Nope," I said. I knew Liebowitz as well. But I figured I'd rather have BeeLine use a chit with him.

Wanda dialed him up on the phone and luckily got him immediately. She told him that she had just heard that her CEO was somehow booked on the Wednesday show but that she hadn't made the deal and no one in her shop knew anything about it. I watched her face to try to discern what she was hearing in response. Her head started shaking left to right, and a slight smile of amusement touched the edge of her mouth.

"Frank, I need your help in killing this," she said. "I'm sure you understand that it is not a good idea for Mr. Sisley, faced with a lawsuit, to appear on national TV. I can get our general counsel to call you or to call Mr. Fallow directly if you need that."

Fallow? Fallow was the president of the network. And now I knew what had happened. Stupid Bradford Sisley had called up his buddy, the head of ABC. Who knows? He might have been fishing for one of the personal testimonials I had asked him to round up, not realizing that the head of a national network would never put himself in such a position. But before the conversation had ended, Sisley had made a deal to appear on *GMA*. He probably thought it was a real coup, the kind of thing that neither Wanda nor I would ever be smart enough or competent enough to do. I wondered when he was going to triumphantly lay it on us.

"Right," Wanda said after a moment more. "That'll be great. No muss, no fuss. I'll tell Bradford."

She listened again and then laughed in a friendly, warm way.

"Wonderful, Frank," she said. "I owe you one. I won't forget this. Best to Betsy. Right. Right. Talk to you soon."

She hung up the phone, her head still shaking in disbelief.

"Well, Jonathan, seems that your client is handling his own PR these days," she said. "He called Mark Fallow and offered to go on *Good Morning America* to tell his side of the story. Fallow was surprised, but he passed it on to Liebowitz at *GMA*. Liebowitz has agreed to say that it just doesn't fit into the schedule this week. As a favor. To me."

A little one-upmanship on Wanda's part. She was bragging to me about what she had just done. I knew I could have done it as well. Killing a story is hardly brain surgery.

More and more I was feeling hostility from her. Not totally unexpected. I wasn't exactly producing any miracles so far or making things any easier for Wanda. Actually, I was kind of in the way. In some ways, I was glad to see her annoyance—it made her more human, less controlled, less cool. I'd pissed her off several times, and now she was trying to stick it to me a little bit. Killing the *GMA* appearance hardly was an important achievement on her part, but she was clearly relishing the fact that I had failed to keep my client in check and she had had to clean up the mess.

"Well done!" I said, as if I hadn't noticed the little barb.

"And I assume you'll let Bradford know about the scheduling problem?" she said, handing me the hot potato.

"Sure thing," I said. "I obviously need to have a broad chat with him about going around me."

"Indeed," she said with a slightly triumphant smile. "You've noticed, I assume, that he doesn't have a Twitter or Facebook account."

I actually hadn't, because I never remembered to think about things like that.

"The lawyers decided that several years ago," she continued. "After he made some misleading financial projections on Twitter. But he's kind of like a tiger on a leash. He has so much confidence in himself and his own judgment that he's constantly trying to break free and regale the world with his amazing insights. Don't feel bad about losing control. He probably figured, since you're not used to his restrictions, he could get past you."

"And he did," I said, trying to use a little humility to once again build bridges with Wanda.

I started to wiggle my way off the couch, which was not easy with Charlie crushed against me. Suddenly, I felt his big hand on the back of my arm, bringing a rush of forward momentum. It was the first time in several years that I felt graceful in leaving a sitting position. It was like having one of those lift chairs I had seen on TV, throwing the old man up and out of his comfortable recliner.

As Charlie and I started to leave Wanda's office, I heard her give an order that would close the loop on her dealings with Frank Liebowitz at *Good Morning America*. "Charlie," she said, "tell the advertising folks that we want to increase the corporate campaign buys on *GMA* next quarter by fifteen to twenty percent. Take it out of the *Today* show buy. Okay?"

"Got it," said Charlie, expressionless as he ushered the old fat guy out the door.

One hour later I got a second emergency summons to Wanda's office. Her TV was tuned to a San Francisco midday talk show. The three hosts were sitting in their fake living room set looking stunned while the unmistakable voice of Bradford Sisley was booming over a telephone hookup.

The tiger was loose again.

"You people in the media are such patsies," he was saying. "You'll believe anything that anyone says. I mean, I'm sitting here watching your show, and the three of you have decided I'm guilty of what this woman has said. You've already convicted me. You're taking everything she says at face value and sitting there—so smug, so smug—passing judgment on me. You don't know me. I've never met any of you. But you hear all this bad stuff from some nobody woman or you read some fucking bullshit on the internet, and you just decide—"

One of the hosts, a classic Fox News–style woman newscaster with lacquered hair and too much eye makeup, interrupted him. "Well, maybe you should come on our show, Mr. Sisley, and talk to us." The producers were probably back in their broadcast booth, thinking how great the ratings would be if Sisley came on. But having already failed to bleep out the words "fucking bullshit," they also knew they'd have to broadcast this loose cannon with an audio delay.

"I don't have time to come on your sad-ass show," boomed the voice. "I've got a company to run—a company which, by the way, does a hell of a lot for this town. Why don't you ever cover that story? I fucking dare you to tell people some good news about me!"

"Gotta stop this," I muttered as I headed out the office door to try to get to Sisley's office. There are times when there are no good options except to pull the plug. This was obviously one of them.

I did the best I could, given all my infirmities, to get down the hallway quickly. I could hear the sound of someone's feet, presumably Wanda's, coming up behind me. I knew I was probably blocking her way, since I had to stretch my cane way to the side to safely make any speed. One woman started to leave her office but dashed back in to avoid the rampaging stampede created by our awkward rush down the corridor.

I yelled at a closing elevator door, "Hold that elevator! Emergency!" The door briefly closed and reopened. As I hobbled in, Wanda pushed me with surprising strength to make room, crushing me against the frightened young man whose quick instincts had held the car for us. The hideous crow's head of my cane was right in his face, its scary red and green eye only inches away, and my bulk had him pinned against the elevator wall.

"Wow, dude. Can I do a selfie with that angry bird?" he asked.

"Later," I said. "We're kinda in a rush here."

"Awesome!"

When the door opened at the next floor, Wanda elbowed her way around my bulk and rushed out. As I struggled to catch up with her, I was imagining an ugly scene where she had to wrestle with Bradford Sisley for control of the phone. But Wanda was smarter than that. She simply stopped at Sisley's assistant's desk and cut the phone call off from there. When there are gatekeepers, just shut the gate.

As I arrived on the scene, Sisley was yelling through the intercom to reconnect the call.

"Don't, Colleen," said Wanda. "I'll go explain it to him. I'll take the blame."

"No, I'll take the blame," I said. "Let's not even tell him that you actually did the dirty deed. All my doing. Get the hell out of here, now!"

She stared at me for a second but was much too smart to hang around for what was about to ensue. Without a word, she turned tail and got out of the executive suite. I looked at the assistant, a no-nonsense middle-aged woman named Colleen whom I had interacted with during previous BeeLine adventures, and put my finger across my lips. She nodded.

Bradford came roaring out the door of his office.

"What the fuck is happening out here?" he screamed. And then he stopped, apparently surprised to see me standing next to Colleen's desk. He strode forward and grabbed the lapel of my dirty suit. *"Did you cut me off, you fucker?"*

There haven't been many moments in my career—although there have been a few—when, faced with an enraged client, I let my own nasty temper explode in equal fury. It's a dangerous thing to do in the job-security department. But when you don't really care whether you keep the job—or, as in this case, if you kind of want to lose the job—it definitely is worth doing. It feels so damn good not to let the other guy shit all over you while you lie down and just take it. And most of the time, yelling back actually works. Screaming bullies hate having someone take them on, but they respect it. And if they are really powerful people—like Bradford Sisley—they can even enjoy the return volley because it happens so rarely.

I slapped his hand off my lapel. *"I damn well did,"* I yelled back. "And I fucking shut down your stupid star turn on *Good Morning America,* as well. What the hell do you think you're doing?"

The expression on his face was worth any price I would pay for my insolence. He was like a kid who had just been slapped in the face. He had thought he could surprise me with his *GMA* appearance, having kept me totally in the dark. Maybe he was planning never to tell, just appear on TV. But suddenly he had been caught—and he had no idea how he had been caught. And I was scolding him—yelling at him—for catching him in the act.

He grabbed my arm and dragged me, stumbling, into his office. He slammed the door behind us.

"How dare you talk to me that way in front of Colleen?" he snarled at me, his face inches from mine.

"What, are you afraid she might see that she can start talking back when you yell at her?" I snarked back. I had already started down a path of two men fighting mano a mano, not of a client and consultant disagreeing. I wasn't going to show any deference.

"You want me to fire you?" he said, keeping his face close to mine. I smelled Listerine on his breath. "I could fire you, you know. Talking to me like this."

"Fine, fire me," I said. "You hired me to help you get through this mess. I've been working my goddamned butt off to quiet things down, get you out of the media, let things cool off. And it was working fine until you went rogue on me. We were fading off into the fucking sunset. Now, with your idiotic talk show appearance, we're going to be a story again. And going on *GMA*? Really?"

"You're not getting my message out!" he screamed. Spit hit my cheeks. I moved quickly to wipe it off. As I raised my hand, he flinched, as if I was going to hit him or something.

"Fuck your message!" I said. "It stinks, your message. Your message is one of the stupidest things I've ever heard. It will bring down the wrath of the universe on your head. We are in the middle of a fucking wave of feminist outrage. This is their 'No more of this shit' moment. Everyone is on their side. Dissenters are eaten alive. You cannot—in the middle of this tsunami—declare that you are being victimized. No man in the world could get away with that right now. And *you*? *You* of all people? You're going to be the guy everyone trusts? Feels sorry for? Are you fucking kidding me? You're nuts."

"Someone has to stand up!" he said, his voice dripping with frustration. For a moment he seemed to have slipped from hot anger to almost desperation. It looked like his eyes briefly welled with tears.

He walked away from me, waving his hands in frustration. He slapped his hands onto one of his windows and started to bang his head against it. The window looked out over his vast corporate campus, the brown California hills in the far background. Big, powerful man looking very little, reduced.

"Not you! Not now," I said, lowering my own anger. "You've gotten caught up in one of the great movements of our life. Settle the case and get out of the way. You've got to get off the list of bad guys as fast as you can. Become invisible. Become forgotten."

He paused. I thought maybe I had broken through.

"*Bullshit!*" he shouted into the window. "I am not giving in to what is complete *bullshit*!"

"Oh, *is it*?" I screamed back at him. "There's a tape, Bradford. The hotel has a fucking security tape of what happened in that elevator. So tell me—who's gonna be the bullshitter when we all see that tape?"

He didn't move. His hands still pressed against the window. I couldn't see his face. I couldn't tell whether the tape scared him or pleased him or whatever. I thought I heard him mutter something like, "Won't that be interesting!"

He spun around and started walking back towards me, shaking his finger at me. "I am not going to fire you right now, Jonathan. Too bad for you. I know that's what you want. Tough shit. I've got other plans for you. I've got some people working on finding out who this Katherine

Davis is and what game she's playing. I'm going to need you to crucify her once we get the dirt on her. You're gonna help me do that."

"Well, Bradford, if you really dig up dirt on this woman, you let me know," I responded. I figured it would never happen. "But in the meantime, I'm not going to stay around if you pull any more shit on me like you did this morning or the fucking *GMA* thing," I threatened. "I'm not risking my reputation on you spouting off."

"Fine. I'll stand down for the moment," he said. "But once I get the dirt on this bitch, you promise me you'll be my guy."

Easy promise to make; easy promise to break. And I wanted to make one more stab at getting him to settle. I had an idea.

I got Wanda to take me to the Executive Dining Room. Unlike the cafeteria I'd gone to with Charlie, it wasn't miles away across hill, dale, and jogging tracks. It was a civilized elevator ride up to the top floor of the BeeLine Headquarters building. Nicely spaced tables covered with linen and fancy place settings. Judging from the expansive view, Wanda's favorite table was directly above Bradford's office. I hoped that maybe it was her favorite table because she had a listening device embedded in her shoes.

Because she was facing out towards the slanted November sun, Wanda put on her sunglasses. So, like the day before with Charlie, I was getting no reading on reactions to what I was saying. I was only seeing a distorted Jonathan in her eyes.

I told her that Bradford and I had had a vigorous conversation about his efforts to grab a microphone and that he had promised to behave. She asked if he had bought the story about a scheduling problem on *GMA*. I lied and said yes. I didn't think I wanted to tell her that I had laid claim to canceling his appearance myself. That was a lie to him that had suited my purpose at the time. Now it was a different lie to her, also for my own convenience.

"And how are you doing getting him to settle the case?" she asked. She had ordered a kale salad, which she actually seemed to be enjoying. Hard to imagine.

"Not well," I acknowledged. "I told him about the possibility of a tape. I gave him a host of reasons why he wanted to get out of the headlights as quickly as possible, and for a moment, I thought I had him. But he slipped away. He says he's got some people investigating Katherine Davis. I'm afraid that until that effort dead-ends, he won't even consider settling."

She chewed her kale in silence, waiting for me to continue.

"But that will take too long," I said.

"What will?"

"Getting to a dead end on Katherine Davis. If I know my private investigator friends at all, they are very good at stretching out their hourly fee arrangements. This could take months."

I paused to take a big bite of the delicious elk meatloaf, which had been served with roasted fingerling potatoes and sautéed broccoli rabe. Not exactly a light lunch, but irresistible.

"And so what if it takes a few months?" she asked.

"Farber doesn't sit still. Every day is a danger," I said. "Another woman will pop up. Another Mary Chan—or a bunch of Mary Chans—will open up a broader can of worms about the company. Plus, even though he's promised to shut up, that doesn't mean he won't say or do something really stupid.

"Think about it. If this case could start to move towards settlement in the next week, the threat of a new disaster lessens exponentially. Until it's settled, the lawsuit is like a pile of dry twigs waiting to be lit into a big fire. If we can throw a bucket of water on the twigs, the fire danger goes way, way down."

She nodded, but a mouthful of kale and walnuts prevented any commentary.

"So here's my question for you," I said. "Who could turn him around on the idea of settlement? Or even force him to settle? Is there a way of taking this to the board or someone powerful on the board and getting them to lean on him?"

That was my big idea. The board. I had seen it work in other cases.

It is very difficult to change the mind of a CEO when he is determined to follow a particular path. Within the walls of a corporation, the CEO is king. There are no internal checks and balances or power centers able to move a CEO in a direction he doesn't want to go. If a CEO is headed for disaster, no one inside can force his hand, particularly in a place like BeeLine, where, over the years, people who had put their heads up had had them cut off.

The only countervailing force in a corporation is the board. In most instances that force is weak, since board member selection is strongly influenced by the CEO. Cronyism is common. Add to that the fact that few board members have the time and energy to really know what is going on. And CEO's rarely do anything to change that situation.

But I had seen it work. I told Wanda about a couple of instances. The auto company where the board forced the CEO to fire his buddy, the executive vice president for operations, whose negligence had led to a record-breaking recall. And the board decision to reverse a chemical company's opposition to new air pollution standards. It could be done; all it took was one or two board members with conviction and guts who would lead the rest of the board in the right direction.

"Have you looked at our board?" Wanda asked. I lied and said that I had.

"It's the ultimate back-scratching board. Look at who's there. The banks we bank with; the universities we fund; the technology geniuses we partner with or whose companies we have purchased along the way. One of those corporate governance watchdog groups gave BeeLine a *D* for the quality and independence of its board."

"Didn't the board care about the poor grade?"

"Mostly they just listened to Bradford's calling the grading process a liberal/socialist plot. No one challenged him on that view. But they went through the motion of asking Carter Shepherd, the general counsel, to prepare recommendations. He did, and, so far, nothing has happened."

Her shrug expressed resigned impotence.

"Okay, if not the whole board, what about an individual

or a couple of individuals from the board?" I asked. "Let me try it this way: If I asked you to convene a couple of folks who might have the ability to pressure Bradford from fighting this case to settling it, who would be in that group? Who would he listen to or, better yet, feel *obliged* to listen to?"

She sat for a second, fork poised in midair. She lowered her head to glance through her sunglasses at my plate. It was hard to imagine, but I had fallen behind her in eating my lunch. In my eagerness to tell my war stories and sell my idea, I had put down my utensils. I think we were both shocked to see how little I had eaten.

"Let me think for a second, okay?" she said. "You finish your meatloaf; I don't want you to go hungry. I need to think this through."

I appreciated the chance to give my plate my full attention. The food in the Executive Dining Room was a whole world apart from the cafeteria fare I had shared with Charlie. While the portions were not generous, at least not by my standards, the quality of the cooking was first-rate. The elk meatloaf was richly spiced and topped with a zesty tomato-based sauce, the fingerling potatoes had been roasted with olive oil and herbs, and the broccoli rabe was done to perfection—just a hint of crunch.

I decided I would definitely want to see the dessert menu.

When I looked up from my plate, Wanda seemed to be looking at me, perhaps mesmerized by my ability to down my food with impressive speed. She smiled.

"I can think of two possibilities, and I'm pretty sure I can get both of them for you," she said.

"Who?"

"Carter Shepherd, our general counsel, and the Board Chair Ben Langerfeld."

"*The* Ben Langerfeld?" I asked. He had been one of the great men of American business when I was first starting out in my career. In the Reagan and Bush years, he was the go-to guy for corporate America. In those days, if Langerfeld endorsed a policy, the rest of corporate America could be counted on.

"I thought you said you had looked at our board," Wanda said. A slight frown appeared above her sunglasses.

Busted. "Sorry," I said. "I didn't connect that it was that Ben Langerfeld."

"Uh-huh," she said in a tone that communicated how lame my cover-up lie was.

"So why those two?" I asked. I was pleased to see Wanda waving for the waiter. She probably just wanted to clear the table before I started devouring the plates. But I was looking for that dessert menu.

"Well, let's start with Carter. He is an absolutely terrific lawyer," she said. "And he has gotten this company out of any number of messes. Bradford knows that Carter is smart and a straight shooter."

She suddenly smiled.

"What's the smile?" I asked.

"Well, it's an interesting story. Carter Shepherd is a blue blood. He comes from a family that stretches back to colonial days in Connecticut," she said with slight contempt.

"Williams College, Yale Law, Jones Day. Classic. Not the typical bio for this industry.

"For years he was the ultimate corporate tight-ass, showing up for work in tailored suits and ties and staying aloof from any unnecessary social interactions," she continued. "Totally an oddball in this place. Bradford used to call him 'the WASP from Wilton.'"

"But Bradford respects him, you said."

"The guy's a genius. You know all the legal trouble we had in the past. It's been a lot quieter the last four or five years since Carter took over. He comes up with brilliant legal and political strategies that have kept us from all kinds of deep doo-doo."

"Okay, so he'll know that a settlement makes sense," I said.

"Hold on," Wanda said, her mouth returning to a smile, which had a slightly wicked cast. "I'm not done. There's more to the Carter story. Suddenly, about six months ago, Carter Shepherd walked out on his wife and kids and is now in a passionate new relationship with, how do I say this appropriately, a very flamboyant younger man."

"Meaning like he wears dresses and heels?"

"Not in public," she said with her wicked smile. "At least not the public places I go to."

"But definitely a major nelly queen," I said. "A sissy boy."

"You've obviously avoided diversity training."

"I don't need it," I said, patting the sides of my belly. "I'm diverse."

"Well, the new Carter Shepherd is proudly gay. The Ivy League haircut has turned curly and redder, and the clothes are more Barneys than Brooks Brothers. And Mr. Antisocial now turns up everywhere holding hands with his boyfriend—sorry, fiancé—and can't wait to get on the dance floor. Now, don't get me wrong. He's still an arrogant, unapproachable guy, but he's maybe more comfortable in his skin. Bradford's new name for him is Bruce."

"Apparently, Bradford could use some diversity training."

"Wait till you see Carter," Wanda gloated. "You'd never know that he used to look like a Young Republican."

"Great, I'll be sure to ask him for his tailor. But where do you think he would be on settling?" I asked, trying to get back to business.

"Oh, he's got to be totally there. He has to be worried that Bradford is damaging the company's ability to operate politically. And he knows his boss well enough to know the very real possibility that he's guilty. I wouldn't be surprised if there haven't been some settlements before, but Carter would never talk to *me* about something like that. He's never been very comfortable with women."

"And what about the chairman?" I asked.

"Oh, the chairman *absolutely* loves women," she said, rolling her eyes. "He's one of those men whose hands just seem to have a lot of accidents."

This is was not where our conversation was supposed to be going. But maybe for the first time, Wanda and I were having a little fun.

"Ben Langerfeld? Ben Langerfeld is a letch?" I asked in amazement.

"Mr. Business, himself."

"Gee, I can remember when he was the biggest name

in American corporate life. I'm actually pretty excited to get to meet him."

"Well, you'll be surprised at what you get. He's not the gray-suited, authoritative person you have in your head. He's more of a slippery, hard-to-pin-down kind of guy. But you'll see. The main thing is he adores Bradford. Ben thinks of Bradford as a twenty-first-century incarnation of who he once was. Bradford has loved having him as board chair for the past four years—they do a father-son thing. Whatever Bradford wants, Ben tries to provide."

"So why do you think he might be helpful? Won't he just go along with Bradford?"

"That would be his instinct if it was a business issue. But this is not. So I think there's a chance he'll see the value of settling the issue. Look, Ben Langerfeld has been around long enough to know what protracted litigation can mean. And if he comes down on the side of a settlement, particularly if Carter is pushing for one as well, Bradford would seriously worry that he could be making a mistake. He might even worry that a Langerfeld-Shepherd duo would sway a few other board members."

"But you really don't know where either of them is right now on the issue?" I asked. The waiter had come to clear off the table and to give us the small dessert menus. Wanda tried to wave them away, but I grabbed one, struggling to stay focused on our conversation rather than look at what were undoubtedly wonderful sweet options.

"I'm pretty confident that Carter will want Bradford to settle," Wanda said. "Langerfeld is more of a gamble. But if you can get him on your side, he has the clout with Bradford to make a difference. Frankly, there's no one else I can think of who Bradford might listen to."

"So Langerfeld's the one we need to focus on," I said.

"Not we," she said. "You."

"What? What about you? What will you be doing?"

"Hey, you're the crisis manager guru. The five-hundred-dollar-an-hour expert. You've got creds. I'm a potted plant in this one. This one's a boys' game."

She pulled down her sunglasses and looked over them. She was reinforcing her words with her beautiful dark eyes. It was clear what she was saying: you're on your own, kid.

She slid the glasses back up. In the direct sunlight, I could see many lines in her face unsuccessfully hidden by her makeup. She had her years on her. But she was still a very attractive woman. At least to me she was.

"You should order a dessert," she said. "Or two, if you want. I'll get working on setting something up as soon as possible. Any scheduling problems at your end over the next two days?"

"Not if Bradford keeps his promise to behave."

"Promises, promises," she said as she stood up and walked away, checking her hair bun with her hand, making an exit worthy of a movie star in her tan pantsuit and black pumps. It was a walk that resonated with me.

That afternoon, a video of the San Francisco morning talk show—ending with the phone connection going suddenly dead—went viral on the internet. I had to admit that the segment, from beginning to end, was hilariously jaw-dropping. Bradford's diatribe, which had become laced with even more obscenities as Wanda and I had rushed upstairs, seemed to terrify the TV hosts, who looked skyward with saucer eyes at this booming angry voice from on high.

And then the voice stops, mid-sentence: "Every fucking crazy woman now thinks that . . ." The hosts look comically confused in the silence. One of them slams the side of his head several times as if trying to clear his ears to reestablish connection. And Bradford's words just hang in the air: "Every fucking crazy woman now thinks that . . ."

The lacquered blonde picks it up. "Well, this crazy woman now thinks that we ought to take a break while we reestablish contact with Bradford Sisley. Apparently, he's mad as hell, and he's not going to take it anymore."

As they break away, you can see the hosts bursting out in laughter. Two of them lift their hands for a high five. It's a perfect ending to a piece of absurdist theater.

Once the TV station had added the necessary bleeps, they put the whole piece up in the cloud for stations everywhere to access. It was great publicity for the show, whose name and call numbers were imprinted throughout the segment. All afternoon, CNN, Fox, and MSNBC made use of parts of it—as an eyebrow-raising example of failed anger management. And failed crisis management.

At one point, one of my competitors in the crisis management field went on Fox to analyze the decision to pull the plug on Sisley. After much "on the one hand" and "on the other," he seemed to come down on the idea that it would have been wiser to just let the rant die on its own. He said that the plug pulling had made the segment twice as interesting as it otherwise would have been.

I had to agree with him. It had been a dumb decision on my part, particularly in a world where social media would carry the clumsy censorship to the farthest corners of the universe. My belated effort to shut off the microphone looked foolish and ham-handed. It added extra spice to an already spicy story, in a Keystone Kop kind of way.

I realized that mine was a tactic from another age, an age when containment was possible. One station, one show: shut it down. But it was no longer possible to contain anything in this world. Every move came with a potential megaphone on it. And that changed everything.

So Bradford was back in the news, star of a very entertaining video. It didn't take but a moment for Wanda and Charlie and me to agree to stay in No Comment mode. I took only about half of the calls from my bemused reporter friends. I told the ones I talked to that the video showed how truly adamant Bradford was about his innocence: he really felt wronged by the accusation. But when they started to ask me about who had pulled the plug and why, I dodged and weaved. I didn't need that kind of story about myself.

Every time my phone rang, I'd check to see who was calling before taking the call or sending it to voice mail. I wanted to talk to Gerald Berger to find out why he wasn't reporting about the elevator tape. But I didn't dare stir up that issue for the media to chew on.

Meanwhile, the video from the morning talk show rolled on and on, providing the cable news channel with lots of good afternoon content.

But then in the late afternoon I saw that there was a call from Ruthie. My Ruthie. My loving until she wasn't anymore Ruthie. My faithful until she wasn't anymore

Ruthie. My supportive until she wasn't anymore Ruthie. My ex-wife. The mother of my only child. Someone who was never easy to ignore.

I really didn't want to talk to her right now. Ruthie was expert at yanking on my guilty strings. It was part of her Jewish heritage. So was the loving warmth that had enveloped me in the first ten years or so of our marriage. It had been like being married to one of Broadway's classic Jewish mamas—a woman full of devotion, concern, wisdom, and chicken soup.

But the last ten years of the marriage were different. They were characterized by reproach and recrimination. And Ruthie's disappointment—her constant bottomless sorrow at how I was failing her and our daughter, Sandra. It wasn't that I had changed; she just became fed up with my single-minded devotion to work. I was absent a lot, and even when I was home, I wasn't. Work was the one thing in my life that had ever made me feel good about myself. And as Ruthie made me feel smaller and smaller at home, I fled even more into the world of work, where I was someone, where people listened to me, where no one made me feel inadequate or guilty.

Oh, Ruthie! Kinky-headed, sharp-eyed, quick-tongued Ruthie. The only girl who had ever looked at me with real love in her eyes. She didn't care that I was fat and ugly. She shared my love of history, my passion for movies, my opinionated take on everyone from world leaders to the guy who owned the dry cleaners on the corner. We talked and laughed for hours, creating our own little world where we were uniquely wise, funny, and interesting. Everyone else was flawed, or stupid, or contemptible. We were way above the hoi polloi who inhabited the rest of the planet.

When Sandra came, things started to change. Ruthie had a new partner in life. And as much as I tried to embrace my little girl as the third side of a solid family triangle, I really didn't know what to do with her. She wasn't funny or witty. She was a child, a mere half person, who, frankly, bored me. I didn't want to play with her; I wanted to get back to the newspaper. I figured that once she grew up, we would become friends. She would become another Ruthie. But my years of indifference did their damage. Sandra saw me as a stranger. Because I was.

When she had turned seventeen, I decided it was time to try to build a bridge. I dug deep into our bank account to take Sandra to Europe, to go on the grand tour to London, Paris, and Rome, with Madrid thrown in because I had a favorite restaurant there. But museums and historical sites bored her. Mostly she wanted to window-shop in the fancy parts of the cities and find expensive cafés for us to sit in.

I actually didn't mind avoiding the long marble corridors of the museums. I'd seen them all, and my feet and knees were already starting to deteriorate. So we worked out a system where we would start at the expensive café. I would sit quietly nursing wine while she explored the high-end stores.

The principal activity that brought us together emotionally during our trip was eating. She ate lightly, but she appreciated food. Lunch and dinner became our bonding moments. We would strategize about ordering, making sure to maximize opportunities for trying multiple dishes on the menu. And then, as we ate, we would reverse engineer what the chef had done, speculating about how the spices and fresh ingredients had been brought together. Exploring French, Italian, and finally Spanish food gave us something to talk about, something where I as father had knowledge to impart, knowledge that Sandra wanted to absorb.

For the last couple of years of my marriage, Sandra and I worked to sustain our special culinary relationship. Eating was really the only pleasurable activity we shared. But by the time she came back from her freshman year at college, she had taken up a vegan regimen, insisting that all the other food groups were dangerously toxic. The aggressive vegan and the obese glutton could no longer be happy dining partners. Instead of bonding over food, we fought about it. And with food gone, we had nothing else to talk about.

Now both Ruthie and Sandra were on their own trajectories. Ruthie was remarried to Nate, the official reason for our divorce, since they had been having an affair for years. They were somewhere out in New Jersey, running their own accounting business. And Sandra was living near her mother, teaching Pilates (or doing Pilates, or practicing Pilates, or coaching Pilates, whatever. I had no idea; the whole thing was a mystery to me).

I knew that a call from Ruthie couldn't possibly be a good thing. And since I was already feeling a knot of guilt in my gut for having made a stupid decision to pull the plug on Bradford's TV-show rant, the last thing I needed was to talk to Ruthie. I knew that guilt was her most potent weapon, her go-to tool. And if she wanted something from me—which she undoubtedly did—she would have a huge advantage at that moment because of how badly I was feeling about myself.

But I couldn't ignore the call. She would only keep trying.

"So, what corrupt corporation are you working for now?" she asked.

"Can't tell you. Then you'd know to hate them. This way I might fool you into liking them."

"It's not Walmart, is it? Are you in Arkansas?"

"No, Ruthie. I'm nowhere near Arkansas."

"So you're not in Texas either. That's near Arkansas, you know."

"Thanks for the geography lesson, Ruthie. Just tell me why you called."

"Not feeling chatty today, Jonathan?"

"Ruthie, c'mon, I'm busy. What do you want?" I found myself staring at a smiling Renata. She was out on some golf course, holding a large trophy over her head. Give me strength, Renata. Make me a winner, too.

"It's about Sandra, your daughter," Ruthie said with a motherly sigh. "She's been working in that Pilates studio for over a year now, you know?"

"Uh-huh." I was surprised it had been that long.

"Well, the couple that own the studio are splitting up, and the man wants the woman to buy him out. But she doesn't have enough cash and doesn't want to stretch out some sort of long-term payout. I've run the numbers for her, and she really can't do this."

Suddenly, I saw myself owning half a Pilates studio in central New Jersey. If I did, I could never dare show my face—and my body—as the proud new owner. Not that

I would ever want to walk into a Pilates studio. The only time I ever saw one, it had looked like a place set up for enhanced interrogations.

"So they're giving Sandra a chance to buy his half of the business!" Ruthie said proudly. "Nate and I can give her some of the cash she needs, but she needs another one hundred and fifty thousand dollars to make it work. With that much cash buy-in, she can handle the bank loan payments."

"You and Nate have run the numbers?" I said.

"Of course," she said. "And it works. For the business. For Sandra. Your daughter."

That little rhetorical twist, "your daughter," was pure Ruthie. I obviously did not need to be reminded that Sandra was my daughter. But the phrase was there for a whole other purpose: to remind me of my parental failure. I was being reminded of how little I had ever done, had ever given Sandra. My daughter.

"Why are *you* calling me, Ruthie?" I asked. "Why isn't Sandra calling me directly on this?" I suspected I knew the answer to that question. Sandra did not have her mother's business sense or any way with numbers. Ruthie was undoubtedly orchestrating this entire deal on Sandra's behalf. And wisely, Sandra was trusting her mother to bring all the pieces together, knowing that she would be protected from any financial jeopardy.

"She would never, ever, ever ask you for anything, Jonathan. You know that. She does not want to be dependent on you."

"But she wants a one-hundred-and-fifty-thousand-dollar long-term loan from me, right?" I asked.

"Very long term," Ruthie said ominously.

"Like how long?"

"Like probably the rest of your life," said Ruthie, pausing for a moment to let me absorb what was being proposed. "Think of it as a down payment on her inheritance. You can help her now when she needs help, rather than her having to wait for some random moment when you drop dead from a heart attack."

"Well, maybe I should just drop dead now," I said. "Then you and Nate wouldn't have to chip in anything."

"Great idea," said Ruthie. "Sorry I didn't think of it myself." She always was such a kidder.

"I don't have that kind of money right now," I said. It was truthful in the sense of cash on hand. Obviously, if I really needed to generate that kind of cash—like if Sandra needed bail money or something—I could sell out some of my portfolio. But that money was supposed to be my nest egg for my retirement. And once I was finally done with Bradford Sisley, retirement might be very appealing.

"Is that a no?" said Ruthie. She knew enough about money and about me to know that what I had just said was a feint.

The truth was that I just was not in a generous frame of mind at that moment, not towards anyone, including my daughter. In order to give Sandra that much money, I would have to sacrifice some of my own security about my future. It wasn't, in truth, an enormous sacrifice, but on this particular afternoon, it was an annoying sacrifice. It made me feel put-upon.

And Ruthie's effort to position the whole thing as simply an early payment on Sandra's inheritance only added to my annoyance. Of course, it was true in its own way. But it took away any joy or self-congratulation that I might have experienced when, as was inevitable, I succumbed to the request.

"No, that is not a firm no," I said. "That is a 'you just hit me with a ton of bricks while I'm in the middle of something else and I'm not prepared to make this decision right now on the phone' no."

"Well, when can you get back to me?"

This was how Ruthie operated. Push, push.

"Next week sometime," I said.

"Okay," she said. "I'll send you the spreadsheet."

"You know I don't understand that shit," I said.

"Due diligence, Jonathan," she said. "Your financial manager will want to see it."

Right. If I could track him down in the Caribbean or Thailand or wherever he had gone that year to escape a New York November.

"But as you think about this, I want you to think about how much this will mean to Sandra," said Ruthie, wrapping up her pitch. "Owning this business will give her a boost up in life, a meaningful stake in something that she loves. It will be an enormous gift to her at a critical moment in her life. Fate is handing your daughter a real opportunity. You can make that happen. Or not."

"I get it, Ruthie."

"I hope you do, Jonathan," she said. "She's really counting on you."

Then let her give me a call, I thought. But, then again, it would be for both of us an embarrassing and painful conversation.

Like Scarlett O'Hara, I needed to think about it tomorrow. Not now. Not when I was feeling very uncomfortable with myself. Disappointed in myself. Score one more for Ruthie.

One of the nice things about working on the West Coast is that the world pretty much shuts down at the end of the workday. Europe is sound asleep, and folks in the rest of the US are settling into their cocktails or their dinners. From a media perspective, most of the stories have been put to bed. And any response you may want to make or any new angle that you want to pitch can definitely wait until morning. Even in today's world of a global internet, there is a "can't do anything about anything right now" lull that starts around six o'clock Pacific time.

And so the calls stopped coming in. The pull-the-plug video had revealed a hard-talking, nasty Bradford Sisley. It was what it was. There was nothing more to add or subtract. And, for the moment, no one seemed to be covering the possibility of a recording of what had gone on in that hotel elevator.

So unlike most other crisis situations, there was no working into the night. No pizzas to be delivered. No huge plastic bottles of Coke. No plastic spoons and paper napkins. No bad Caesar salads in huge containers. No teeth-shatteringly sweet sheet cake with chocolate frosting.

So I had to find a bar.

Now, this is no easy task for a guy like me. In some towns there might be a quiet hotel bar that offers the homeless businessperson some room service–quality food in a place other than one's room. But over the years, those bars have gone downhill by trying to go uphill. First they installed flat-screen TVs silently broadcasting various sports events from every corner of the room. And then some of them started to offer live music—usually some local wedding pianist or sad-assed jazz trio with a housewife singer trying to make an extra buck.

Some of the national chain hotels that traditionally never offered liquor decided they were missing out. So they began to stick bars in the lobby or in the ugly room used for the complimentary breakfast. The result: a lot of socializing and sexual prowling underneath fluorescent lighting. These are not places where a guy can quietly nurse a scotch and then order a good hamburger or a plate of spaghetti.

When I was ambulatory, I could wander a neighborhood and look for the right kind of place. The search was actually part of the pleasure—even with the occasional adventure of wandering into a gay bar. Lesbian bars are okay, although they almost never have anything to eat. Gay men's bars are far too friendly and chatty. And some very scary men can approach a big, fat guy.

Now, on the fringes of San Jose in my corporate apartment, I was stranded. The flat was comfortable in a highly decorated sort of way: everything was tastefully sleek, covered in subtle tones of gray and sepia. The concierge service—which took care of all my personal needs, like laundry and shopping—had an extensive menu of order-in food of excellent quality. And the bar in the flat was always stocked. But drinking and eating in solitude can be lonely, even in luxury surroundings.

On Monday night, I had tried the fancy place where

Wanda and I had met. It was obviously a hangout for Silicon Valley executives. A clubby place, filled with people who knew each other and who loved talking shop. I didn't speak Silicon, and their ambitious maneuverings didn't encourage conversation with a stranger, particularly one whose appearance made him obviously irrelevant.

But on Tuesday, I was rescued by Frank Ferricelli.

He popped into my little office at the end of the day and said, "Hi, Jonathan. Frank Ferricelli. You probably don't remember me."

It took me a moment, but I most definitely remembered him. He had been in the Public Affairs Office of the SEC. In one of the BeeLine/Sisley crises I had weathered, Frank had been the government guy to coordinate with—the guy to approve when and how we could talk about the settlements and their meaning. Smart, straight talking, and super, super thorough.

"Of course I remember you, Frank," I said. "The only government guy I ever trusted." I reached my hand across Renata's desk, now covered with my clutter. I knew Frank wouldn't be offended if I failed to lift my butt in respect.

"Have a seat," I said. "Just throw that stuff on the floor." I had a habit of using chairs as temporary filing cabinets—easy access.

"What the hell are you doing here?" I asked as he sat down. He looked the same. A kind of classic DC bureaucrat look. Graying goatee trimmed around the mouth, wireless glasses, and a closely shaved balding head of hair. The button-down shirt and the khakis had probably served as his Washington outfit for casual Fridays. He definitely had not gone native in California.

"Been here nearly five years," he said. "Sisley had them recruit me. He said it was on your recommendation."

News to me. But then I thought I might have casually said they would be lucky to have a guy like Ferricelli.

"So, is it working out?" I asked. I wasn't going to deny my role in his changing his life if it had turned out for the better. I'd long ago learned that since you rarely get credit for the good stuff you actually do, you may as well take credit for good stuff you didn't do. Or in this case, didn't really mean to do.

"Yeah, it's good," he said in a neutral way, implying that it was not a triumph but also not a disaster. "My family loves being in California, the kids are doing well in school, and my wife found a consulting firm to join."

"And you?"

"It's fine here," he said with an expression of ill-disguised dishonesty.

I thought, this is a man who needs a drink.

Frank drove us to a place called The '49er Saloon. It was about twenty minutes in the opposite direction from the corporate campus, in a part of the urban sprawl that I had never seen. On my own, I would never go to a bar with a name like that. I'd figure it was meant for people who costumed themselves in Western clothes and played pool. In my worst nightmare, they might have even had one of those bronco-busting machines or a dance floor for couples doing the two-step.

The décor was, in fact, along those lines. But it was less about horses and lassos and more about mining. Lots of pickaxes on the wall, as well as huge metal sculptures that Frank later explained were pieces of mining equipment repurposed as art. It was definitely a saloon, with a long, polished wood bar and handsome vintage leather-tooled bar stools. Over the bar was a huge mural of people, horses, and covered wagons struggling through a mountainous snowstorm. No one had to tell me it was the Donner Party.

We were shown to a table by a lady in period costume, complete with a low bodice revealing the tops of pushed-up boobs. I was thinking this place belonged in some old restored ghost town selling itself to tourists as the Old West. But as we settled in—and I got my Macallan neat in a very respectable glass—I realized that the crowd in the place were just local folks out for the evening. There were families, older couples, clusters of both office workers and blue-collar folks.

I hadn't been in such a place in many, many years. My hangout in New York was a place for journalists. This wasn't like that. It was more like a London pub—a neighborhood tavern that had, for some reason, a mining motif, including small ore-laden rocks holding down the paper napkins. Someone had had a vision.

Frank was clearly glum. Something was making him discontented. So I started with the obvious—the topic I was most interested in.

"So how is it working for Wanda?" I asked.

"Fine. She pretty much leaves me alone," he said. "She knows I know what I'm doing, and I keep the BeeLine financial guys off her back about communications stuff." It didn't seem like Wanda was his issue. But she was mine, so I kept on.

"So, does the pretty lady have any kind of personal life?" I probed.

"There was, I'm told, a husband once, a Mr. Fletcher," he said. "But that was before she ever got here, back in her IBM days. Or before. Apparently, he was an artist of some kind."

"An artist as in paintings in a gallery?" I asked. I had trouble seeing Wanda hanging out with an artsy crowd in New York.

"Dunno," he said. "What I heard was that it was a short marriage when she was pretty young."

"Kids?"

"None that I know of."

And, I was thinking, no pictures in the office. Just pictures of Wanda at BeeLine events, smiling at Sisley's side or standing at some podium making a speech. The only relaxed and candid photo showed her cracking up with a bunch of people all holding cocktails at some resort. It probably had been an off-site meeting.

"You know that she's a skydiver," Frank suddenly offered, out of the blue, so to speak.

I probably said something like "No shit!" since this news blew me away. I really loved the audacity of the idea—the sheer incongruity of the carefully controlled woman I knew putting on one of those bulky, goofy uniforms with the crotch straps and the space cadet helmet and then throwing herself out of a plane. It was such a "fuck you/fuck this" kind of thing to do to wipe the corporate grime away. That was the photo I wanted to see—Wanda standing in her skydiving uniform, hair askew, helmet under her arm, smiling broadly in triumph at the end of the skydive. Wanda the queen of the skies. Wanda the test pilot. It was so hot!

"I hear she's also really good at chess," he added. "She's part of the company chess club, one of the only women. You can imagine the kind of chess players we have at BeeLine. I mean, we have a really serious geek brigade. But she apparently holds her own with the boys."

Which probably infuriates and embarrasses some of them, I was thinking. Good for her.

"What else? This is interesting stuff," I said.

He shrugged. "Nothing else that I know. Like I said, she leaves me alone, and we don't talk a lot. Just transactional things. I don't cause her any trouble, and she makes sure I get my just rewards."

"So you're satisfied with the pay and stuff?" I asked.

"Absolutely," he said. "I never dreamed I'd be making this much money, plus all the stock benefits. Amazing stuff."

So what was this guy's problem? We ordered another round of drinks, and I decided to do a test run on the Gold Digger Burger Platter, complete with both fries and onion rings, plus coleslaw. Frank said he was expected home for dinner. But his second beer got him talking.

Turned out that part of his discontent was classic to people who moved from government to the private sector. Working in government was deadly in many ways, the pay was never great, and promotions were glacially slow. But for someone like Frank, working in government also meant being a player in power games where the stakes were very high. And when you're on the government side, you're on the team that has most of the chips. Now, even though Frank was working for one of the hottest companies in the global tech sector, the stakes were only about money. He missed the feeling of the government's authority running through his bloodstream.

"And besides all that," he said, "It didn't take me long to figure out that a big reason that they wanted me was because I had such good contacts with the SEC staff. It's not like I'm a registered lobbyist or anything, but I sure have spent a lot of time checking out information for the company with the people I used to work with. And now that it's been five years, my contacts are drying up. So I'm feeling less and less secure."

"Hey, a guy like you who knows his way around financial communications can always get a job," I said, after swallowing a huge bite of the nearly rare hamburger covered in bacon, tomato, avocado, cheese, and a rich, spicy barbecue sauce. Good bun—sourdough, of course.

I was hoping that what I had said was true for someone of Frank's years. It's funny how years of experience work so well for a person's career until suddenly they equal "too old."

"Yeah, but my family wants to stay here," he said. "The demand for my kind of work in this area is pretty lean."

I knew he was thinking narrowly. He had had only one job outside of government, the job at BeeLine. And he thought his only possibility was the same kind of job in some other company. This was not a man ready to explore a change of life—a leap into some new situation where he could develop some other facet of himself, some hidden passion that lay waiting in his soul. I always called this the "open a cheese shop" option, since that was the dream I had never had the guts—or the energy—to pursue. Who would be able to resist buying cheese from the jolly fat man in the big, colorful apron standing behind tiers of counters brimming with cheeses from all over the globe?

"Jonathan, there's something more," he said with a sigh.

"More what?" I asked.

"More that makes me uncomfortable with my job," he said.

Uh-oh, I was thinking. Frank had been waiting to tell me something. He had been working up to it.

"Look, I know you're here for the sexual harassment suit—" he started.

"Sexual assault," I corrected him. One more man who didn't really understand distinctions that were not just little nuances.

"Right. I know you're here for that. But there's another crisis coming at this company—and at Sisley." He suddenly hesitated.

"I'm listening," I said to prod him forward.

"You understand about insider trading, right?" he asked. "'Cause what I'm about to tell you will make you an insider."

Did I understand about insider trading? I had seen two of my bosses hauled off in handcuffs in my first year at the big PR agency. I was fresh out of school and was serving as the lowest man on the totem pole in a project about a corporate acquisition. I had heard these guys talking about taking positions in the company to be acquired, and I had no idea that they were doing something illegal. So I told my brother-in-law, who always dreamed of becoming rich in the stock market, about the opportunity. I didn't have any money to invest myself; otherwise, I would have invested too. Who knew?

When the shit hit the fan and the Feds slapped the cuffs on these guys right in front of me, I figured my days were numbered. But no one thought to look at the kid who was doing the Xeroxing and putting the press kits together. And since this was long before e-mails, my name was on nothing that was gathered up. I was invisible in the investigation. But I had gotten my lesson in the topic of insider trading.

My stupid brother-in-law never did. For years, he continued to bug me for "investible information." Finally, he struck it rich in a biotech stock without my help.

"I know what it means to be an insider," I responded. "I never invest directly in anything. I'm in funds." This was true. It was a safe-haven decision that had made life very simple for me.

"Well, they cooked the books this past quarter. They've prebooked a lot of income and are hoping the next few months will be better. And I don't think it's the first time they've done it. I think they may have a hole that keeps growing and never gets filled in. Now everything is pinned on the Christmas season going gangbusters, but so far the retailers aren't making big orders. They're already sitting on lots of BeeLine products in their inventories. It's not good out there."

"So you're saying that a big write-off is coming," I said.

"More than a big write-off, Jonathan," he said. "You've heard of Sarbanes-Oxley?"

"Yeah, kinda, sorta."

"It came out of the Enron mess. It says that a CEO and a CFO have to sign all quarterly reports, attesting to their accuracy. If they lie, they can get up to ten years in jail. It's serious shit."

"And you're saying they've lied?"

"Yeah. Sisley and Bashari, the CFO. Certainly this past quarter. Maybe several quarters."

"Who knows about this?" I asked.

"They do—Sisley and Bashari—and a couple of people in the CFO's shop, one of whom clued me in. I'm telling you, Jonathan, if there isn't a bang-up fourth quarter, the whole house of cards is likely to come down," Frank said. He gulped down the last of his beer.

"Sisley will survive," I said. "He always does."

"He's the one who's been pushing it, Jonathan. The CFO has consistently advised against it. He can prove that. When fingers start pointing, they'll all be pointing at Bradford Sisley."

"He'll survive," I repeated. He was, after all, an expert at shifting blame and avoiding responsibility for bad things.

"He's a bad guy, Jonathan," Frank said, looking hard into my eyes. "Your client is a really bad guy."

Tell me something I don't know.

4

WEDNESDAY MORNING

Wanda had managed to gather the necessary people for a nine o'clock strategy session on Wednesday morning. As her security card opened the leather-covered door that led to the boardroom, she made a prediction.

"Langerfeld will already be there. Carter Shepherd will be late and come bursting in talking on the phone. And we'll have to make Bradford show up."

"Make him show up? We're discussing a strategy for *his* problem!" I lamely protested.

"He hates strategy meetings. Just comes in at the end and pronounces what he wants. That's how it works around here."

I love boardrooms. Almost as much as I love Gulfstreams. I remember my first boardroom—at the great chemical company DuPont when it was in its heyday. Lush green carpet, a huge mahogany table surrounded by luxurious leather chairs, gold-framed painted portraits of past corporate leaders, back to the original family founder.

Boardrooms are designed to express authority and

sage deliberation. They are the ultimate inner sanctum of corporate power and, occasionally, wisdom. They're sexy.

BeeLine's boardroom somehow lacked the magic. Blond wood everywhere. (Could I never escape it?) It looked like some designer had headed in an ultracontemporary direction but got redirected down a sidetrack of midcentury modern. The combo didn't work. I wondered if one of Bradford's wives had had a hand in creating the room. It had a slightly feminine feel.

And true to Wanda's prediction, the legendary Ben Langerfeld was already there, seated at the far end of the huge wood table. He was staring at his tablet. Except for occasional TV interviews, I hadn't seen him since his glory days. His once great square jaw was now softened by sinking jowls, but when he looked up at our entry, his bright eyes were untouched by the passing decades. They gave him a look of slight joviality. Also, intense intelligence.

"Wanda, my precious!" he said, spreading his arms. "Give the old guy a proper kiss."

As Wanda headed down the table, he smiled across the long span of the table at me. "Ah, the famous spin doctor. Nice to meet you."

Wanda dutifully gave him a two-cheek air kiss—apparently a ritual between them.

"Come on down and shake my hand, Dr. Spin," he said. "Old men don't have to rise, even for people with canes."

There was a definite royal feel to what was going on. His graciousness was tinged with an edge of condescension as he asked me whether I was being treated well and told me how honored he was to meet me. I replayed the compliment of feeling honored, as we acted out a Kabuki dance of flattering remarks.

Someone had ordered up breakfast pastries, fruit salads, cereals, yogurts, lox and bagels, etcetera, all displayed on a sideboard. It was enough food for ten people, creating an obligation for me to attack it with abandon. Free food at a meeting is a temptation I can never resist. I filled up a plate with goodies, even though I had enjoyed a bacon-and-egg breakfast at the corporate apartment only two hours earlier.

Langerfeld quickly directed our conversation to the matter at hand.

"How do you think this is going, Keaton? From a spin perspective?" he asked as I launched on my second chocolate croissant.

"I think we both"—I gestured at Wanda—"think it's going as badly as we expected." I didn't think it necessary to point out that it had worsened the previous afternoon because the tiger had gotten out of its cage and I had screwed up in my attempt to contain the damage.

"I assume it will quiet down for a while, at least until the trial starts," he said, totally ignoring my effort to include Wanda as a partner.

"A trial?" I responded. "Mr. Langerfeld, you don't want to even think about a trial. Going for a trial would be a public relations catastrophe. I would say that avoiding a trial should be a number one objective."

"I think our number one objective is to clear Bradford's name," he responded in a slightly contentious tone.

Wrong, wrong, wrong, I thought. That might be what Bradford wanted, but Langerfeld was supposed to be thinking of BeeLine and its reputation. How was I going to get him there?

"So you don't think there's a chance he might be guilty?" I asked.

"If he's guilty, he's only guilty of doing what men and women have always done. Flirting and petting is hardly a capital offense," he said. "I think Bradford's doing the right thing. It's time for someone to put his foot down and stop this harassment thing from demonizing what's been normal behavior from time immemorial."

I wondered for a moment whether Bradford had already spoken to Ben Langerfeld, had given him Bradford's party line. Maybe yes, maybe no. Maybe Ben and Bradford were just instinctually on the same sexist wavelength. Either way, we were not starting from a good place. I glanced at Wanda. She was watching Langerfeld with a blank face, as if he had just made a comment about BeeLine's balance sheet.

"I agree, sir," I said, hoping that Wanda would know that my agreeing with Langerfeld was a tactic. "But here's my concern. BeeLine sells a lot of products to women as well as men, and the last thing you want is for something to get in the way of anyone's loyalty to the company."

"You're thinking boycott?" he asked. "You know, my company ACM went through a whole boycott thing back in the seventies. Polluting the Susquehanna. Let me tell you about boycotts—they mean nothing. No impact on sales. Nothing."

I remembered the whole story about ACM and the Susquehanna River. His company had ended up paying an enormous fine and having to close the plant.

"Actually, I wasn't thinking about a boycott," I said. "You remember, I'm certain, how that Susquehanna River issue hung over ACM and its reputation for so many years. Even after the issue was settled. I'm certain you and other people at the time were positive you were right in fighting the government—and maybe you were right in a narrow legal sense. But in the long run, choosing to make a stand on the Susquehanna cost the company a lot of goodwill and money."

"There's no parallel to this situation," he said grumpily. "Solving this is much simpler and cleaner." He leaned forward and poked his wrinkled finger at me. "You want to solve this problem? Just make that woman disappear!" His hand made a shoo-it-away gesture.

This all had a definite Godfather feel to it. Like we should deep-six her in San Francisco Bay? Kidnap her, give her a brainwashing and plastic surgery? Sell her into slavery in Saudi Arabia?

I wondered for a second whether, in the murky days of Langerfeld's rise to power, there had been some nasty business. Maybe not murder, but how about bribery and extortion? Threats. He was clearly good at threats. I had no idea what he meant by those words about making a woman vanish, but I could see an opening for me.

"I totally agree!" I said. "Bradford should make a settlement with her, bind her to confidentiality, and be done with the whole thing. She disappears!"

A slight confusion crossed the old man's face. This apparently was not what he had had in mind. But I really didn't want to know what he had had in mind.

"Settlements are for when you're guilty!" he growled. "The only times I let my people make settlements were when some nincompoop had screwed something up. I never just gave in on a fight. Unless I absolutely had to because someone had really done something wrong!"

I was getting nowhere. In Langerfeld's world, Sisley had done nothing wrong; groping a woman was just a form of flattery. So settlement made no sense to him. It was only for when they had you dead to rights.

Okay, I had a card to play.

"There may be a videotape of what went on in that elevator," I said.

"What?" Langerfeld said with some alarm.

"A security system is in the elevator," I said. "If it was on, there could be a tape."

"But you don't know for sure," he said. "And you don't know what it would show."

"No," I acknowledged.

"Does Bradford know about the tape?" he asked.

"Yes," I said.

"And he still doesn't want to settle," he said.

"Correct."

"Well, that's good news," the great lion of business concluded with a sigh of relief.

Pivot, turn, go in another direction.

"Mr. Langerfeld," I said. "You know how dangerous the jury system is. I'm sure you know. Particularly these days. Bradford Sisley is a very rich, very powerful guy. There are juries that would love to take him down. I'm sure you've been seeing the media coverage. Bradford has a lot of enemies, people who want to bring him to ruin. You must understand what that's like. That kind of vicious envy that people can have towards a powerful, successful man."

Finally, I had pushed a button. The old man's bright

eyes squinted, and his mouth turned down. Something was rising up from an old memory bank. He sat quiet for a couple of seconds, his liver-spotted hands shaking slightly and his eyes gazing off to nowhere. His lips moved in some silent conversation he was having with himself, or maybe with some demon buried inside.

I asked if anyone wanted some coffee or food. That seemed to break his trance. He turned to Wanda and asked for some coffee. Then he turned to me.

"Listen, spin man," he said to me with clear annoyance. "You need to stop all this negative stuff in the press. You should be taking those stupid reporters out to lunch and plying them with booze or something. Or calling their publishers. I used to pull advertising from the newspapers I didn't like. Always worked."

Then, in an angry voice directed at Wanda, he demanded, "Where the hell is that pouf lawyer?"

Thinking about his "pouf lawyer" gave Ben Langerfeld a chance to escape the memory I had coaxed him into. His annoyance with me was, I knew, a good sign. I had touched a nerve. In his head, he had just replayed a tape where something had spun out of control because of hostile forces that tried to bring him down.

Powerful people can sometimes feel terrifyingly vulnerable. Often justifiably. It's something that goes with success and fame: a fear that everything can just be swept away. Gone in a flash.

I had no idea what had spooked him. I had never

heard a whisper of a scandal, personal or professional. But he clearly was spooked.

I was glad he wanted the lawyer to join the conversation. I needed the lawyer too, pouf or no, to build up the pressure for a settlement. And as if on cue, the door opened with a high-security whoosh, and in walked Carter Shepherd, barking orders on his cell phone. He wanted some kind of document forwarded to him by end of day.

"Sorry," he said absentmindedly as he ended the call and headed down the table to shake hands with Langerfeld.

"Ben, good to see you."

"Carter, how's your dad?" said the old man as he added his left hand to their handshake in a show of affection. I haven't spoken to him in weeks."

"Well, I haven't spoken to him in months. He and I are not seeing eye to eye much these days." Shepherd extricated his hand in a way that implied he wasn't terribly interested in Ben Langerfeld's bonhomie.

He turned to Wanda and then to me, pronouncing each of our names with a polite nod of greeting. He and I had never met before, but apparently none of the usual introductory niceties were on the agenda.

Since I had painfully risen to my feet at Carter Shepherd's entrance, I figured I might as well head for the sideboard and refill my plate. Why waste such a massive effort when there was free food a few steps away?

After Wanda's description of Carter, I had expected that he would cut a fairly outlandish picture. But to me he just looked like a slickly dressed California guy. All in black, with comfortable-looking buckskin shoes. His hair, which she had commented on, looked natural enough. There were a lot of flashy rings on his fingers, an opal stud in his right ear, and a delicate gold bracelet. But, of course, that meant nothing about sexual orientation in the twenty-first century.

It was all a little self-conscious, however. Sort of artfully drawn. The pants a little too closely tailored to his butt, the shirt opened almost too far, the glasses a little too hip. Okay, he did look a little gay. But he walked and talked like the straight Connecticut blue blood who still undoubtedly lurked inside his new persona. It looked to me like you could take the boy out of prep school but you couldn't quite take the prep school out of the boy.

He joined me at the sideboard to survey the spread of breakfast goodies. I noticed the flash of a big diamond on his left-hand fourth finger. I pointed to the glazed brioche and raised my eyebrows to signal "Delicious!" He frowned slightly and turned to the fruit bowl, picking out a piece of pineapple with his fingers.

"So, this morning we got a call from one of our biggest institutional investors. Not at all happy about the negative press," he said as he sat as far from Langerfeld as the long table allowed. This was not going to be a cozy meeting. Two of the principals had already decided to sit at opposite ends of a very long table.

He turned to Wanda. "Did you see the story this morning on CNBC?"

"Yes," she responded quietly.

"I didn't see it," said Langerfeld from the other end of the table. "What did they say?"

"It was about the rough-and-tumble culture at

BeeLine," responded Wanda simply. Actually, it had been a pretty devastating piece where several female ex-employees talked about the super-macho culture that spread out from the very top of the organization. Either Mary Chan or Sandra Farber, or perhaps the two of them working together, had stirred up some unpleasant stories and accusations. It was a very ugly picture that they had painted.

"Wait till some of the gay employees get interviewed," said Carter Shepherd. "Our anonymous e-box for diversity complaints has been filling up over the past few days. It's starting to feel like someone turned over a rock and all the maggots are scurrying around."

"Why should women or even the gays be complaining about this company?" asked Langerfeld with indignation. "Look at the two of you!"

No one knew exactly what to do with that one.

"Okay, but here's the other thing the institutional investor called about," continued Carter. "He wanted to know if corporate resources were being spent on this thing—lawyers, PR people, personnel, blah, blah. He even mentioned you, Jonathan, and asked who was paying your fee."

I happily couldn't respond because my mouth was full.

"What did you tell him?" asked Wanda.

"The truth, of course," Carter said huffily. "For the moment we're paying for everything. But I'm having someone check our contract with Bradford to see what it says. I have no idea if corporate staff is obliged to handle this mess he's made. Or, for that matter, if he does have to use outside legal resources, whether that would be on our nickel or on his."

Carter Shepherd's words and tone suggested that he had not been involved to date on the legal side of

Bradford's problems. I still didn't know who the guy had been using for legal advice. Or if he had any legal counsel at all. It was possible that he had made his own decision not to go see Sandra Farber the previous week. It was possible he was out there on his own, winging it, because he believed that he was doing the right thing and didn't want to hear otherwise from any lawyer.

"Well, there's an argument to be made that this is corporate's responsibility. Bradford was on company business at the time," said Wanda. "He was checking out a possible location for his global senior management off-site."

"Yeah, and Clinton was on company business too when he had Monica Lewinsky on her knees in the Oval Office. But he had to get his own lawyer and pay for it," said Carter.

"Bad analogy," barked Langerfeld.

I put my plate down midway on the table, leaving all of them at the two ends—Ben and Wanda at one end and Carter at the other. No one was asking my view, but I had seen it come out both ways. Sometimes the corporate officer was left to manage his situation, and sometimes the company took care of him. It actually said a lot about the person's perceived value. The fact that the BeeLine folks immediately went for the corporate checkbook was natural. Sisley was BeeLine. BeeLine was Sisley. But the institutional investor who had called Carter—the big shareholder—apparently saw the world differently. Little tremors signifying nothing? Or a potential earthquake?

"The board will stand behind our CEO! I promise you that," Langerfeld declared as if he were at a microphone.

"For Christ's sake, Ben," said Carter Shepherd, clearly

annoyed. "We're only talking about who acts as the lawyer and who pays the bills. No one's talking about Bradford's position in the company."

I wanted to steer the conversation away from this topic of who would pay the bills. It was something that they needed to discuss, but better without me. Also, it was not the topic we had gathered to discuss. I wiped my napkin across my lips to make sure that I didn't have any encrusted crumbs or distracting bits of brioche glaze as I entered the conversation. I wanted to take things in a different direction.

"If I might, I'd like to point out here a near truism in situations like this," I started. I looked down the table at Wanda and Langerfeld, knowing full well that Ben's reaction was going to be critical. "This is not likely to be the only such allegation of misbehavior. In fact, it is almost inevitable that someone else is going to pop up. And maybe more than one."

"You're making a very big assumption when you say that, Mr. Keaton," said Langerfeld, once again sounding threatening. "Bradford Sisley is a very honorable guy."

I turned to look at Carter Shepherd. I could see from his face, however, that I was on track. "Have there been other cases before, Carter? Have there been settlements before?"

There was a long pause while Carter, the pedigreed lawyer, considered his words. "You know, that is not the kind of information that I consider appropriate to share with an outside consultant who does not have legal privilege."

"Fair enough," I said agreeably. Lawyers love to do

stuff like that—secret cabal kind of thing, keeping out the riffraff who must not have been smart enough to go to law school.

I had been smart enough to go to law school. But I wasn't dumb enough to want to spend my life doing legal work.

But Langerfeld felt free of legal constraints. "Those cases were just disgruntled employees," he said. "Women who couldn't take a joke, or that one woman who didn't like that he touched her waist."

So fuck you, Carter, I was thinking. I got my answer. "So how come Bradford agreed to settle those cases?" I asked Carter.

He stared back at me, seemingly annoyed that his legal wall had been breached. After a brief pause, possibly to consider asserting legal privilege again, he responded. "He didn't have a choice. These were company employees, which means the cases were company matters. The company settled the cases, not Bradford. But this one is different. The accuser is not a company person. And the company is not named in the suit that's been filed."

"So the company cannot force Bradford to settle?" I asked.

"No. And, then again, yes," Carter responded in good lawyerly fashion. "No, in the sense that it is a personal matter and, in some ways, none of the company's business. But, of course, the board could insist that they want the issue to go away through a settlement."

"And fire him if he refused?" I said to complete Carter's thought.

"No one is firing Bradford Sisley from BeeLine," grumbled Ben Langerfeld from his end of the table.

Carter shrugged and slightly lifted his fingers. His expression said, "See? That's where we are."

"But, Carter," I said. "What do you honestly think he should do?"

Carter straightened himself up in his chair and folded his hands together as if to make sure that we understood whatever pronouncement he was about to make was well thought out and important.

"I am the general counsel of this company," he started. "My responsibility is to the shareholders of this company. Not to Bradford nor to anyone else who is currently filling any particular leadership role in this company. Speaking from that position, I strongly believe Bradford should settle this case quickly. Otherwise, it will be like a cancer that will spread throughout everything. This morning's CNBC story is the tip of an iceberg. We need to contain things by moving quickly."

"Have you told Bradford your view?" I asked.

"He hasn't asked me," Carter responded with a cold edge to his voice.

"He probably will when he gets here," I said.

"We'll see, Mr. Keaton. Won't we?" he responded.

Again, Wanda was right. Sisley had not shown up for the meeting. She, Langerfeld, Carter Shepherd, and I continued to sit in the boardroom accomplishing nothing while we waited for him to appear. I had gotten the answer I needed from Carter Shepherd. He had said the case should be settled. Ben Langerfeld had heard him say it.

The two of them restarted the argument about whether

the company should be footing the bill for Sisley's scandal, including my fees. Never did a 350-pound man try to look as unobtrusive as I was trying to be during that conversation. But they yelled up and down the long table as if I were invisible anyway.

Shepherd spoke on behalf of the institutional investor who had phoned him earlier. It was Sisley's mess: he had made it, and he'd have to pay to clean it up. Langerfeld was more benign towards his protégé. People make mistakes, but if they have been loyal and have made major contributions to the company, they deserved company support. It was, I decided, a generational difference between them. Langerfeld came from an older, postwar corporate world, when great companies were paternalistic towards their employees, tried to avoid layoffs, and provided generous pensions. Shepherd was the champion of the new corporation, which cared primarily about shareholder returns and had only a transactional relationship with employees.

But I also sensed a subtext running through Carter Shepherd's argument. He really hated Bradford Sisley.

"Think about it, Ben," he said. "Bradford doesn't settle. So, like Mr. Keaton here says, more and more dirt starts flying. Farber digs up more women. That e-box complaint line we've got is suddenly the lead story on SFGate.com. Other women in the company who he has offended through words or deeds start to come forward. And because we're still paying the bill, we deal with all the flak. Our lawyers have to work on it, Mr. Keaton becomes a permanent San Jose resident, and Wanda spends half her time on cleaning up messes. But we're supposed to be running a company.

"If we just stay away from it, we can put a wall between

us and Bradford. He can do his rant and rave and bad behavior as much as he wants, and all his ugliness goes on public display, but we just shrug it off. Not our business. And guess what? It's not our business."

I was thinking Carter was actually making a case for firing Bradford Sisley. I didn't really agree with him. Keeping an arm's length away financially from Sisley's legal and image morass was not going to keep the company out of trouble. I had a funny feeling he knew that as well. But, obviously, he couldn't openly make the case to the company's chairman that they should fire the founding father.

I wondered how much Carter actually hated Sisley. He undoubtedly had taken severe abuse over the years. And his transformation from "the WASP from Wilton" to "Bruce" had to have included many moments of Sisley's cruelty. He probably had a million reasons to want Sisley gone—including, maybe, knowing of the financial shenanigans that Frank had told me about the night before and the fact that Sisley had broken federal law.

Bradford had said there was a conspiracy to get him out. Could Carter be part of such an effort? Nothing he was saying in this meeting gave obvious evidence of that. But his antipathy was clear, as was his desire to put a protective wall between BeeLine and its founder. His little speech about only owing loyalty to the shareholder and not to any particular corporate officer was telling. Brutus killed Caesar to save the republic.

"I don't think you do that to your CEO," said Langerfeld. "You don't hang him out there because it could be messy. My company didn't do that me when I needed their support."

Man, I wished I knew what that was about. I looked over at Carter to see if he knew something I didn't. He had stood up and was staring down the long table at his board chair.

"I'm betting they supported you because you settled," he said, leaning forward on the table like it was the rail of a jury box. "I'm betting that they knew you would never drag your company into a swamp filled with alligators."

Ben Langerfeld sat immobile at the end of the table. He obviously did not wish to pursue the subject any further.

"I'm going to text Bradford to tell him to get his ass in here already," he said angrily. "I'm tired of waiting for him."

Five minutes later, Bradford Sisley, in the guise of Master of the Universe, threw open the door and headed for the now badly diminished banquette of food.

"Well, I see you all have been busy chewing things over," he said with scorn. He turned to Wanda and demanded, "Call Corporate Services and tell them to bring in more coffee and take the rest of this shit away."

He noticed the pile of plates and the sea of crumbs in front of me. "Unless you want to pick at the leavings one more time, Jonathan. I wouldn't want you to deliberate on an empty stomach."

"You really should have that last glazed brioche," I said. "They're amazing!"

He picked it up and smashed it on the plate in front of me. "No, fat man, it's all yours. In appreciation for all the good work. Did you see that piece of shit on CNBC this morning? Did you have anything to do with that?"

Before I could answer, Wanda bravely cut in. "Charlie

on my staff worked with them yesterday. The problem was all those women who came forward to be interviewed."

"Losers. They're all losers," Sisley grumbled. "They all deserved to be fired." Actually, I remembered from the show that most of them had quit in disgust.

Then he went directly at Wanda. "I bet they all were in your stupid Women's Network," he sneered. "I should just shut that damn thing down. It's just a bunch of bitches sitting around carping about how sad their lives are."

"Look, Bradford," I interjected. "You're up against Sandra Farber. This is how Sandra Farber works. It's her MO. She holds a press conference, women start calling her office, and she connects them with the reporters she knows."

He leaned down and put his face right in mine, literally spitting on me with his sarcasm. "I am so glad, fat man, that I pay you for such useful insights. Apparently, you don't know how to *do* anything to stop shit like that. But you sure can explain it well after it's happened. You're a fucking fraud, you know that."

He turned to Wanda, who was phoning in his coffee order. "Tell Charlie to pack his bags. I don't care if he's black. He's totally over his head." She spun away to finish her call.

Finished with us, he turned to Ben Langerfeld, who was watching the scene like a sphinx. "Ben, how are you?" he asked in a pleasant tone, a totally different person.

"Not so bad, considering."

"How's the golf game?"

"I'm losing it, Bradford. Old age has really fucked up my swing."

"We should go out while you're here."

"Didn't bring my sticks."

"Well, just as well. We seem to have a situation here. What do you think?"

The old sage of corporate America leaned forward to clasp his hands on the table. Throughout the morning, he had defended his boy and opposed making a legal settlement with Katherine Davis.

"Well, here's how I see it, Bradford," Langerfeld started. "I'm assuming you're an innocent man."

"You're damn right I am," Sisley insisted. He still had not sat down but stood rigidly with hands fisted at his side. "All I did—"

Langerfeld put up a hand to stop him. "Bradford, I don't want to know what you did or did not do. That is not my business."

Smart cookie. Easy to get through a deposition if you know nothing.

"As I said, I'm assuming that you're innocent. But you are a rich and powerful man, and when you are a rich and powerful man, people try to bring you down."

Bull's-eye! What was coming out of his mouth had come straight from mine! I actually *had* hit a hot button. One of the great leaders of American business was saying my words as if they were his own. In a consultant's world, this is as good as an orgasm.

"So you have a choice," he continued. "You can pay them to go away, or you can fight. Me, I paid more than once, and, trust me, it's a decision you'll go over and over again in your head for the rest of your life. But that's what I did."

"And you regret it, don't you?" Sisley probed.

"It was a different time and place," Langerfeld replied

somewhat ruefully. "In those days, we all had to be respectable, be a Boy Scout. Nowadays, you're not expected to be perfect. People can live with imperfections and peccadilloes. Look at Trump. Look at Clinton. He got away with it. So did Kobe."

I'd forgotten that Langerfeld had been a partial owner of the LA Lakers. He had to have been involved when basketball star Kobe Bryant was accused of rape and had to make a settlement.

"The problem is, Bradford, that there are lopsided upsides and downsides in something like this," Langerfeld continued. "You think there's a huge upside in winning a case, and there may be from a narrow perspective. Look at OJ. He won! He kept out of jail. But he didn't really win. He never could show his face in public again, and his life spiraled downhill anyway. So the upside thing can be an illusion.

"And then there's the downside. What if you go to court and you lose? Now the shit really hits the fan because a jury has stamped you a guilty man. And that will stay with you forever. A settlement, on the other hand, takes away all the risks. In our world, no one gives a damn about settlements. They shrug them off. Make excuses. Oh, he just settled to avoid the hassle. Oh, he just settled because it would be too expensive to win. Oh, he just settled because he has more important things to do with his time. Life goes on. No win, no foul."

"So you think I should settle this bullshit case?" Bradford asked.

"I think you should do whatever you think is best for you," Langerfeld said. "Were it me, I'd probably settle, just to get it out of the way."

The chairman and the CEO were not having what I would call a business conversation. Rather it seemed like one guy giving another guy some personal advice over cocktails or in the golf cart. Langerfeld still was failing to act as the chairman of BeeLine by speaking on behalf of the company's interest and telling the CEO to back off from a damaging confrontation. He was avoiding that responsibility.

But at least, in a convoluted way, he was encouraging a settlement.

Wanda grabbed her phone, looked at it, and headed out of the room. "Got to deal with this," she said. The security door whooshed shut behind her.

Langerfeld and Sisley continued their conversation, with Sisley insisting that his case was different from anything Langerfeld had ever faced. We were living in a time of mass hysteria about sexual harassment, and it was time to stand up and stop what Sisley called "reverse harassment." By switching to this narrative, he clearly got Langerfeld's attention and sympathy. They bantered back and forth about several great and mighty men who had fallen in recent months, and they shook their heads in sadness at their undeserved passing.

But every time that Sisley tried to bring his argument home that he was the man and this was the case to bring these injustices to an end, Ben Langerfeld would slip out of the noose that Sisley had tried to construct. He kept insisting that he wouldn't want to be the guy who went out there to win for mankind. It was a dangerous mission, and failing at it would be catastrophic.

So Sisley finally turned to Carter Shepherd, who had

been keeping himself busy on his BeePad. "So, counselor of counselors, ready to go to battle for me?"

Shepherd put the BeePad aside and leaned back on one chair with his long legs stretched out onto another. In this position, his outfit made him look like a lounge lizard settled into the celebrity room at a dance club. His was not the posture of a sycophant. He stared back at Sisley with what looked to me like malevolence, not a deep regard for his boss.

"Why didn't you call me immediately when you heard from Sandra Farber?" Carter demanded. "I could have made this go away if you had called me in the beginning."

"Because I knew what you would say. You would say I should make a deal. You always settle," Sisley sneered. Sweeping his arm around to include me and apparently noticing for the first time that Wanda was missing, he felt free to lay it on the line, "You two don't know how to fight for what's right. You buckle under. You're just pussies. You just open your legs and say, 'Fuck me! Fuck me! Oh, baby, fuck me!'" He demonstrated his point by thrusting his hips and jumping in Carter's direction. The point he was making to "Bruce" was more than obvious.

At least Langerfeld looked uncomfortable with that one. But Carter Shepherd was taking it in stride. He pulled in his legs and sat up in his chair. The lounge lizard had transformed himself into a schoolmaster.

"Well, you're going to have to settle this one too, Bradford," he said sternly. "We've got investors on our backs, employees grumbling, bad publicity for the company—not just you but the company. I have no idea why you're so keen to fight this, but—"

"Because I'm innocent, you asshole," spat Sisley. "All I did was—"

The lawyer put up his hand as quickly as had Langerfeld. "I am not your attorney on this, and I have no desire to be drawn into it, Bradford. You need to get your own attorney if you want to fight. If you want to settle, I'll help you. If you want to fight, you're on your own. Your own lawyer; your own money."

Sisley spun around to Langerfeld. "Did you decide that before I got here, Ben? That if I want to fight, I'll be on my own?"

Langerfeld slid by the question by responding, "It was discussed, yes." In truth, they had never reached a decision on how to handle the bills. Carter Shepherd had just made up a corporate policy. And Langerfeld was letting it happen.

"Well, it's all bullshit," Sisley said. And then, pointing at the door, he added, "And she's the one who's been stirring up all this trouble with the employees. She's a fucking feminist agitator."

I looked at Langerfeld and Shepherd to see their reactions to his assault on Wanda. Langerfeld kept his eyes on the table, his hands still clasped in front him. Shepherd was shaking his head silently but wasn't contradicting his boss. I guessed it was my turn to speak.

"Are you talking about Wanda?" I asked.

"No, I'm talking about the lady who brought in all the food you've been stuffing down your face," he snarled. "And where is the goddamned coffee?"

"Sorry, I don't understand what you're saying," I said.

"You wouldn't, would you?" he responded. "Why do you think I brought you into this, numbnuts? I can't trust that bitch. Who do you think sent me over to that hotel that morning to scout that room? Who has never once—never, ever once—defended me when these sad-ass women employees complain about how unfair and miserable their work life is? She's always on their side, always carrying water for them against the men in the company."

I looked again at Shepherd, and he gave me a shrug. I couldn't tell if it was a shrug of "what he says is true" or a shrug of "this guy is nuts." Maybe it was both.

"Well, Bradford, I've been working with her for nearly a week now," I said. "And she has never once bad-mouthed you or said anything negative about the company or you or anything."

"Oh please," interjected Carter Shepherd. "Don't tell me Wanda the Witch hasn't bad-mouthed me."

What the hell, I reached for the truth. "Well, maybe she had some fun at your expense, but, c'mon, you've provided a lot of fodder for that."

Oddly, he looked pleased at my dangerously honest—and inappropriate—comment.

We were so far off track! This was supposed to be a meeting about strategy. It was supposed to be a session to convince Sisley to settle, to discuss the pros and cons of that, and then to explore how best to do it with dignity. I knew I had to abandon my defense of Wanda since it wasn't going to get us back to where we needed to be. And besides, it was a hopeless cause in the face of Bradford Sisley's deep paranoia.

I went back to Crisis Management 101. "Look," I started to say. "We need to be agreeing on some goals here. Let's go back to what Ben said about the downsides of losing . . ."

But I was overwhelmed by buzzers going off. The devices that were on everyone's belt were suddenly dinging, and like Pavlov's dogs, all three men were reaching for their holsters, pulling out their devices, and gazing at the screens. A suspended moment of silence while they read.

"Fuck," sighed Sisley.

"Double fuck," said Shepherd.

Langerfeld was shaking his head.

Wanda had sent out a press release announcing her resignation from BeeLine. She described "a poisonously hostile work environment" that was "sexist, racist, homophobic, ageist, and dictatorial." She said she would be consulting with legal counsel about a class action suit by all the people "who have been victimized by the management of the company."

"Gee, was it something I said?" Sisley joked. Ha, ha. I could think of several possibilities in just my brief few days in the company. I could think of several things just this morning.

"Well, you did say you were going to shut down the Women's Network," said Carter Shepherd.

"I never said that," said Sisley.

"Yes, you did," said Carter, looking to me and to Ben Langerfeld for confirmation.

"I don't recall that," Ben said vaguely.

"I think you did *threaten* to shut down the network," I said to Sisley.

"Well, I probably should," he responded. "They've been nothing but trouble. It's like having a union—bitch,

bitch, bitch, demand, demand, demand. And Wanda's been the worst of them. Good riddance."

My mind was racing through all the reasons why this was anything but "good riddance." From a purely practical perspective, I was screwed. I had lost my partner, my highly competent pilot who knew how to get stuff done. I had helped navigate the plane, but she had been the one keeping the damn thing in the air. And now Wanda the skydiver had strapped on her parachute and jumped.

And then there was the image side to all of this. Here was a CEO who had been accused of accosting a woman in an elevator and was smeared from head to toe with the detritus of a lifetime of bad behavior, including his recent verbal tirade on television. Now one of his most senior woman executives (the most senior? I didn't know) had resigned. But not resigned quietly. She had sent out an angry, accusatory press release saying the whole company was rife with abuses of all types of people.

Carter Shepherd was carefully reading the press release, making highlights on his BeePad. Lawyers, I'd learned, love to pore over documents and mark them up. They are probably the last people alive on earth who think that specific words matter. I'm in public relations; I know better. It's much, much more about tone.

And Wanda's tone was bad—very bad.

"Shit," Carter said, face down in his pad. "She even says that Asians are being dissed here."

"Well, that's totally bullshit," said Sisley. He had finally stopped pacing around and plopped in the chair at the other end of the table from his chairman. "Asians are practically running this place top to bottom. No one—no one—can ever blame me for some sort of bias against Asians.

I've been in this with Malcolm from the beginning. He and I built this place from nothing. Together. Like brothers. We are like brothers. Like family."

Sisley was talking about Malcolm Wong, the BeeLine technical genius who had turned ideas into hardware and software that actually worked. Bradford and Malcolm had started the company not in the proverbial Silicon Valley garage but by splitting off from Dell in the eighties because Michael Dell wouldn't pursue their idea for what ultimately became the hugely popular BeeLine video game console.

Up until a few years earlier, Wong had been the chief technical officer in the company. But then Bradford Sisley kicked him upstairs to a non-job called executive vice chairman for strategic development. Wanda had told me he was an unhappy guy who spent most of his time traveling the globe. He had become, like Sisley, insanely wealthy and didn't need to work for a living. And with his seat on the board guaranteed by his holdings, he actually didn't need to work for BeeLine to have a voice. But for some reason, he wanted to continue to collect a paycheck, even though he had been shoved aside.

While Wong had been "family" to Bradford Sisley in the past, everyone on the inside and outside knew that nowadays he was being treated as excess baggage. And whether or not prejudice had anything to do with it, undoubtedly Asian employees had to be very aware of Wong's expulsion from power. And who knew what glass ceilings and other obstacles Asians might be facing at BeeLine? Certainly none of the white guys in the room—Carter Shepherd, Ben Langerfeld, Bradford Sisley, or I—would have the foggiest notion.

"Listen," I said, "I think there are going to be some really big reverberations from Wanda's press release, given where we are right now in the press."

"And in social media," added Carter.

Shit, I kept forgetting that part. I hate social media. I really should have stopped working altogether when Facebook and then Twitter took off. I should have done a Wanda: sent out an angry press release saying that the situation had become intolerable and that I was suing Mark Zuckerberg for making me obsolete and ruining my career.

"And internally with employees," I shot back, not wanting to leave Carter any satisfaction for having caught my omission. "Right now, every employee in the company is poring over her words just like you are." Carter looked at me, taking this in, and then he shut his eyes with a sigh. He knew the full implications of twenty-five thousand BeeLiners reading the angry and probably accurate description of their workplace, written by Wanda Fletcher, senior executive.

"Forget it! No one's going to give a shit about Wanda leaving," said Sisley. "We've had lots of senior people leave over the years, some of them openly unhappy about it. A little rumbling for a couple of days, and then life goes on. It's not like she would win any popularity contests among employees."

"You're right," said the sphinx called Langerfeld. "People come and go in any company. Folks will see she's just being a spoilsport, sniping on her way out the door."

"Where the fuck is the coffee?" demanded Sisley, looking at Carter Shepherd. With Wanda out of the room, he was counting on his general counsel to make the coffee happen. Carter ignored him and with a shrug went back to his BeePad.

Over the next half hour or so, I tried to monitor media coverage of Wanda's resignation without leaving the sanctity of the boardroom. I didn't want to leave my three musketeers alone since I knew they were capable of generating not only bad ideas but also completely alternative realities. Also, I was really comfortable in my chair and had access to the remaining breakfast food. (Everything was good except the lox and bagels. I was definitely on the wrong side of the Hudson River; the lox was tough, and the bagels were soft.)

Most important, I didn't want to go down to sit among Wanda's staff. God only knew what was going on down there.

Bloomberg caught the story first and sent out the entire press release without much commentary. Then their broadcast network took it, as did the CNBC and Fox Business folks. I texted down to Charlie, whom Bradford had said he wanted to fire, not to answer any media calls. I'd be down soon to discuss messages and strategy. If I could figure out what the hell to say or do.

Meanwhile, the topic of settling or not settling the lawsuit had been abandoned. My great strategy session had collapsed. Langerfeld was tapping out messages on his

BeePad while Sisley and Shepherd were discussing what to do to fill Wanda's job.

The logical choice was Charlie. Sisley really disliked the guy, which I half understood because Charlie wasn't very good at hiding how he felt. If you said something he didn't like, his face would broadcast his disapproval. Not a good approach when dealing with Bradford Sisley.

But they were ignoring this obvious solution. Instead, they were having a stupid conversation about finding a woman for the job, since hiring a woman would show that there was no sexist bias at BeeLine. In their mind, losing Wanda was like losing a Jew or a black person on the Supreme Court. Token slots could not be ignored. Of course, they also believed that no seriously ambitious man would want the job. They discussed various candidates who had no background or experience in communications. Bradford was pushing some woman from Finance, who he said was pretty good but not as attractive as Wanda.

Then, without warning, Ben Langerfeld seemed to wake up. Up until now he had been passive in the conversation and seemingly uninterested. Suddenly, his eyes were sparkling as he explained a wonderful new idea, namely that he would convince Wanda to come back. He blithered through two lengthy stories about how he had convinced senior executives who had written angry resignation letters to rescind their plans to leave. He was proud to say that one of the two had become his successor. (I was thinking that Langerfeld had probably flipped the guy with the promise of that promotion.)

I pointed out that this situation was a little different

from Ben's stories, since Wanda's resignation had already gone public. Very public. The idea of her now returning seemed far-fetched. Unless she got something big in return. Something that would also have to go public.

I knew from experience that few people have as much leverage as a valued employee who decides to quit. I had used this twice in the years when I worked for a large public relations agency. I built up a clientele (i.e., lots of billing) and made myself uniquely valuable. Then I announced that I was quitting. Suddenly the red carpet was rolled out, and the boss was asking, "What would make you stay?" Worked like a charm twice. But when I tried it a third time, they showed me the door. You can overdo extortion.

"Public turnarounds in resignations happen all the time in politics," Ben said. "The secretary of state offers his resignation, and the president refuses it. That's what you could do, Bradford. Refuse her resignation."

They were talking across the long expanse of the table. Sisley was looking slightly defeated, slumping in his CEO chair. Langerfeld, on the other hand, was leaning forward from his chairman chair, engaged in selling his idea.

"No fucking way, Ben," said Sisley with an air of disbelief. "She's shown how completely disloyal she really is. She's always worked to undermine me in sneaky, sneaky ways. Now she's shown her true colors. I don't want her back. And like Jonathan says, I'd have to offer her something. And I don't want to give that bitch anything!"

"Just take her back for a while, Bradford. Until things blow over," said Langerfeld. I was wondering what "until things blow over" might mean. Until Sisley won his sexual assault trial? "I can act as a go-between," he continued.

"I've got a great relationship with Wanda. I can reach out to her."

Yeah, I thought. She told me all about your ability to reach out—inappropriately.

Ben was truly animated by what he seemed to see as his opportunity to participate, to prove his worth. He would be the great negotiator, the Henry Kissinger shuttling between the implacable enemies. He wanted to throw himself into the fray.

But so far it wasn't going well. Bradford Sisley was done with Wanda. He sat glowering in his chair, shaking his head no, no, no.

Eventually, Ben realized that he was getting nowhere. But that didn't signal defeat. Not to Mr. Corporate America. "Okay, okay," he said. "I'll reach out to Wanda and talk to her. She adores me. She trusts me. I'll see if I can bring her around, and I'll let you know." I could only imagine Wanda's reaction to the opportunity to return to the BeeLine happy family.

Bradford's face turned red with anger, but before he could lash out at his chairman, buzzers started going again, and everyone grabbed for his holster.

BeeLine's stock price was tanking. Rumors were flying, supposedly based on a conversation that a financial analyst had had with an unnamed board member. The board member had told the analyst that the board was going to have to fire Sisley.

"Who the fuck would say something dumb like that?" said Sisley. Then he put his firepower on Ben Langerfeld, who was not as bright eyed as moments earlier when he was fighting for Wanda. "You're the goddamned chairman of the board, Ben. Who the hell on your board would be dumb enough to say something like that to an analyst at Deutsche Bank? For fuck's sake!"

The body language at the board table had flipped. Langerfeld's enthusiasm had disappeared. Meanwhile, Sisley, red in the face, was energized by anger.

"I can't imagine *anyone* on the board who would say such a thing," said Langerfeld. I wondered whether he was being honest or he was tracking down a list in his head, looking for the weakest links in the chain. "Everyone supports you, Bradford. Down to the last man."

"Or woman?" said Sisley.

"What?" asked Langerfeld. "You can't for a minute think that Wendy would do something like that. For one thing, she would never, ever talk to a financial analyst. She's an academic, for God's sake. Probably doesn't even know what an analyst is."

I made a note to myself to find out who board member Wendy was. In the meantime, I'd just listen.

"She and Wanda are pretty chummy," piped in Carter Shepherd, his face still down in his tablet. "Fuck, the stock is down by almost thirty percent."

"You're kidding," said Ben.

"Better cut back on those big wedding plans of yours," Bradford said to Carter.

Carter glanced up with an angry look on his face. He started to say something but then seemed to think better of it.

I wondered at the randomness of this nasty remark.

Everyone in the room—except me—was experiencing a financial debacle that, if not reversed, could ruin their lives. Why, in the midst of such mutually shared anxiety, would Bradford pick on Carter's wedding plans? Maybe he hadn't received an invite?

Sisley returned to his pursuit of the Judas on his board. He aggressively peppered his chairman with various names, citing for each one a negative comment that the person had delivered in the past. He apparently had a prodigious memory for slights, carrying them in a mental sack as large as Santa's bag of toys.

But Ben Langerfeld kept swatting the accusations away, citing particular board votes or other signs of loyalty. He kept reassuring Sisley that the board loved him.

"I don't need their fucking love!" Sisley exploded at one point. "I need their support! This is a question of the survival of the company, Ben. Imagine BeeLine without me! BeeLine cannot exist without me. I made this company! I am the company! Anyone who believes that BeeLine can survive without Bradford Sisley has his head shoved up his ass. And you've got a board member whose head is apparently right on up there. You need to find out who that person is and get them off the goddamned board!"

I let this useless conversation continue for a while as I developed an action plan in my head. Like most people faced with unexpected and largely uncontrollable events, these titans of American business were engaged in a pointless blame game. And their lawyer was burrowed into the internet, eager to read every bad piece of information floating around the public sphere. I call it "Bad News Addiction" (BNA). It's a common response of corporate types who are used to the controlled environment of the office suite. They lose themselves in the wonder of what a hostile media environment can do. Can't get enough of it.

It was time for my magic wand, a rhetorical trick taught to me by an eccentric college professor who had reveled in pricking the muddled logic of undergraduates.

"Okay, guys," I said. "Let's try this. I wave my magic wand, and I tell you exactly who talked to the financial analyst, and I wave it again, and Ben gets that person to resign from the board. Now exactly what have we accomplished? Does the stock bounce back? Does everyone decide to ignore Wanda's accusations? Does the Katherine Davis lawsuit disappear? Do all the employees feel good about working here? All the bad press stops?"

"Fuck you," responded Bradford. "You know what you can do with your magic wand."

But I had their attention. Even Carter was looking up from his tablet, BNA-free for the moment. Once again the spin doctor was working to stop the spinning of panicked people. I was the cool head in the room. Easy enough to do. I was the only one with nothing to lose.

"We have to get focused here," I said. "Ben, you keep saying that the board stands behind Bradford. Great! And that they know he is essential to BeeLine. Great! Let's get that out there."

"Good idea!" said Ben, happy to stop being badgered by Bradford, who was acting as prosecuting attorney. "Bring in a secretary, and I'll dictate a statement that says all that."

I wondered if there was anyone in the building with a title of secretary, a moniker that had disappeared sometime in the late twentieth century, when all the secretaries became personal assistants. And when was the last time that someone took dictation?

"Actually, I think a board resolution would be a better way to go," I offered. "Then it's not just you, but it is a real, recorded action by the board. You could organize a conference call this afternoon."

"*Yes!*" said Bradford, banging his fist on the table with enthusiasm.

But neither Ben's face nor Carter's was glowing with eagerness to proceed to organize a board conference call. For each, such a step represented both work and some risk. Carter's office would have to track down everyone, negotiate a time, and ensure a quorum. And Ben would have to organize an impromptu meeting on a tricky topic. Not enough time to lobby everyone towards a set decision. Having made the claim that the board stood behind Bradford, he now would have to deliver. And both he and Carter knew that any board meeting could wander off into uncharted territory.

But I had let the cat out of the bag, and Bradford Sisley just loved that little kitty. He wanted his board meeting, he wanted a statement of unconditional support, he wanted to crush the person who wanted him fired under a tidal wave of board confirmation of his leadership.

And so everyone got to work. Carter went off to organize the meeting. Ben went to his guest office in the building to start lobbying board members. And I was tasked with writing the draft of a board statement of support. Also with getting the communications folks around the company to make calls to various key people—inside and outside—to alert them that the board would be putting out a statement of support. I knew that my buddy Frank

Ferricelli would be particularly important here; he needed to call the crucial financial writers and tell them to expect a strong board endorsement of Bradford Sisley, founder and CEO of BeeLine.

As for Bradford, I encouraged him to contact his senior managers around the globe and tell them that it was business as usual and that the board would be putting out a statement of confidence in management. I figured he'd probably call only the folks he liked and trusted and would spend most of each call spilling out his grievances, bad-mouthing Wanda, reminding people of his indispensability. But whatever. In a way, Bradford telling his managers about how important he was would be Bradford conducting business as usual.

As Bradford started to leave the room, I tried to check off the last thing on my action plan. This one was more for me than for him or his company.

"Hey, Bradford," I said. "Think about giving Charlie a chance for Wanda's job, will you? He's there in Communications already, he knows the ropes, and for the moment, you don't have a good other replacement. Give it shot. Why not?"

"I think he's an arrogant prick," he responded.

"Hey, so am I, and you put up with me, right?" I said. He stared at me for a second.

Then he walked out without a word.

I sat in the silence of the boardroom for a few more minutes in order to tap out a two-sentence statement from the BeeLine board. They would express "unanimous full and complete" support of Bradford Sisley and look forward to years and years of his continuing leadership. Sent it off to Carter Shepherd for legal approval.

As I started to gather my stuff, the coffee service that Sisley had ordered finally arrived, complete with sugar cookies. I wasn't really hungry, so I stuffed all the cookies into my sports coat pockets. Knowing that I was armed with sugar fixes on an as-needed basis, I felt fortified to go down to Renata's office, down the hall from what used to be Wanda's.

5

WEDNESDAY AFTERNOON

I expected things to be in chaos down in the Communications Department. Their boss had quit in a blaze of angry words. And assuming that Wanda was liked by her staff, there were probably tears and even thoughts of following her out the door. Mostly, there would be a lot of emotion—and concern about the future.

I felt I should try to step into the void, gather the troops, and offer soothing words of comfort and reassurance. But then again, why should I? True, I was far and away the oldest person, and from my several days with this crowd, I was confident I was the wisest. But it wasn't my job to play shrink to all the needy psyches. Plus, I was lousy at that kind of stuff anyway. I have a philosophy that personal shit should stay outside the office. Business is business. Get over it.

Happily, Charlie was way ahead of me. I don't know if he had done the soothing-words thing, but he had done the smart thing: he had focused everyone on work. He had gathered the whole department in a conference room, where they were brainstorming ideas for restoring market confidence in BeeLine. At a glance I could see that there were two groups of charts stuck on the wall: one for external communications and one for internal communications. Good work, Charlie, I thought. Otherwise, these folks would be wandering aimlessly, traveling down all the highways and byways of gossip land.

Charlie wanted to review all the ideas for me, doing a stand-up presentation to show how much he and "the team" were on top of things. I guessed that normally he would do such a show-and-tell for Wanda. There was really no point in doing it for me, but I wanted to support Charlie, particularly in front of the rest of the department. But before I let him get started, I took Frank out in the hallway and told him about the upcoming board meeting. Then I sent him off to get out the word to the Investor Relations folks and to his contacts in the financial press.

Back in the conference room, I sat patiently in a very uncomfortable chair while Charlie ran through every idea on the flip charts.

One of the principal mantras of brainstorming is that "there is no such thing as a bad idea." It has to be one of the stupidest notions ever articulated about creative thinking. It couldn't be further from the truth. In every brainstorming, there are usually twelve stupid notions for every good one. But everything gets put on the flip charts.

These flip charts definitely proved my point. Example: the company should make a major donation to Planned Parenthood to prove it cared about women. Example: the company should run TV ads showing happy female and minority employees. Example: Bradford should do a series of town hall meetings with consumers around the country, a listening tour where he could show what an open and friendly guy he was.

I sat there quietly. I didn't want to interrupt the parade of stupidities with my own brilliant idea that was in the process of being implemented: a board resolution of support for Bradford Sisley. I waited until Charlie was done with his presentation. I told them what was afoot. I could feel the disappointment and deflation in the room. So why had they done all this good work? To assuage all the wounded prides, I suggested that maybe some of the ideas might be useful as follow-on steps. As if.

That was when Miley spoke up. I had seen her in the hallway over the past several days, a petite attractive Asian girl with owlish glasses who always seemed to be rushing to put out a fire and for whom I was an invisible whale-sized presence. Miley was in charge of internal communications, whose flip charts were on the wall behind me. Her eyes bored into mine. She was going to lay it on the line. She wanted to make sure that I got the picture straight.

"Well, you may think your board statement is going to calm things down, but when employees hear that Bradford is staying, there's going to be a very mixed reaction," she said. "Wanda has touched a big nerve inside this company. She's opened up a Pandora's box of bad stuff that has been shoved under the rug for years. Everything she said about the corporate culture—sexist, racist, homophobic, ageist—is true. This company operates like a big locker room of arrested male adolescents."

I'm afraid I smiled a little smile. It actually was a smile of admiration at her bravery and candor. But she misunderstood.

"It's not funny, Mr. Keaton," she said. "I've been getting

texts all afternoon from people—not just women—who are leaving early today and plan to phone in sick tomorrow. They agree with Wanda. They want something to change in this place. If the board says they're one hundred percent behind Bradford, that'll be a slap in the face to thousands of concerned employees."

"So what do you recommend?" I asked.

"There are a bunch of ideas on the flip charts behind you," she said, gesturing over my head.

I couldn't stomach another "all ideas are of equal value" presentation. So I challenged the young woman. "No, tell me what *you* recommend. You're telling me that a bunch of employees are going to be boycotting their jobs tomorrow. What do you think we should do?"

"It's on the wall behind you," she said defiantly.

"No, give me your best idea," I said defiantly back. Don't play Tiger Mom with me, I was thinking.

"Tomorrow morning Bradford does a Sisley Show."

Already I was lost, and I threw up my hands to signal my confusion.

Miley explained. "A Sisley Show is a live broadcast direct to everyone's computers. We do them when Bradford tells us important stuff like product launches, earnings, big management changes."

"Got it," I said.

"So tomorrow he does a Sisley Show, and he announces some kind of culture-change initiative."

"Like what?" I asked.

She looked around at her colleagues. "Well, we've ideated about a lot of things," she said. I refrained from complaining about her turning the noun "idea" into a verb form. I had spent years trying to swat down this particular intrusion into the English language. But I had lost that battle, along with so many other linguistic skirmishes.

"Like firing the Nazi," I heard a voice down the table say. I knew who he was talking about. The head of Human Resources was a German guy named Winkelmann, who seemed to be universally hated. I hadn't run across him yet. That would happen the next day.

"Is that on the wall behind me?" I asked. "'Fire the Nazi'?"

Miley allowed herself a small smile. "No, it's written down as 'high-level personnel changes.'" The smile was then replaced by a wicked squint as she added, "Which could be more than one person."

"Is that what Bradford is supposed to say in this broadcast thing tomorrow?" I said. "Heads are going to roll!"

"No, I think he needs to announce a new board committee, a Diversity Committee. It would investigate what's going on here—the corporate culture—and recommend solutions that would be adopted explicitly by the board," she said. "Including that some heads would roll." No smile.

Well, I thought, this one goes big when she goes for it. She was sitting down there in the Communications Department, deciding that the board needed to wake up and create a new committee to shake up the culture at BeeLine. Not exactly a communications recommendation. But it was probably a good one. Other companies had created such structures when similar issues popped. If the right board people got involved and actually put some time and effort into it, change could happen.

It was the kind of thing a company would do if they didn't fully trust the CEO and management team to solve the problem. Which was why Bradford would probably hate the idea. It would take control out of his hands.

"But, whenever I talk about the board, people think I'm talking about my father," Miley added.

Whammo! Now I knew who Miley was. Frank had told me about her in our evening at the '49er. She was Malcolm Wong's daughter, the scion of the original—now sidelined—cofounder of the company. She had anglicized her real name, Mai Li, to Miley as part of a youthful obsession with Miley Cyrus. Frank had told me she was a sharp cookie. And he had warned me about her. Said she was an advocate for her dad and carried his wounds and resentments on her person. She also was an open-mike to her father, so one needed to be careful with secrets, such as the upcoming major write-off.

So now I had to consider who I was dealing with. Was her passion for corporate culture change a subterfuge for hurting Bradford Sisley and resurrecting her father's role in the company? Was she seeing in Wanda's public rebuke of the company an opportunity to stir the pot of resentment among employees? Were a bunch of employee texts and e-mails about boycotting work the result of spontaneous combustion, or was Miley Wong lighting fires around the company?

The thing was, I liked her. And I liked her idea of a board committee. Wanda didn't leave on a whim, and I had no reason to doubt her accusations. Something, someone, undoubtedly needed to drive some badly needed change in the work environment at BeeLine. Miley's idea was a good one—but it would not exactly be easy for her, or for me, to pull it off.

I asked Charlie and Miley to stay after the meeting to discuss "moving forward with some of the creative ideas on the wall." In the absence of Wanda, there was no real way for them to make any decisions. For the moment Charlie and Miley were reporting to an empty office. I wanted to see if I could be helpful in channeling their energies in useful directions.

Actually, that's a lie. What I needed was some intel about what was going on at BeeLine that might have triggered Wanda's resignation and, worse yet, might amplify her attacks on the company. I felt pretty confident that once the board had made its full-throated endorsement of Bradford, he would be okay. At least until the next woman popped up. But the Wanda thing had opened up a new avenue of trouble. And I needed to understand what was lying underneath the surface.

"So," I asked, "how are you guys doing? How's everyone doing with Wanda's departure?" They were seated side by side across the table from me.

Miley sat silent. She wasn't going to go first. She pretended to be shuffling papers.

Charlie, never one not to speak his mind, opened up. "Well, none of us saw anything like this coming, you know? I mean, I was with her yesterday. You were with her too, Jonathan. She was normal Wanda—cool, calm, collected. Something big must have happened in the meantime."

Something big. There had been the strategy meeting in the boardroom. As my mind scrolled back through it, I was having trouble finding anything truly monumental. True, I thought, her boss had told her to order coffee. But I knew that couldn't be it. That kind of disrespectful behavior couldn't have been a first for Wanda. And it hardly was the kind of thing to qualify as a straw that might break a camel's back.

"Well, what are people speculating?" I asked, directing my question more at Miley than at Charlie.

She looked reluctant to open up but couldn't ignore my question. "Most people seem to be assuming Bradford said or did something that was so terrible that she finally had had enough."

"So they're assuming that this is about Bradford?" I asked.

"Of course!" Miley said in a tone that suggested I might be an idiot if I didn't know that.

"I'm not assuming that!" interjected Charlie. "Her statement is much, much broader than just Bradford. She talks about the culture of the company. She isn't just attacking him; she's attacking everyone. All of management. She's joining the Mary Chan bandwagon."

"Of course she is," said Miley, keeping her disrespectful tone, but this time directed at Charlie. "Mr. Keaton asked what triggered Wanda's resignation. It had to have been some terrible thing that Bradford Sisley said or did. She's been living with this corporate culture for a long time. We all have. Nothing changed this morning. But once she made the decision to leave, she knew she finally had to speak out about what goes on in this place."

"Which is?" I asked.

Charlie waved his hand dismissively. "Oh, it's this whole thing about the fraternity-house culture at BeeLine, how women are dissed, how blacks are discriminated against, how Asians are held back. Oh, and probably, the disabled don't get full access to the gym. Everyone is suffering under the yoke of white techno-nerds who wear Mickey Mouse sweatshirts and never shower."

I looked over to Miley. She was shaking her head in disbelief and disagreement. But she wasn't going to speak up without a prod.

"Miley?" I said. "You look like you disagree."

"Look, Mr. Keaton," she began. "Charlie and I don't agree on a lot of things. He eats meat. He likes the Dodgers. He doesn't see—he chooses not to see—the things that have been going on around here. He thinks that people like Mary Chan are making things up—"

"Mary Chan is a psychopath!" Charlie interrupted. "She sees ghosts and goblins in every corner."

Miley stopped speaking and threw her hands in the air.

"Well, Miley," I said. "In the meeting just now, you said that Wanda's resignation is kicking open a Pandora's box of stuff. Do you think there is a really widespread problem, or is it a narrow group of people?"

Charlie interrupted again. "It's a narrow group of people, located mainly in this building," he said. He was staring at Miley like she knew exactly what he was talking about. "If you go further out onto the campus, if you visit with the R & D folks, the marketing folks, the operations people. If you leave the campus and you go to the manufacturing sites or the sales office. If you get beyond the politics of this tower, BeeLine is a responsible, respectful, diverse bunch of people. But here in this building there is a little cabal of angry people who want to drag the company into the whole #MeToo thing and tear down a bunch of people who aren't perfect but also are not monsters. And you know why? So they can get those jobs!"

Now if I were a responsible person, I would never let Charlie get away with such a diatribe, such a thinly veiled attack on the person sitting to his left. But I wanted to see how Miley would respond to him.

But she didn't. Instead, she responded to me. A brilliant strategic move, straight out of classic communications strategy. If your opponent is implacably opposed to you, don't even bother to argue with them. Argue to the audience—which in this case was the big fat guy across the table.

"There are, Mr. Keaton, two realities in this company," she said in a calm, even voice that made me realize that Charlie had become loud and shrill. "There are a lot of Charlies who think that things are just fine. They know that Bradford can be weird and sometimes crude, but he's our guy. He brought us to the promised land. And these people are sorry to see him caught up in that woman's lawsuit. They think he should be forgiven his trespasses.

"These same people also think that all the diversity training and touchy-feely videos have made us one big, happy, respectful family. They actually believe the annual diversity report with its ever-improving numbers and the pictures of laughing interracial groups of people. Things are great and are getting better.

"But there is another group of us—people like Mary Chan, like me, and, obviously, Wanda—who thinks that a happy picture has been painted over a boiling cauldron of sexism, racism, homophobia, all of it. It's a Potemkin village, a façade. Behind the façade there is corruption, discrimination, and deceit.

"You asked us how everyone is doing with Wanda's resignation, Mr. Keaton. It depends on who you talk to. Talk to the one group, and they see Wanda leaving as just one more departure. It happens; this is Silicon Valley. People come; people go. And if she left in anger, she's probably just angry with Bradford Sisley. He can get under anybody's skin. But if you talk to the other group, they see Wanda's resignation as a call to action. The most senior woman in this company has walked out because she says she's disgusted with what she sees going on. And when I told you there will be a boycott, there will be a boycott. And there will be more complaints filed. If some newspaper or TV station wants to poke around here, they will find a lot of people ready to talk. People are not going to be silent anymore."

I was staring through Miley Wong's thick round glasses into her eyes. And I knew that a whole new front was opening up in the battle. Suddenly, I wasn't feeling so good about my strategy of a board endorsement of Bradford. As Miley had already said, Bradford's victory this afternoon could be the spark of a new explosion.

I heard my phone ding with a new text message. I glanced down to where it lay on the table in front of me. It was a text from Carter Shepherd. The board would meet by conference call at two o'clock. He also said that he had approved my draft message for the board to adopt.

That timing would mean that the stock market would close before the board would have a chance to issue its endorsement of Sisley. So the stock would sit in the tank overnight.

I suddenly flashed on Miley's idea of a Sisley Show in the morning. The board statement would come out in time to be comfortably absorbed before the markets opened in New York. Then we could add a kicker—a Sisley Show where Bradford speaks to his employees, telling them he appreciates their support *and* then adding comforting words about addressing critical issues in the company, exploring avenues of change, blah, blah, blah. He would say things that would take some energy out of the motivations of Miley's crowd. Show him as a guy who gets it, who hears the message from Wanda, who wants to fix any problems and to make sure that BeeLine is the best damned workplace in the world for every single person!

"Okay," I said to Miley and Charlie. "Let's put on a show!" I waved my hands in the air to show enthusiasm.

They looked at me blankly. My weird attempt to imitate Mickey Rooney and Judy Garland rallying all the kids to put on a show was a nonstarter. So I had to explain myself.

"Miley, I'm talking about your idea. A Sisley Show tomorrow morning. Bradford talks to employees. He thanks the board for their support, and he acknowledges the need for change."

Her face brightened and then clouded over. "I suggested a lot more than that. I suggested creating a Board Diversity Committee." Push, push. Had she taken lessons from my ex-wife, Ruthie? A wave of anxiety swept through me as the issue of $150,000 for Sandra escaped from the dark corner where I had left it. I shoved it back in.

"I know, I know," I acknowledged. "One step at a time, okay? Bradford can't create a board committee. Only the board can do that. Right now, I just want to get Bradford to acknowledge the problem. I'll talk to him about how far he's willing to go right now, what he's willing to promise to do. I'll mention the board-committee idea as one possibility he might want to bring to the board later, okay?"

"Words alone won't do it, Mr. Keaton," Miley said

ominously. "He's got to do something concrete. Right now!" She poked her finger on the table to make her demand very clear.

Whoa, girl, I was thinking. I'm not negotiating with you. Bradford Sisley is not negotiating with you. I've heard what you said. I'm responding to what you've said with something that actually may be doable.

"Fine," I said. "I'll tell him you said that. I'll tell him that Miley Wong says he's got to do something *right now*!" I repeated her gesture of poking a finger on the table.

She looked frightened that I might not be joking. I might actually quote Malcolm Wong's daughter giving him an order. Charlie was smiling at her discomfort. I wondered if they fought a lot and how Wanda might have handled that.

Wanda! Why did you whip up this morass and then leave me to deal with it?

Charlie, Miley, and I agreed to have a working lunch in the conference room starting in one hour. I put Charlie in charge of ordering the food, since he had seen me eat and would hopefully take care of my needs. Miley looked to me like a soup-and-salad person.

I called up to Colleen, Bradford's assistant, and begged for a five-minute audience. She put me through to him on the phone, not my favorite communications mechanism for selling an idea.

"So I hear the board meeting is at two," I started. "How's it going with your phone calls?"

"It's going great!" Bradford responded with genuine

enthusiasm. "Great, great, great! Just like I told you. No one is sorry to see Wanda go. She was a downer, everyone says. A real sourpuss. A regular bitch on wheels."

I had to wonder how much Bradford was leading these conversations. I knew enough from corporate life in general to know that if the CEO is bad-mouthing the employee who is headed out the door, the tribe becomes an echo chamber. Why defend someone who's already gone? If the boss wants to trash the person, just pick up a tomato and throw it at their disappearing shadow.

"Things are pretty good down here in Communications," I said. "It was a bit of a shock, but these folks have been busy developing ideas for ways to tamp down the negatives of Wanda's statement."

"Everyone I've talked to says her statement was crap!" he said. "A crock of shit."

"Well, folks down here think she has an audience among employees," I said. "Not a big audience, but an audience, particularly among the women. Have you talked to any women?"

"Of course I have," he lied. "No different than the men."

"Well, it's probably at the lower levels," I said. "I got a bit of an earful from several women." Okay, I was lying too. I had only heard Miley. Whatever.

"Here's the best idea, I think," I pressed on. "They want you to do a Sisley Show tomorrow morning. The board will have given you their full support, and the stock will have bounced back. You'll be king of the hill. You go before your employees, you act graciously for the huge wellspring of support, and we craft some words for you about willingness to take any steps that need to be taken to address any concerns that any people may have about fairness and nondiscrimination in the workplace."

"I don't want to make any promises I can't keep," Bradford said.

"Agree, agree," I said. "We'll find the right words that express openness, concern, willingness to listen, blah, blah. And then over the next few months you can figure out if there's anything you have to do. The other thing is that this Sisley Show will be picked up outside the company. We'll make sure of that. So the whole world gets to see you face-to-face, acting as a gracious and caring leader. That visual replaces the lawsuit and Wanda and your stupid TV rant in the media space."

"Fine," he said. "Let's do it. I've got a slot at nine tomorrow morning."

"Perfect!" I said, having no idea what had to happen to make it perfect. "I'll draft the script for you."

"No promises, no commitments," he repeated.

"Understood," I said. I'd done enough verbal gymnastics in my life to know it would not be a difficult assignment to sound committed without being committed.

Charlie, Miley, and I reconvened in the conference room whose walls were still covered in the stupid flip charts. The room was a cavernous interior space with hideous fluorescent lighting. Four cheap conference tables were scrunched together in the middle. I wouldn't have been surprised if, underneath the flip charts, the walls were displaying bad poster art. (Later on, I learned that it was worse than that: the walls displayed the various awards the department had won for best product launch and best multimedia campaign, etcetera, from various public relations associations.) Corporate décor at its most banal and oppressive.

Charlie arrived with an uninspired lunch of tuna salad and egg salad sandwiches on indifferent white bread with accompanying bags of potato chips. Even worse, he brought ugly red apples for dessert. Last time I would trust him on an important assignment.

We sat at a corner of one of the tables. The veneer was discolored and chipped.

I decided I wanted to try to soften Miley up a little before I let her know that I would be writing Bradford's remarks for the broadcast and that there would be nothing close to a Board Diversity Committee in what he would say. So, as we unwrapped our sad sandwiches and popped open the small bags of chips, I told her about my interaction with her father some fifteen years earlier.

It had been the kind of corporate crisis that makes a great story at the bar. The story of Darren Dragon's Boner.

Back in the middle of the video game mania of the eighties, when BeeLine was emerging as a major competitor to Atari and Sony, the company had released a new game cartridge called *Dragon Wars*. The hero was a young dragon named Darren, a prince of the Blue Dragon Kingdom, which was constantly having to defend itself from attacks from the Red Dragon Kingdom. For no explicable reason, Darren was usually fighting off hordes of Red Dragons by himself—spouting fire, whipping around his massive tail, swiping with his long claws, using his pointy wings effectively to lift off when a Red Dragon attacked or to swoop down in an aerial ambush.

Every time Darren killed off a Red Dragon (winning points for the player), he would stand up on his hind legs and howl with maniacal glee, great fireballs spouting from his mouth. His skin would light up in a kind of chartreuse, and all his scales would rise up in excitement as his little wings lifted him off the ground and spun him around. But, lo and behold, the scale that rose up between Darren's legs was unusually long and tubular and revealed beneath it two distinct orbs.

Apparently no one in the fast-moving, get-it-to-market BeeLine company had noticed the sophomoric joke that some programmer had embedded in the software. The game went through beta testing, and other glitches were noticed and repaired. Launched with great fanfare, *Dragon Wars* hit the market for the Christmas season with Darren Dragon's boner still intact.

Letters (this was before e-mail was widespread) started coming into BeeLine from concerned mothers whose sons—and whose daughters—were having just too many giggles from Darren Dragon's gleeful triumphal performance. The howl and the tremor of his entire body suddenly took on a whole new complexion. Darren Dragon was feeling more than just the joy of triumph.

When I arrived on the scene as the head of a horde of people from the big public relations firm where I worked, the media had not yet discovered the issue. It was the first time I ever met Bradford Sisley, who was becoming one of Silicon Valley's superheroes. A techno-megastar. He was somewhat less grandiose than the person I met ten years later in the SEC crisis or the person I was dealing with now. But all the personality traits were there: a huge ego, an unwillingness to listen, an insistence on getting his way, and a foul mouth.

It was obvious that neither Miley nor Charlie had ever heard this story. As we chewed on our sandwiches and chips, Charlie kept guffawing, enjoying every flourish and double entendre that I had developed in telling this tale over many years. Miley, on the other hand, sat silently, keeping her eyes steadily riveted on mine. I was careful with my language because of Miley. I'd noticed her own lack of profanity in an office environment where almost every nasty word seemed to be allowed. So I carefully used the words "penis" and "erection" to describe the problem.

At the time, Bradford had kept referring to Darren's affectation as a "stiff dick." He insisted that people were just imagining it. In the beginning, he had instructed the small consumer relations group to ignore the concerned letters from parents. Then, he had them craft a form letter telling parents that BeeLine's designers wanted to assure them that Darren Dragon did not have any genitalia.

But the letters kept rolling in. Finally, Miley's dad, Malcolm Wong, had made the call to the nation's biggest PR firm to send in a crisis management squad. He had gotten the reference from a buddy who worked at one of the biotech companies that had had to explain the outrageous price it was intending to charge for its new cancer drug.

"I remember my first meeting with your father," I said to Miley. "He was very cordial to us, almost deferential, which, believe me, was not something we were used to. He seemed pretty clear about the issue: he completely rejected the idea that there was no problem. He showed us the visuals. He made a very persuasive case and begged us to help him overcome the blindness of the many executives who were following Bradford down a path of denial.

"We met separately with Bradford, and he was absolutely on another wavelength altogether," I said. "He kept insisting that people were imagining something that wasn't there, and he saw no reason to change anything. He claimed that changing the program would be hugely expensive and pointless. He was convinced that the complaint letters were the work of agents employed by Sony.

"As we continued our interviews, it was obvious that your father was very isolated, a bit like the kid who kept pointing out that the emperor had no clothes. Operations people, marketing people, even legal people had bought into Bradford's narrative. There was no erect penis; there was no penis at all. This was just a big hoax being played on BeeLine."

"And what did you think?" asked Miley.

"I believed my eyes," I said. "I rationalized that maybe it was an unintentional visual effect, but it certainly could be mistaken for an erection. I tried to run a middle path between your father and Bradford. Okay, so maybe it wasn't a real penis, but it could be mistaken for a penis." (Oh, how difficult it was for me to keep to this clinical language. The real story—the good story, the unexpurgated one—included the line, "Okay, so maybe it wasn't a real prick; maybe it was only a dildo.")

"But, eventually, your father won the argument."

"How?" Miley asked.

"Your father is a scientist," I said. "He went looking

for the truth. He became his own detective, walking back through the documentation of the game's development. And finally, he homed in on the culprit—actually it was two meatheads in the Coding Department. Your father forced them to confess. So Bradford had no leg to stand on in all of his denials of a problem. And now the choice was clear: fix the problem or run the risk of walking right into an inevitable scandal about an erect penis."

"Which seems to be a habit with Bradford," said Miley, revealing for the very first time a sense of irony. I laughed overly heartily to show my appreciation for the joke. She didn't seem to find it quite as funny.

Why did I want so desperately to please this young woman? I think it was totally instinctual on my part—a gut feeling that, like her father fifteen years before, she was motivated by integrity and high moral values. She was tougher and less polished than her father, but she was clearly a chip off the old block. She seemed to carry within her the same kind of no-nonsense honesty that I had felt from Malcolm Wong many years earlier.

So, ladling on the praise, I told Miley Wong how her father had wrestled the issue out of Bradford's hands. He became BeeLine's Darren Dragon, the lone warrior fighting a horde of enemies. And one by one he took them down, tore them away from the Red Dragon King's refusal to address reality. And finally, the board asked for a remedial plan of action.

Malcolm Wong insisted that the company take the highest road possible, asking our crisis team for its recommendations. What we came up with cost the company millions of dollars to clean up the mess. BeeLine pulled the product from the stores, destroyed tens of millions of dollars of inventory, and took a huge revenue hit from the several months' gap before they could put the new version of *Dragon Wars* on the shelf. Millions of game cartridges went into crushers, and never once did the media know that it was all about crushing little dragon penises.

The recall was officially positioned as a technical problem, and every player who wanted to trade his Version One for the "new and improved" Version Two could do so. Despite the huge publicity campaign our PR company ran, few kids wanted the new version when it finally became available. By then, Darren Dragon was yesterday's game. The world had moved on.

This was one of those crisis stories that one could never publicize, because the secret had been so well contained. Even Malcolm Wong's daughter had never heard about her dad's battle to do the right thing. She told me she had only vaguely heard about an expensive recall of an early video game because of a technical glitch. She was glad to hear the true story and was not surprised to learn that her father had done what he had done.

When I would recount the tale of Darren Dragon's Boner, it was only among friends. And I would swear them to secrecy about the company and the particular game. It was actually sad that the story could never be told in public, because it was every bit as good as all the famous crisis stories, like the successful Tylenol recall or the botched BP oil spill in the Gulf of Mexico. It was the kind of story that belonged in a Harvard Business School case study. A founding executive became the whistleblower against his own company, against his own financial interest. I was glad to be the one to tell Miley about what her father had done.

I only wished that someday someone might tell my Sandra such a story about me. If I could only think of what that story might be.

Softening Miley up with her dad's heroics did not help a lot when I finally let her know that I would be writing the script for the next morning's Sisley Show and that it would not include the Board Diversity Committee idea or any other specific remedy to the problems of the BeeLine employee culture. I told her, truthfully, that Bradford had been very clear about avoiding commitments or promises. I told her, untruthfully, that he was totally on board with recognizing the existence of a problem and the need for change.

I could see in her face that she wanted to argue with me. But she held back. Instead, she stopped eating her egg salad sandwich, wrapped it up noisily in its white paper, and threw it into the wastebasket. She looked at her watch and announced that she had to get going on all the logistics of a morning Sisley Show: booking the studio, getting the crew, sending out the notice to employees, etcetera.

She marched out the door. I was hoping she would pop back in and thank me for the story about her father. I'm such a foolish, vain man.

Charlie started peppering me with questions about who had been around during the Darren Dragon's Boner drama and about any other juicy gossip I might have. I realized that I had probably made a mistake in telling the story in front of him; he was not necessarily a person inclined to keep a secret. So I put on my sternest face and swore him to secrecy in the name of protecting both Bradford and the company.

Once the sandwiches were gone, I was done with the grim conference room. I picked up an apple and took a bite. It was as mushy as a pear, and I spat it out into a napkin. What I wanted was a pint of chocolate ice cream to wash away the cheap mayo taste. A cigarette would also be good. I had had to quit three years ago. But I wanted one now, even though I'd probably have to hike miles before I could find a smoking area beside a dumpster somewhere.

I told Charlie to stay in his office so we could get out the board statement as quickly as possible. Only later did I remind myself that Charlie probably didn't have to literally be in his office to do this. He could probably disseminate a statement to the entire universe from a seat in a downtown Starbucks. Or from his stationary bike at the gym. But I knew he understood what I meant. "Stay in your office" was a twenty-first-century metaphor for "be available."

I went back to Renata's office and shut the door, thinking that I would start to draft Bradford's remarks for his morning video broadcast. It was one thirty. In a half hour, the board meeting would start. With any luck they would approve the statement quickly and we would make the TV evening news in the West and late TV news in the East.

I started typing, but the muse wouldn't come. Instead, Sandra was in my head. I knew I had no choice but to find the $150,000 for her. But, selfishly, I wanted to get something back. I was jealous of Malcolm Wong. He had a daughter who admired him. He had a daughter who, at some level, wanted to follow in his stead, to be a part of something that he had created. I sensed that Miley and Malcolm had a deep bond of affection and respect.

Was that something I could buy for $150,000? Probably not.

I phoned my account manager in my financial adviser's office. He always seemed to know the details of my situation, unlike his boss. I told him that I might need to lay my hands on $150,000 in the next couple of weeks. He didn't sound thrilled. He gave me a long-winded explanation that had to do with maturities and EDFs and short-term capital gains. His bottom line: it would be better to wait until the new year. Maybe I should consider taking a short-term loan.

I told him to keep thinking and said I'd call him again next week. Then I put down my head and went to sleep at my desk. At Renata's desk.

When I woke up, it was already three o'clock. No messages on my phone about the board meeting. This was worrisome. Telephone conference calls are not supposed to drag on, and the task before the board was a simple one: approve the damn statement.

I again tried to write the script for the Sisley Show broadcast. But now I was too worried about what the board might be up to.

So I convinced myself it was stupid to write the script before the board had done its work. Who knows? Maybe there would be more for Bradford to comment on. I could be spinning a lot of wheels writing in the dark about the outcome of the meeting. I would have plenty of time to write the script once I had their statement in my hand.

I decided I wanted to talk to Frank Ferricelli. He had been phoning folks all afternoon to prep them for the statement. Maybe he had something interesting to report.

I went searching for Frank's office, waddling through the maze of cubicles stretching around me. I remembered the airy, spacious office Frank had occupied at the headquarters of the Securities and Exchange Commission. I hoped that BeeLine hadn't reduced him to being a cubicle person. That would have been reason enough for his discontent. But when I finally found him, he had a modest but windowed office with an actual door. It was closed but covered with cartoons, mostly from the *New Yorker*, which made fun of financiers and of government.

I knocked on Frank's door and put my head in. He was on the phone, but he waved me in with an apologetic nod towards the small functional chairs he had for visitors. Still talking on the phone, he leapt up from his own office chair and gestured for me to sit in that. I was exhausted enough from wandering the maze of cubicles that I didn't refuse.

Done with his call, he sat down in one of the visitor chairs placed across the desk from where I now sat.

"So?" he said.

"So, how's it going?" I asked.

"So where's the board statement?" he asked, glancing at his watch. "It's already past four. I've got reporters waiting in New York. You're keeping them from their drinks."

"I'm betting I'm not," I retorted.

"What's going on?" he said.

"I wish I knew," I said.

"Maybe the rumors were right. Maybe they're firing him."

"Langerfeld was pretty adamant about board support," I said. "I think he'd resign before letting them fire his boy."

"Langerfeld's a fraud," said Frank. "He was a fraud all those years at ACM. Windbag with no guts. He won't stand with Sisley if the winds are blowing the other direction."

"You've had experience with him?"

Frank smiled. "More than you know. Or will ever know."

Damn, I hate confidential sealed settlements. Frank obviously knew some really juicy stuff about Langerfeld, and I didn't.

"Okay, then tell me this: Does what I don't know or won't ever know about Ben Langerfeld have any relevance to this situation? To BeeLine and Sisley?"

Frank stared at me for a moment while he considered his answer.

"No, only for what I just told you. Langerfeld's a fraud. He won't stand by your guy in the end. And I've already told you what the endgame will be about for Bradford Sisley—not sexism in the office. It'll be financial misstatement and Sarbanes-Oxley."

"But they couldn't be talking about that right now, could they?" I asked.

"Dunno. Depends on who's on the call and who knows what."

"No, you told me they still had a couple of months to

work with, Christmas and all that," I said. "They can't fire him without seeing all the financial information tied up in an incriminating package, right?"

"Maybe yes, maybe no," said Frank with a shrug. Then he added, "Probably no."

So what the hell were they still talking about?

At five thirty, playing solitaire on Renata's computer, I finally got the statement from Carter Shepherd. I shot it over to Charlie to get it out over the wires and the various social media that someone on his team undoubtedly understood.

My original draft of the statement had been mangled to pieces.

The statement now started with "The board met to discuss critical issues concerning the BeeLine's workplace environment." It went on to express "strong support" for Bradford, not the "unanimous, full, and complete" support written in my draft. And my words about the hope for years and years of his leadership had disappeared without a trace.

Then came the kicker. "The board has asked Board Director Wendy Smith-Kenyon, president of Caltech, to work with Mr. Sisley and BeeLine senior management to explore new initiatives to improve the work-life environment for all BeeLine employees."

Miley! She hadn't pulled off her official Board Diversity Committee, but she certainly had moved her ball forward. Did it happen by chance, or had she and her father been working off a predetermined game plan?

And now I knew who Wendy was, the board member that Bradford had mistrusted and Ben Langerfeld had disparaged as ignorant of financial analysts. She was their token academic and one of their token women. Well, she had certainly taken on an interesting assignment: to "work with" Mr. Sisley and his merry band of ruffians. But she probably had the fortitude to deal with those monkeys. After all, she had been handling a university faculty. She had experience dealing with nasty, petty, egotistical, manipulative people.

I had had my own experience with academia on an assignment a few years earlier. It was about the firing of a female black assistant professor at a private college in the South. I had helped the president of the college try to bring logic and a reasoned process to a perfectly hysterical situation. The professor had incited a small riot on campus against budget cuts. She had been cautioned to step back from confrontation and then had proceeded to lead another disturbance. The faculty was split down the middle. It became a food fight of flying accusations of racism, sexism, fascism, anarchism. I'm telling you, you don't want to see an angry faculty up close and personal, as I did. It makes kickboxing look like ballroom dancing.

My text message signal dinged. It was Bradford asking me to come to his office right away. This did not sound like an appealing prospect, given how the board meeting had come out. So I told him I could be there in ten minutes. Keeping him waiting would probably make him madder than he already was, but I needed a moment to pull my thoughts together.

I had been the one who suggested the board conference

call. I had known there was a risk—there always is a risk. But I had assumed from what Wanda had told me that the board was under Bradford's thumb. And that Langerfeld was in Bradford's court. But apparently things had run away from the chairman during the call. The Wanda and Mary Chan issues—picked up by Malcolm Wong and maybe Wendy Smith-Kenyon and possibly others—must have taken over the meeting.

Deep down inside, I was not unhappy with what had happened. When Miley had described two realities—hers and Charlie's—I had had a strong feeling that hers was the more credible. Actually, both were credible. Guys like Charlie thought everything was fine; women like Miley knew that there was an ugly underbelly to Charlie's world.

I also thought it might have been better if Miley's original idea of a full board committee had carried the day. Wendy Smith-Kenyon had a pretty vague mandate. Plus, she had to work with Bradford. A board committee would have had independence.

But this compromise—and it clearly was a compromise, in all its vagueness and messiness—was better than just ignoring the elephant that Wanda had left in the middle of the room.

Good for the board. Good for BeeLine.

But Bradford was my client. Not BeeLine. Not Wanda. Not Miley, for God's sake. And Bradford had just gotten a slap-down. Not a big slap-down. But a slap-down. And knowing my man as I did, I knew he would turn his anger on me.

I went to the men's room to wash my face and hands, take off my suspenders and reset my shirt into my trousers, and run a comb through my thinning hair. I looked at the large man in the mirror and decided he had no reason to feel guilty. If he had really been a bad guy, he might have set this situation up; he would have knowingly betrayed his client by walking him directly into the buzz saw of the board meeting. But he didn't do that. He did the best he could with the imperfect knowledge of the moment. Shit happens.

And in my heart, I knew it wasn't really shit that had happened, even though my client would think so.

Fine. I had convinced myself I didn't need to feel guilty. But I did need a strategy to defend myself from Bradford's anger. I needed to turn this lemon into lemonade—find some words that would somehow make Bradford see opportunity in his new partner Wendy Smith-Kenyon.

How clever I had been not to write the script for tomorrow's Sisley Show. Now it would be so easy. What would a magnanimous, wise leader say at this point? He would welcome Wendy's help; he would agree with the board that the time had come to take a close look, to maybe make a new start. It was time to ask tough questions and get down to the truth, even if it was uncomfortable. No one was more important to BeeLine than its people. Bradford was excited to work with Wendy on this critical project to make sure that everyone at BeeLine felt supported.

And then he would fire the Nazi, whoever he was, as the head of Human Resources. And do some other housekeeping. Maybe that was the lemonade I could offer Bradford! He could fire some people.

At night, Bradford's floor-to-ceiling windows became mirrors. It was a kaleidoscope of endless reflections of reflections. The art wall was repeating itself in several directions. So was I. As I stood with my crow cane in front of Bradford's enormous, clean desk and let his vitriol spray over me, I could see myself in several versions. There was Jonathan from the side, resembling the old cartoon of Alfred Hitchcock, a large parabolic line running from his chin to his crotch. There was Jonathan from the back, with his surprisingly small ass. There was Jonathan from the front. Why did he look so serene and bovinely contented in the midst of Bradford's diatribe?

"I'm surprised you don't see the upside here," I finally said while Bradford paused for a sip of whatever fine Scotch whiskey he was drinking.

"The upside?" he said with disdain. "I'm going to have that pompous dyke popping in and out of here with lamebrained ideas for making all the girlies happy while I'm trying to run a business. You have no idea what I'm facing here. I've got some serious issues coming up that I've got to deal with."

I assumed he was talking about his financial can of worms. But I showed no sign of knowing what he was talking about. He would tell me when he was ready.

"But that's the upside," I said. "Let her do her thing. She can take the pressure off of you on all this culture stuff. Wanda's farewell address can't be ignored or shoved under the table. The board just handed you a gift. They've anointed Wendy as the Joan of Arc to save the day. You don't have to wade through all that shit. Let her do it. If she wants to run focus groups and hold group-grope sessions, let her do it. Let her take on the problem. Meanwhile, you can keep your eye on the ball."

He stared back at me. "I don't trust her."

"I get that. She probably doesn't trust you, either," I said. "But you're stuck with each other and can probably make an unhappy relationship into a productive one. Listen, I'll write a great script for you for tomorrow's—"

"Oh, fuck! I forgot you convinced me to do that Sisley Show tomorrow," he said. "Cancel it. I don't want to do it."

"You have to do it," I said. "Your board just gave you their endorsement and asked you to work with Wendy. Tomorrow you go up in front of all your people and show them you are totally on the same page as the board and you're eager to fix anything that's wrong."

"But I'm not."

"You have to be. That's what the board wants; that's what a bunch of your employees want; that's what the outside world will want to hear. If you go silent, if you say nothing, there will only be trouble. Big, big trouble. Speculation about why you're being silent. Rumors of disunity at the top of the company. Swirling controversy with the lawsuit included in every story. You have to embrace this. That way it will quiet things down."

He was listening. He actually was listening. He took another big sip of his drink.

"You know how you can help me?" he asked. The tone was weird. It wasn't plaintive—that was probably impossible for a man of such ego. He had something in mind. Was I supposed to guess it?

"I *am* helping you. Right now. I'm giving you good

advice. And I'm going to write you a hell of a speech for the broadcast tomorrow."

"No, I have another idea," he said.

"What's that?" I asked. "And can I please sit down? My knees and feet are killing me."

He leapt out of his chair and pointed over to the couch area. "Yes, of course, I'm sorry."

Mr. Hyde was suddenly Dr. Jekyll. "I'm sorry"? He said "I'm sorry"? Bradford Sisley just apologized to me and sounded sincere. Now I was worried. I fell into the couch, immediately knowing that I would have a hell of a time getting out of it. Maybe that was his plan—to trap me in expensive upholstery until I gave him whatever he wanted.

He sat down across from me, still holding his scotch and offering me none.

"How about you taking on Wanda's job?"

The man had just finished excoriating me. And now he was offering me a job. I really needed some scotch myself.

"I told you I think you should give Charlie a chance, even if it's as 'acting' while you look for someone," I said. "I was very impressed today when I got down—"

"I hate Charlie," he said. "He was Wanda's boy, and I doubt he'll last very long now."

"Bradford, can I have some scotch?" I asked.

"Not unless you say yes," he said with a smile. "Jonathan, I need you. I trust you. You are smart, much smarter than Wanda, and you're not afraid to push me. You've got guts. You're not a pussy like she was. Miserable cunt."

I was hoping that Bradford didn't, like Nixon, have a

taping system in his office to capture everything for his memoirs.

"Look," I said. "I'm not a corporate animal."

I knew that for a fact. I had once taken the top communications job for a food company that had gotten to know me in a salmonella crisis. I lasted only a month in the job. It only took that long before both they and I became aware of how incompetent I was at the mundane aspects of corporate communications—employee communications, annual reports, management speeches, corporate events. You don't put a sprinter into a marathon. It doesn't work.

"Fine, I'm not a corporate animal either," he said. No truer words were ever spoken. He was truly that classic case of the entrepreneur who should have been kicked out years ago when his company needed to become a serious, functioning corporation. "I need you to help me with this corporate-culture shit and with Wendy and with Winkelmann."

"You need to fire Winkelmann," I interjected. Why did I say that? I hadn't even met the guy. Maybe Miley worked by witchcraft and she had possessed me. "Throw him under the bus to take the rap for all the culture problems."

"It's not that simple," he said.

Oh boy, another corporate intrigue.

"C'mon, Jonathan. Say yes. Big office. Big staff. I'll start you at six fifty plus a signing bonus of a hundred fifty. And a great options package. All the executive perks and benefits. Nice town to live in. You're single again, right? Lots of lovely ladies."

"Yeah, but is there a chubby-chaser bar?" I asked. He had no answer to that one.

But I sat there thinking about the proposition. Had Ruthie called him and given him that exact figure for the signing bonus? How perfect was that? With that signing bonus, I could be a hero to my daughter and, after a couple of years, be really flush and ready for retirement. And I'd have a Charlie and a Miley to do all the work.

Besides, I actually had nowhere else to go at the moment. The single life that had been rudely thrust upon me a year ago when I separated from my so-called girlfriend had so far been barren. I had hidden so long in the comfort of a relationship—first my suburban marriage and then my girlfriend—that I had lost the ability to manage on my own: to make an apartment livable, to devise my own entertainments, to make a new friend, to take a vacation. I hated my bachelor pad in the city. It was as cold and austere as my lonely existence. I could transfer that existence to California without losing anything. Perhaps the change would spark something inside me. Some buried normal human being.

What the hell? I could always quit if it didn't work out with BeeLine. And go back to the hotel living of my consulting life.

So I collected on the scotch.

For almost an hour, Bradford was charmingly gracious to me as his latest hire. He ordered up a huge plate of appetizers, probably meant for a group of ten or twelve people. Cheeses, salamis, guacamole, and chips, as well as hot things like nachos, wings, and tater tots to be dipped in a creamy horseradish sauce. I love pigging out on bar food.

We chatted amiably about the next day's broadcast

and my new role. Somewhere during my third glass of scotch, I raised, once again, the issue of his settling the sexual assault case with Katherine Davis. That ended our cozy tête-à-tête. I was dismissed.

I went down to Wanda's office—my new office.

Naturally, I snooped into every drawer and cabinet. But either Wanda or her personal assistant, Diane, had removed all the personal items. All the photos were gone. Several empty drawers suggested that a great sweep had occurred sometime after the late morning resignation.

I couldn't sit in Wanda's desk chair—it was too small and ergonomic for me, so I sat on her couch. I found the last of the cookies I had stashed in my pockets as I had left the boardroom. I had no recollection of eating all those other cookies, but it had been that kind of a day. I promised myself that I would savor this last one, actually paying attention to what I was eating. I only recall the first dainty bite.

My mind was racing, reliving moments of the crazy day. The totally worthless strategy meeting, sabotaged by Bradford Sisley's aggression and then Wanda's resignation. The Wall Street rumor sparking a sell-off of the stock and internal panic among top management. The waiting, waiting, waiting for the board and not knowing when or if they would come through. Miley and her secret powers.

But in the silence of her office, what was haunting me was Wanda. I looked around for some sort of clue about what had happened after she left the meeting in the morning. The office told me nothing: the corporate art was still on the walls, the array of company publications untouched on the shelves. I reached over to pick up the previous year's annual report from the coffee table and searched for her photo. The carefully composed corporate photo made her look younger than she did in life. Her eyes—again vaguely familiar—belied the smile.

Something in the unfolding of the morning's events was wrong. What had sparked her angry resignation? Miley said everyone assumed it was something Bradford Sisley had done or said. To be sure, Sisley's behavior towards her at the meeting had been rude and dismissive, but his meanest remarks had been aimed at me. His real nasty denigration of her came after she had gone, when he attacked her loyalty and then acted out his crude "fuck me, fuck me" performance. For the life of me, I couldn't reconstruct the conversation and pinpoint a moment when something was said or something happened that could have been a trigger for her.

Obviously, the tension between Wanda and Bradford was much greater than anything I had understood or felt. Or that she had let on to me. But I couldn't find a motivator, an obvious provocation in that morning's meeting. All I could recall was that she had been there very passively, and then she had announced she had to deal with something.

If my sense of time was anything close to accurate, the speed with which Wanda had left that boardroom, returned to her office, composed and released her statement, and then cleared out her office was simply too fast. And the statement was too tightly written to have just spilled out of an angry person, particularly a person as generally deliberate as Wanda.

So this was not an impetuous decision. It had been planned and prepared for. All of which suggested that my wonderful collaborative partner, working so hard to protect BeeLine and save Bradford Sisley's skin, might have been like a terrorist wired up for a suicide mission. She had seemed an ally, but apparently she had made all the preparations to blow everything to bits.

But why? And why that day? Why not the previous week? Why not the next week? Next month?

I decided to give her a call and ask to get together for a drink. Ostensibly, it could be about work, her job, the things I needed to know about upcoming events, and the quirks of the people I now had to supervise. But then once we were huddled in a corner table with ice cubes clinking in our glasses, I would ask her for the truth about her relationship with Sisley and about how and when she had decided she would leave in such a destructive way.

I pulled out my cell phone, swiped down to Wanda's personal mobile number, and poked it to call her. It immediately went to voice mail, which had been changed from its previous personal message to one of those mechanical responses. I hung up.

I rolled to a prone position on Wanda's couch and promptly dozed off in a scotch haze. A cleaning lady shook me awake around one o'clock in the morning and sternly told me to get on home. I called an Uber and stiffly headed to the front door to meet it.

6

THURSDAY

Thanks to the remnants of my jet lag, I was able to be refreshed by a couple of hours' sleep. At six o'clock, I was back in Renata's office. Having comfortably settled into her space, I was reluctant to abandon it as my own.

Besides, I had no idea whether I was now the senior vice president for communications or not. Sisley was crazy enough to have forgotten about the whole conversation. He was also sly enough to pretend to forget it if, in the light of a gray Thursday morning, he decided to change his mind.

It didn't really matter for the moment. I had plenty to do. I had to rewrite the script for the Sisley Show to reflect the Wendy Smith-Kenyon factor. Then I needed to get it to Carter Shepherd for legal clearance and to Bradford as soon as possible. We were supposed to rehearse at nine and broadcast at nine thirty.

Plus I wanted to be available when the stock market opened at six thirty. I checked all the important news sites. Because the statement had gotten out so late, it was pretty much taken at face value without commentary. Generally, reporters read the words as a clear endorsement of Bradford Sisley and implied that Wendy's assignment was something the board had to do. How little they understood. Probably both decisions had been contentious.

I saw that Gerald Berger had filed his story about the board actions. But in the buried paragraph discussing the lawsuit, he still did not mention the possibility of a security tape in the elevator. That made me suspect that he was working on a separate story with the tape as a centerpiece.

I needed to head that off, or at least blunt it. So I called him. I would give him an update on Bradford—how good Bradford was feeling about the board's action, how confident he seemed when I had told him about the possibility of a videotape of the encounter.

"Apparently, there's some sort of technical problem with the security tape," Gerald said.

"Technical problem? Like the camera wasn't running?" I asked.

"Dunno," he responded. "The guy got suddenly very tight-lipped about it. Like the hotel lawyers had gotten to him. He said they were looking further into the matter."

"Did you ask him directly to confirm or deny the existence of the tape?" I asked.

"You telling me how to do my job, Jonathan?" Gerald said. "Of course I did. He said, 'No comment.'"

"What do you think is up?"

"Oh, probably your boy sent in some goon squad to foul up the recording," he said. "Sort of a combo of the Watergate burglary with a Rose Mary Woods seventeen-minute-deletion kicker."

All I could think of was Bradford saying he had some

people checking out Katherine Davis. Gerald had no idea how scary his joke was.

"I told you," I said. "Bradford is very cool about the tape. He says it will work in his favor."

"Fine," he said. "I'll use that if the tape ever makes it to prime time. In the meantime, no tape. No confirmation that such a tape exists."

As I hung up the phone, I tried to remember how many people I had told about the tape. Bradford, to be sure. Wanda, I thought. Definitely Langerfeld. Definitely not Carter Shepherd. Except for Bradford, there was no need to give any of them the amended information about technical problems. And, of course, it was possible that Bradford might even know about those problems already.

After the market opened, there wasn't a thrilling bounce-back for the stock, but it was respectable. Hopefully, by the end of the trading day, most of the lost ground would have been regained. Maybe the worst was behind us on that front.

A knock on my closed door. I was engrossed in writing the Sisley Show script and preferred not to be disturbed. A second knock. And then a third even more insistent one. Okay, I'm doomed, I thought. I yelled, "Come on in."

It was a ridiculously tall man with a head of rich, gray-specked hair. The hair had been gelled to allow stray strands to fall across his forehead like that of a movie-star idol arriving at a screen premiere. The clothes were expensive and obviously tailored to the man's enormous height. The shirt had been fitted to accentuate the fact that his middle-aged body was in good shape. Did I see cowboy boots peeking out the bottom of the pants? Why would someone that tall be wearing cowboy boots, particularly at work?

He marched forward, hand outreached, and flashed a set of perfect teeth.

"Vell, Mr. Senior Wice President, I belief congratulations are in order."

The German accent was pronounced, almost comic. Claus Winkelmann, senior vice president for human resources, had come to call. Miley's Nazi.

I extended my hand without taking all the actions that would lift me from my seat. My hand felt like a child's in the embrace of his enormous fingers.

"May I sit down, pleasse?" he asked in a formal European way.

"Actually, I'm on a very short deadline for Bradford right now," I said. "Perhaps we could chat later today. Things are likely to be calmer by this afternoon."

"Vell," he said, clearly annoyed by my priorities, "ve need to discuss all zee terms of your employment. And you must sign many, many documents. You cannot start your yob until the paperwork ist done." This last was said with the severity of a judge handing down a sentence.

"Fine," I said. "I'll just continue as a consultant until we get the paperwork signed."

"Bradford vanted zee paperwork to be completed this morning," he said in a slightly threatening tone.

"I'll be seeing him at nine, and I'll explain," I said.

"Yes, pleasse," he responded. "Ve don't like to disappoint Bradford."

Really, I thought, this guy is a comic. He's seen *Hogan's Heroes* or *The Producers* or something and decided to be the

German stereotype that makes people laugh. Where were the lederhosen?

And to continue his laughable performance, his face, which had been deeply stern, now turned warmly friendly, and the perfect teeth reappeared. "Und, off course, I vant to make your acquaintance and learn to know you bettah. Ve vill be vorking togethah on many things."

"I look forward to that," I said pleasantly. "But right now, I really can't talk. I'll call you around midday to set up some time for me to come to your office."

"Wery goot," he said. He turned, and without a good-bye, he opened the door, stepped through, and closed it again. He did not click the heels of his cowboy boots as a finale to his comedy routine.

I wondered what the hell this guy was doing heading up a Human Resources Department in a Silicon Valley corporation.

Once I had hit the Send button on the script, I gave Charlie a call. I thought I should give him a heads-up about his new boss. Plus, by coming in to see me, he would open my office door for me without my having to do it myself.

Apparently, the office grapevine (which probably ran through Miley's office) had already alerted Charlie to my being hired. He offered me a polite congratulations. He also said he had some bad news: Wanda had made an appearance by Skype on *Good Morning America*. I recalled how, several days earlier, she had easily killed Bradford's appearance on the show. She obviously knew folks over there pretty well.

Charlie showed me the segment on his BeePad. It could have been worse. The extreme anger of her press release had given way to a demeanor of sad regret at the situation at BeeLine and other Silicon Valley companies. It was a tragedy that so much human potential was being wasted when, in so many other industries, men and women were able to work together with mutual respect. She praised the board for the Wendy Smith-Kenyon assignment but said, with a rueful smile, that Wendy would need a lot of help from the inside to really change the situation. She carefully dodged a couple of questions about Bradford, declining comment on the Katherine Davis lawsuit. She said that sexism was systemic at BeeLine and was not about one person only. When asked about the possibility of a class action suit, she smiled enigmatically and said, "We'll see."

When the segment was over, Charlie said, "Not too bad, huh?"

"So why do you think she did it?" I asked. That was the question in my head. The day before, she had thrown a huge grenade at the company. Now, she was soft-pedaling her critique a little, making it a broader industry issue, praising the board, avoiding an attack on Bradford. The *Good Morning America* producers were probably disappointed; it was all pretty vanilla.

"Sorry?" Charlie was confused by my question.

"Why was Wanda so careful about her criticism of the company today after yesterday's atomic blast?"

Charlie thought for a moment. "Maybe because of the Wendy thing?"

I could never tell whether people of his generation

used that question thing at the end of a sentence as a real question or as a way of making a statement that they couldn't quite bring themselves to present as an assertion.

"So you think that maybe Wendy is enough, as far as Wanda is concerned?" I asked.

"Well, maybe not enough but a good start?" he said, again inflecting upwards on the last word.

Maybe, I was thinking. Maybe skydiving Wanda was not really an angry fist-shaking revolutionary. Maybe all she really wanted was for a reform process to begin. And maybe the others—I was thinking about Miley—would also be satisfied with Wendy Smith-Kenyon leading a reform effort.

But, exactly on cue, Miley appeared at the door to dispel that hope.

"I hear congratulations are due," she said without a trace of a smile.

"Actually, you should be congratulated as well," I said. "That was quite a little victory the board gave you."

She wasn't going to take the bait. I really wanted to know whether her father had been a driver of the decision to anoint Wendy Smith-Kenyon. And whether she had played a role in that. But she, wisely, wasn't going to let me in.

Instead, she told me that no one should think there had been a victory the day before. Employees were finding the board's action inadequate. According to her network, there were probably between nine hundred and one thousand people who had called in sick that morning. Most—but not all—were women.

"Is this organized?" I asked, wondering if the person I was asking was the organizer.

"Well, people have been communicating with one another through Facebook and stuff, if that's what you mean by organized," she said. Once again, I had been caught flat-footed by the paradigm shift of social media. I was back in the Stone Age, where if you wanted to organize something like a sick-out protest, leaders were required. You needed flyers. You needed a mimeograph machine.

"What are they saying?" I asked. "Through Facebook *and stuff*?" I hated phrases like "and stuff," particularly from a communications person.

"That the board doesn't know how big the problem is. And that they're wrong if they think that Wendy—who has her own job at Caltech—can solve these issues by working with Bradford, of all people. This is rubbing a little ointment on something that needs major surgery."

Major surgery? Like "high-level personnel changes"? This girl wanted to see blood on the corporate carpets.

"So, what would make these folks happy?" I asked. "What do you recommend?"

Miley stared at me for a moment, and then a little smile appeared. "You know, Mr. Keaton, you gave me a little lecture yesterday about how a corporation's structure works. What the board does. What management does. What I do. I don't think it's up to me to recommend solutions here. Sounds like a board problem to me. Don't you think?"

I loved this young lady's pluck; I really did.

She turned to leave. Then she turned back, a smug little smirk on her lips.

"You know, you really need to have an all-hands department meeting. Introduce yourself. Say nice words about Wanda. Set a tone."

Of course, she was right. But I really had other priorities right now.

"Great thinking," I said. "Why don't you write up some message points? And once my announcement is officially made, we can talk about timing."

And by then I'd have thought of some other way to delay an all-hands meeting. I hated shit like that.

The corporate TV studio was impressive. I could recall the days when companies would designate some inside conference room for shooting a video, slap a couple of fake potted plants behind a desk, and run cables and cords down the hallway from the nearest outlets. Here at BeeLine a multistage studio with a high-tech control room had been constructed behind the cafeteria, and best I could tell, the technical staff was first rate.

And the whole operation was undoubtedly part of my new empire as senior vice president for communications. Hey, I had a studio in California!

When I arrived at nine o'clock, Miley was already there checking the setup for the Sisley Show. Bradford would be remotely miked, could use the stool if he wished, could wander if he wished. The backdrop was, inevitably, a warm blue wall with a bunch of BeeLine logos on it. The ubiquitous potted plant was there. The makeup lady was ready for Bradford, and the teleprompter was only waiting for the script. So was I.

Bradford and Carter Shepherd came flying in with the script at about nine fifteen.

"We've taken out the mention of Wanda," Carter told me as he handed a memory stick to the technician to transfer the script to the teleprompter.

"I think that's a mistake," I said.

"Instead, we've inserted an announcement about your appointment," he said. "Moving forward and all that."

I got the logic of what they had done. But I was annoyed to have it handed to me as a done deal. Presumably Wanda had faced a lot of this: the "boys" would make their decisions on communications materials and not consider her as an equal partner with, perhaps, useful input.

"Maybe I could see what you're saying about me?" I asked with clear annoyance.

"Sure," said Carter. "Just ask Mark over there, who's doing the upload."

While I would never be so petty as to note that Carter had offered no congratulations or best wishes, I was definitely feeling the cool air from him. He and I had been working together effectively in the last twenty-four hours, but something had clearly switched with my taking Wanda's job. I tried to remember the person he had recommended for Wanda's job the day before—some guy from his own department, I recalled.

I went over to the teleprompter technician, but Bradford had already started his rehearsal. So I had to wait while he rattled off 80 percent of the statement before getting to what had been the Wanda part and now was the Jonathan part.

It was okay. I could have written it better and would

have left out mention of the work I had done years ago for Morris Feldstein, the Wall Street crook. Not only was it sleazy to be involved with Feldstein, but it also didn't speak well for my PR skills. I had failed at my image-making with Morris; he went down in history as one of the greatest scumbags in the history of Wall Street. Great PR job, Jonathan.

But the statement did a nice job of talking about my past work for BeeLine and the deep respect that management had for me. They even made up a quote from Ben Langerfeld saying how thrilled he was to have me on the team. I wondered if anyone had even told him about it yet.

We were in the final moments before broadcast. Carter came up behind me and asked if I was okay with what they had said about me. Just for the hell of it, I said no. He didn't respond.

Bradford's delivery was good enough. It was clearly a strain for him to show enthusiasm for Wendy Smith-Kenyon's mission. But he put a little oomph into the sections where he talked about his personal commitment to the people of BeeLine and to addressing any concerns they might have about the workplace environment. He also sounded positive on the subject of me. I was glad there would be a digitized record of that moment; it undoubtedly would provide amusement in later years.

After sign-off, I approached Bradford, who was perched on his stool, to give him a quick update. The stock was coming back, and the press coverage was good. But I also told him that according to Miley, some nine hundred to one thousand employees had not shown up for work that day.

"Sure, it's Thursday," he said. "Bunch of lazy shitheads are going to take a long weekend and pretend it's a protest. Get me a list of any executives who didn't show today. This could be my chance to do some housecleaning."

"Bradford, I have no way to get you a list," I protested. "Shouldn't that be Claus?"

"Sure, whatever," he said. "Have him give me a list of these lazy assholes who haven't shown up for work. I want to see who's involved."

I made an appointment to see Claus Winkelmann at eleven o'clock. But I never made it. I was hit by two shitballs.

Around ten fifteen, Sandra Farber sent out a new press release, claiming to have another victim of an aggressive Bradford Sisley sexual advance. Having predicted several times that other shoes would drop, I felt a secret satisfaction at seeing this happen. I'm bad that way.

The new accusation seemed a little lame, and significantly, Farber wasn't trotting out a victim at a press conference. Officially, that was because the woman wanted to remain anonymous. But you can always hold a press conference with a person behind a screen—makes great TV. The accusation was over ten years old, and just too conveniently, it included an elevator, which presumably was an erogenous zone for Bradford Sisley. I particularly noted the carefully chosen words of the accusation: it sounded more like a late-night, clumsy drunken pass rather than something that would hold up as a real assault case.

I knocked out a one-sentence absolute denial and ran it by an apoplectic Bradford. He had no recollection of any such event, not that he would, particularly if he had been drunk or high on cocaine. Carter Shepherd frigidly approved the statement. Apparently, they still had not worked out who would be Bradford's lawyer on these tawdry matters. Not my business.

Charlie put the statement out. But I knew that a statement alone was not enough. A statement's clean and simple denial needed to be tarted up. I needed to provide some elaboration, some context with the most important reporters. BeeLine and Bradford were headed back in the news cycle again. And the new news would drag up all the old news of earlier in the week. The goal had to be to make this latest accusation seem not all that interesting—keep it from being the next bombshell.

So I had to hit the phones again. I had to convince all my dear reporter friends that Sandra Farber was pulling a shenanigan to keep up the pressure. But she was playing a very weak card. And I wanted to make sure that when they wrote their stories—which would inevitably include the Wanda accusations—they also included the Wendy initiative. The company had responded; the company was addressing any issues.

I canceled my eleven o'clock with Claus and starting dialing. I took each reporter through the careful wording of the accusation, suggesting that there probably was no case. I talked about the piling on that happens in these kinds of situations, particularly when there is a chance for significant money. I said everything I could to make the story unnewsworthy.

I was holding my breath on the employee sick-out. Eventually, it had to come out, but I didn't want it to happen that day. Then the negative story would have more hooks. I could see the headline: "BeeLine Faces Mounting Challenges."

Wanda's assistant, Diane, kept trying to entice me into Wanda's office to do my phone work, but I had grown truly fond of Renata's office, surrounded by the mementos of a young woman's life so different from my own. As I talked on the phone, I was still enjoying all her photos—in the mountains, under the seas, trekking through the jungles, bicycling through green countryside. I had never once considered doing things like this—except for one snorkeling misadventure, when the backs of my legs, arms, and neck got sunburned to a painful lobster red.

Obviously, I couldn't tell Diane that I had fallen in love with Renata's life and didn't want to leave it. Instead I told her that Claus Winkelmann would send in the storm troopers if I stepped into Wanda's office before I had signed the "many, many papers" that had to be signed. She clearly appreciated the dig on the German. She was trying to make me feel welcome in my new position, and I felt bad that I wasn't responding appropriately. But I really had other stuff to do besides build my relationship with Diane.

So she took another tack—much more effective. About twelve thirty, when I was halfway through reaching out to my list of contacts, she brought me a plate of excellent spaghetti Bolognese from the Executive Dining Room. Smart lady. She also brought me a small bottle of wine—but I knew better than to take that risk. Besides, it was crappy screw-top California merlot.

As I was just settling in to enjoy my lunch, the second shit-ball hit me. Veronique, the gorgeous European pop singer, had lobbed an explosive shell at us from across the ocean. And because she had done it as a tweet to her millions of followers, it was instantaneously viral. Now there was no hope of keeping the next round of BeeLine stories low key.

I was vaguely aware that Veronique was used in ads for BeeBuds, the company's high-powered Bluetooth earphones. I'd seen the billboards in airports—a stunning black woman in a slinky, shimmering gown throwing back her head with joy, presumably because of the quality sound of the music in her ears. The tagline was something like "I found the music when I found my BeeBuds."

So it was with ironic flare that Veronique had sent out her tweet: "Bad news! I've lost my BeeBuds and I don't know where to find them."

An emergency meeting was called. All hands to Bradford's conference room.

I wolfed down the spaghetti and the accompanying bread and salad. I texted Charlie to come see me, figuring that if I took Charlie to the meeting, I could hand any work off to him so I could get back to my phone-a-thon. He arrived just as I switched over to the dessert—a generous bowl of rice pudding with raisins.

Charlie seemed pleased by my including him. He told me he had managed the publicity for the Veronique endorsement.

"So you know her?" I asked.

"Not really," he replied. "I usually was in the room, but it was Wanda who had the lead on this."

"But does Veronique know you well enough that if you reached out to her, she'd recognize the name?" I probed. I knew I was playing the race card. Charlie was probably one of the few black faces—maybe the only black face—Veronique would have encountered within BeeLine. Maybe they had sent sympathetic signals to each other or something. I knew I always did that with any fat person in a room—little smiles that said hey there, look at us stuck in this room of skinny-asses.

"Doubtful," he responded. "She's a major space cadet."

I finished my pudding and used my crow cane to lift my bulk to a standing position. As we headed out the door, Charlie kindly removed my napkin, which was tucked into the top of my shirt, a fat man's protection against stains. At least someone was looking out for me.

There was a crowd in Bradford's sleek conference room. Like me, everyone had brought their entourage. The head of Global Marketing—a short gray-haired guy who kept biting his nails—had brought three people. I had no idea who any of them were. Carter had four young lawyers in tow, all men, all very nice looking. I had heard talk of Shepherd's Flock of Pretty Boys, how he seemed to recruit only the handsomest of the smart lawyers who wanted to work at BeeLine. Collectively, they made a ludicrous sight, like a casting call for the next legal drama on Fox TV.

Bradford was agitated, yelling at the gray-haired guy about how they never should have made the deal with this piece of Euro-trash, how it had never made a dime, and how he should have known better.

He hadn't noticed that Charlie and I had walked in. For a second, it sounded like Bradford's diatribe against Veronique was going to include the N-word. Everyone looked at Charlie as Bradford raced up to the word. But he turned and saw who had just entered and awkwardly changed the structure of his sentence.

Charlie gave him a big grin that seemed to say, "Nice catch, dude!"

"You're late," he growled at the two of us.

"My fault," I said. I refrained from telling him that I had been delayed by rice pudding. Mainly, I just didn't want him to blame Charlie.

I sat down without a further word, ready to hear where the discussion was.

A movie-star-handsome young attorney, in a ponderous, classically lawyerly way, reviewed the terms of Veronique's contract. After extensive hedging and the repeated use of the word "pursuant," he finally concluded that she had not violated the terms of her contract. It stipulated that she could not denigrate the product, and she hadn't. All she had said was that her BeeBuds were lost.

"She had help on this," opined Carter Shepherd.

"What do you mean?" Bradford asked.

"Well, from what I've heard, Veronique is a bit of an airhead," said Carter. He looked around for confirmation, and several heads nodded, including Charlie's. "So an airhead doesn't craft something as clever as this tweet—both from a legal perspective and from a PR perspective."

No glance in my direction. No sought-after confirmation from the expert in the room, the corporate officer in charge of PR. Was I being overly sensitive? Maybe. But I wouldn't make legal judgments; why should Carter Shepherd be talking about PR? I felt disrespected. So I butted in.

"Well, if the lawyers say she's legally clean, I assume we're not going to sue her or cancel her contract or anything really dumb like that," I said. "I mean 'dumb' from a PR perspective. I wouldn't think to make a legal conclusion." I said these last words with an evil-eye stare at Carter Shepherd. "But what we do need to do, from a PR perspective, is say something. And fast."

The golden boys from the Legal Department sat stony faced. The gray-haired guy suggested maybe we should state that we were willing to send Veronique a new set of BeeBuds if hers were truly lost. That would call her bluff. His staff all lowered their eyes at the stupidity of his suggestion.

"I like that," said Bradford.

"I don't," I said. "It would be a stupid thing to do. Like a fifth-grade response."

I could see that neither Bradford nor Mr. Nail-Biting Gray Head understood what I meant. So I had to go further.

"Plus, it would give her a chance to refuse the BeeBuds—throw them back in our face. That would not be good. Even more bad press. From a PR perspective."

Carter must have gotten the message that I needed a little ego-massaging, because he politely asked me to tell them what exactly I thought we should say.

So easy.

"We send out a statement that we hope to meet shortly with Veronique to discuss any issues she has and to talk to her about what Board Director Wendy Smith-Kenyon will be doing to ensure cultural change at BeeLine."

"Well, who the hell is going to do that—meet with Veronique?" Bradford demanded.

"Wendy?" I suggested.

"No way!" said Charlie.

I looked at Carter for confirmation of Charlie's adamant objection and saw that both he and his flock of boys were smirking. I could tell it wasn't about the idea of Wendy Smith-Kenyon and Veronique having a tête-à-tête. It was about the effrontery of Charlie putting down my suggestion. The suggestion of his new boss. Apparently, in the land of the sheep, one didn't disagree openly with the shepherd.

Stupid corporate bullshit.

I knew it was just Charlie being Charlie. Which is what drove Bradford crazy about him.

"Why not?" I asked Charlie.

"Humorless Lesbian academic meets space cadet rock icon," he said. "Not a match made in heaven." He gestured with two hands passing right by one another.

My first thought was that Charlie might need a little brushup on his diversity training. My second thought was that I still needed to find out the scoop on this Wendy person. When Bradford called her a dyke, I had assumed he was just being Bradford. But, apparently, she was actually gay. Interesting.

"Okay then," I continued. "Who is best equipped to talk to Veronique? Who has a relationship with her?"

The silence was deafening. I looked at the gray-haired guy because I knew enough about corporate structure to know that the responsibility for the relationship with someone like Veronique was in the marketing area. He wasn't talking. He was working on the nail of the fourth finger of his right hand. Bite, examine. Bite, reexamine.

"C'mon," I said. "I'm new here. I don't know her. But you all have paid her a lot of money, and someone has to know her, be her handler, or whatever."

Still silence. So, with all my dramatic flair, I did my angry outrage routine. One of my favorites. I swept my arm around the room and yelled, "*With all the high-paid talent in this room, no one has anything to say?* The question is simple, people. Who the fuck knows this woman?"

I was glad that Charlie had removed my napkin from my chest—it would have significantly reduced the power of the moment.

Charlie, good old direct Charlie, finally broke the silence with a question to the Global Marketing folks, who were following their boss in his silence.

"I thought that was Jasmine's job?" Question or statement, Charlie?

From the name, I was guessing that they had put a black woman into the relationship with the black celebrity. Typical. Not stupid, necessarily, but typical.

"Let's get her in here," demanded Bradford.

"Jasmine's not in today," the gray-haired man said

somewhat sheepishly. "She sent me an e-mail this morning that she has a family emergency and won't be back till next week."

Hmm, I thought. A boycotter.

"Fucking track her down," demanded Bradford.

"Martin here has been trying," said the gray-haired man, nodding to a young man to his left. "Martin?" he said, handing off the hot potato.

"She's not responding," Martin said. "Maybe she's on a plane?" Same upward inflection at the end of the sentence as Charlie. I hate it. Everyone talking like a Valley girl.

"What about the ad agency?" I asked. "They must have someone who was designated to deal with her."

"Yeah, but we fired them last week," said the gray-haired man.

"Well, maybe that's what she's mad about," I said, hoping that I might be right. "Maybe this whole thing is about the ad agency. Maybe they're even helping her—writing the tweet and shit. Maybe it has nothing to do with Wanda or Bradford or any of that."

Everyone seemed to perk up at the prospect of my straw in the wind. "So how do we talk to her?" I asked again. "Who else has a good relationship with her?"

"What about you, Charlie?" asked Bradford. I knew, Charlie knew, probably everyone in the room knew that Bradford was now playing the race card. Just as I had done earlier with Charlie. It looked so stupid, so obviously inappropriate, when someone else did it.

"She's maybe said two words to me," Charlie said.

"Yeah, but she'll recognize you, at least," said Bradford, digging his hole even deeper.

"What about Francesca?" asked Carter Shepherd. There were various expressions around the table—ranging from "not a bad idea" to "Jesus, are you kidding?" to "whoa, do you really want to go there?" to "who the hell is Francesca?" I was definitely the leader of the pack on the last one. The gray-haired guy bit off a satisfying piece of his fourth fingernail and pulled out an emery board to smooth the mess over.

"They *are* close friends," said Bradford.

"Who is Francesca?" I asked.

"Claus's wife," said Carter Shepherd. "She and Veronique were jet-setters together. They went to school together in Switzerland and did some modeling together in London."

Finally, the gray-haired guy had something to say. "Francesca helped us seal the deal with Veronique."

I sat quietly letting everyone ponder this possibility. I was hoping that someone would pick up the ball and carry it across the line. It was completely weird that no company person had the right relationship with Veronique to serve as an ambassador to her. But with Wanda gone and Jasmine going AWOL and no one ready to designate "*the* black person" or "*the* woman" who might be appropriate, maybe Claus's wife, whoever the hell she was, was the best bet.

Finally, Bradford moved the action forward. "I'll call Claus," he said. And then he added mysteriously, "She owes us one, anyway."

Charlie did a nice job of drafting the response statement to Veronique's tweet, saying that we hoped to meet with her soon. Out it went. And Bradford went off to put the machinery in motion to have Francesca reach out to the great superstar.

I could tell there was a big backstory I was missing about Claus and his ex-model, ex-jet-setter wife. But I could get that from Frank or, if I had to, from Carter. For the moment, I could get back to my phone and talk to all my buddies about the story they would be writing below the now inevitable headline I had wanted to avoid: "New Challenges for BeeLine."

Foolishly, I thought I was finished with the rock star drama.

Around four o'clock, as I was wrapping up what had been a fairly unsuccessful afternoon of trying to minimize all of BeeLine's issues, Diane came in and said that Claus and Francesca needed to see me. "Why me?" I asked. Bradford was supposed to be dealing with this Veronique business—him or the nail-biting guy. Diane rolled her eyes.

"Francesca gets what Francesca wants," she said. "And right now she wants you. Claus told me she needs guidance about dealing with Veronique."

"What the hell does that mean?"

"You'll have to ask her," Diane said. "I can only tell you that Claus was 'wery' adamant that you 'moost meet' this afternoon." Were Diane and I going to start our bonding by both making fun of Claus? Whatever. But it didn't seem very nice. I wondered if diversity training included a module on not mocking accents.

I tried to reach Frank to get a quick tutorial on Claus and Francesca, but he was on the phone. A few minutes later he texted me that we had to meet that night at the '49er—a big issue had come up. Just what I needed.

Claus had ordered up a corporate car to take me out to a fancy golf club south of town. As I slipped into a short snooze in the sumptuous back seat, I thought about how I might actually get to like my new corporate life. Apparently, BeeLine executives had many services at their fingertips—fine lunches at their desk, cars to chauffeur them wherever, the corporate jet. Probably club memberships as well. Maybe there was a club for gourmands that I could join.

Claus, dressed in a handsome golf outfit with a Scottish tam on his head, was standing under the porte cochère to greet me as the car pulled in. This was odd. The driver must have phoned ahead. I knew that honored guests were greeted this way at the White House or whatever, but as I struggled to get my bulk and my cane out of the car, I decided it was actually a cruel thing to do to an honored guest. No one wants to be watched as they struggle out of a car. Luckily, my driver knew how to leverage my heft a bit, although he was so strong that there was a brief perilous moment when I almost fell face-first on the pavement.

Claus quickly dispelled any thoughts I had had that he was standing there to honor my arrival. He took me by the arm and whispered, "Ve must talk for a moment. Then ve meet my vife."

He guided me to a sitting room on the right of the entry. It held at least a dozen clusters of chairs for chatting opportunities—deep stuffed chairs, card tables with chairs, settees with leather side chairs, little circles of straight-backed chairs. It looked like a used furniture warehouse with so many styles scattered about. A few seating clusters were taken. Claus guided me to a corner with two stuffed chairs. He wanted privacy.

I wanted to keep standing; he was offering me a deep, low chair I would never escape.

Claus's news was not unexpected. A female employee had filed a sexual harassment complaint about Bradford.

"Harassment or assault?" I asked.

"Harassment," Claus answered, with a certainty that suggested he absolutely knew the difference. "It is yust like the other ones. She says he told her she was wery pretty and that she would be vell rewarded if she vould come home wiff him."

"You said just like the other ones. How many other ones have there been?" I asked.

Claus's eyes rolled up to the left as if to indicate it was hard to keep count. "Bradford alone or all of them?"

"All of them?" I asked with real trepidation.

"My dear new friend," he said. "Vanda was not making things up, you know."

"Okay, let's focus on Bradford," I said. He was, after all, still my client. "I was told there were only a couple of Bradford settlements in the past."

Claus smiled enigmatically. "Settlements are for ven ve fail. Ve haff a process for handling such things. It is a wery good process that keeps many troubles from getting too far."

Looking up at the giant smiling German, I could only imagine the worst about his process. Threats, intimidation, kidnapping women's pets, keying their cars, hacking into their computers, sending texts in the middle of the night. I have a flair for the dramatic.

"It's called delay, deflect, demotiwate," he continued. "I vorked on it wiff Carter Shepherd. It's all perfectly legal. Wery legal. Complaints go into—how does he call it—a Rube Goldberg machinery. Most the time the voman gives up. Or she just leaves. Poof! Gone!"

Suddenly, "Fire the Nazi" had a whole new meaning for me. It was not about this strange Teutonic robot wandering the BeeLine halls like an alien from outer space, a clown with a German accent. This was an evil clown—the bagman who had a process for getting rid of the dirty laundry. He was protecting Bradford and the other men from the consequences of what they were doing. Keeping them free to continue to do it.

I thought back to my conversation with Bradford when I suggested firing Claus, thinking it would be a good gesture. And he had responded, "It's not as simple as that."

Fuck. This all was something I needed to think about and digest. It wasn't like I was a stranger to hellholes or shit swamps. But I was always the stranger in town, the Lone Ranger coming in and fixing the short-term mess with no responsibility for fixing the real problem. Here I was in danger of becoming part of the problem. In fact, as of this moment, I *was* part of the problem. What exactly was I supposed to do now? I had just been informed that there was an organized system at BeeLine for shoving sexual complaints under the rug or sweeping them out the door.

Francesca was a display of Latin fireworks. In the context of the golf club grill room, where the other women wore subdued suburban golfing clothes—and far too many logoed visors—Francesca was ablaze in bright orange and purple. Her luxuriant black hair was pulled back by a matching orange scarf, which trailed down to deep cleavage between her voluptuously raised breasts. Gold bracelets and bangles were up and down her arms.

I decided she had definitely not played a round of golf that afternoon.

She beckoned me to a chair next to her, which had a wider girth than most in the room. Before I sat down, she reached out a bejeweled right hand, displaying her long deep-magenta fingernails, which matched the lipstick on her collagen-overdosed lips. She wore artfully applied makeup: copious mascara, eyebrows darkened to a Frieda Kahlo thickness, and perfectly rosy cheeks. It was exotic, but I couldn't help wondering whether the face beneath the mask—the face she woke up with in the morning—was simply ordinary.

"I set a special chair for you, my friend," she said. "My darling Claus told me you were large. And you are." She was smiling a rich, inviting smile.

"And he told me you were beautiful," I lied. "And you are." It was clear she was a woman who went out of her way to be noticed. Why wouldn't I feed her vanity?

Her Spanish accent was thickly delivered in a low throaty alto voice. As Claus and I sat down, they spoke to one another briefly in French. I wondered if that was to keep me out of the loop or because it was their easiest common language. I actually knew enough French to understand that he was telling her to keep it short because they had a dinner reservation at six, and she was annoyed because she had thought the reservation was later.

"I have ordered a mojito," she said to me. "You *must* have one. I have especially trained the bartender on making a true mojito. Eet ees excellent here. You will have one, yes?"

I actually hate mojitos. Mint has always disgusted me. As a kid, it grew wild behind our family's garage, and the dog always pissed on it. My friends and I pissed on it as well. So when I smell mint, I smell piss.

But for the moment, I would comply with the señora, who never encountered an *R* she couldn't roll. She waved two fingers at the bartender and mouthed the word "mas," apparently deciding the issue for Claus as well.

"So," she said, crossing her long-nailed fingers together in a let's-get-down-to-business clasp. "My husband tells me you want me to visit my old friend Veronique."

"Maybe Bradford could explain it best. Why don't you talk to him?"

She rolled her eyes. Her right hand disengaged from the schoolgirl clasp to carefully pat her hair, checking that everything was in order. Her left hand remained on the table to exhibit its large display of diamonds.

"Bradford ees afraid of me," she replied. "He runs away when I come into a room. I theenk you must learn why." Her hand, finished with her hair, landed gently on my forearm to suggest how close we had become. She leaned in, her perfume enveloping me, and whispered conspiratorially, "Thees is why you are here." My eyes were drawn to her beautiful bosom, which was even more exposed in her twisted position. When I finally looked back into her face, she was smiling coyly at me.

Over the next few minutes, with much hand gesturing and an occasional tear, Francesca took me back many years to when she and Veronique first met. They were both in a Swiss boarding school meant to train young women to be refined. She, with a Moroccan mother and a Spanish father, was the only girl to befriend the half-African, half-French girl. Together, they would sneak off to Geneva to go to bars and discos and get men to buy them hashish.

They went together to London to break into modeling and lived together in a "rrrat's nest" south of the Thames. Veronique, with her exotic looks and tall, lanky body, did better in the modeling game and soon was flying off to Milan and Paris. Francesca's body grew "more womanly" (hands fluttering around her breasts in case I hadn't noticed), and she knew that modeling was not for her.

"So I married!" she said. I glanced over at Claus, whose head was in his phone. "No, not heem. I married my Yew! My New York Yew!"

I wondered what his Yewish mother had thought when he brought this exotic *shiksa* home.

And so the two friends drifted apart. Francesca lived on the Upper West Side of Manhattan with a husband who made "millions and millions of dollars selling electronic things in stores all over New York." Veronique became famous as a model and then branched out into her singing career. The ladies would have occasional lunches in New York or London or Paris because "we were always the best of friends, always, always!"

"And then I met my wonderful Claus," she said.

We both glanced over at her amazing catch, but he was still absorbed in his phone. "Eet was in Frankfurt of all places—the least romantic city in Europe. One of those horrible electronic trade shows. I saw him at the BeeLine display. He could have been a model, he was so beeg and handsome. Eet was love at first sight. So I left my Yew, and I married heem."

This time Claus looked up from his phone and shared with us his well-crafted pearly whites. In the shadowy corner of the golf club, he did look quite handsome. They looked at each other. It was obviously a love affair that was still continuing, probably both of them in love with each other and with the glamourous couple they made.

"And so I came back to Europe and yoined my new husband in Frankfurt."

Now the story started to get relevant. Apparently, someone named Roger from BeeLine had started to negotiate with Veronique about an endorsement/advertising deal. But Veronique hated Roger. She said he was slime. Since her dear friend Francesca's new husband was running the German subsidiary of BeeLine, Veronique decided to create a back-channel line of communication. She would keep Francesca informed about what was going on. Francesca could then tell Claus, and Claus could tell people at BeeLine whether Veronique was happy or sad about progress in the discussions.

As the negotiations dragged on, the back channel tended to make things worse rather than better. Finally, Claus had to become a kind of intermediary between Roger and Veronique, who weren't even speaking directly.

"Roger is a *goniff,*" Francesca said, pronouncing it as

"gon-eef." At least the Yew had left his mark on her vocabulary. Claus looked up from his phone in confusion at the word. I explained it meant "thief" in Yiddish. Francesca explained to him she knew I would know the word because I was from New York. Then she asked if I was a Yew. I explained that, like her, I had been married to one.

Finally, when it had looked as if the deal might fall through, Bradford took matters into his own hands. He flew to Paris to talk to Veronique one on one.

"Naturally, Bradford believed he could solve all problems," said Francesca. "Besides, he wanted to meet the glamorous Veronique."

At that moment, our mojitos were delivered. Claus quickly grabbed his and excused himself to make a phone call. Now Francesca and I were alone. We toasted "Salud" and sipped the mojito. It was excruciatingly sweet, happily masking much of the mint. But it still tasted like sugared piss.

"Delicious!" I assured her.

She picked up the story, but with Claus gone, she was free to get down to the real dirt.

"At first Veronique was charmed by her tycoon from Seelicon Valley. He took her out to the best restaurants in Paris. Their photo appeared in *Paris Match*. He loooved being seen with her."

She awakened a memory I had buried. It was one of Bradford Sisley's marital scandals, since at that moment he still had wife number three back in San Jose. The *Paris Match* photos showed a radiant, tall Veronique with her short, unattractive escort. It all had a vague resemblance to the old days of Jackie and Ari. What was *she* doing with *him*? Counting the dough, stupid.

"Naturally he was eager to take her to bed. But she kept pushing him away. She told him eet was her time of the month, which was a lie. My dear friend was at a time in her life when she had lots of fame but not enough money. So she and her agent wanted to make the best possible deal with BeeLine. They both knew that the enticement of her body was part of the negotiation. Eet should not be given away until the deal was done. Consummation *after* the consummation, yes?"

Where on earth had that phrase come from? Where had that word come from? Something the young girls had learned at their Swiss finishing school? It sounded like something that the wily Swiss might teach.

"Finally, the deal was done. The contract, eet was signed," Francesca continued with a sigh. "But by thees time Veronique had had enough of hees ego and hees crudeness. He ees a very crude person, you know."

She stopped so that I could agree. It was, I knew, a test of my empathy and loyalty that would affect how she told the rest of the story. I gave her a strong nod of agreement, which was not hard to do, because he truly was a really crude guy.

"So the night of celebration turned into a deesaster. She tried to keep him off, first with words and then with fists. But he was a man who wanted hees prize after finishing the race."

Francesca took a long sip of her mojito. It was not just for dramatic effect; she was fortifying herself. In a thin voice, she muttered, "So she let heem have what he wanted."

"So he raped her," I said, just trying to get clarity on the story.

"Poor Veronique," answered Francesca, taking another swill of her mojito. I stared at mine and couldn't imagine taking another taste. "She has never called it a rrrape, because she gave in. She says that she made the deeecision to give him her *chatte*. That ees the word she uses. I think in English, you might say 'pussy.' She says that was what he wanted and that was all he got—he got nothing from the rest of her. She lay there, she says, like a corpse."

I knew—and certainly Francesca knew—that this was rape. But my good buddy Bradford probably would be shocked to hear it described that way. If, God forbid, he ever did describe it to someone, he probably told them it was great sex.

Now I was ready to take a sip of my drink—I needed that foul taste in my mouth.

"When eet was over, she called me," Francesca said. "She was deestroyed by all thees. Sobbing on the telephone, threatening to harm herself. So guilty! So I dropped everything and drove all night from Frankfurt to Paris to get to her side.

"I conveenced her to leave Paris, and we went down to her villa outside of Antibes. We were several days there, lying in the sun, drinking vodka, talking about the past. We shopped and cooked together, like we were back in our London flat. We cried a lot. We laughed a lot. And she slowly pulled herself together. And finally, she became angry. So was I. So we hatched our scheme—our jewelry heist."

Francesca paused to let me dangle on those words. She took another large swallow of her mojito and looked around the room, as if to make certain no one was listening to us. Claus was outside on the patio, staring at the golf course. If he had made a phone call, it was apparently over. It dawned on me that his exit had been planned. He needed to be offstage for this conversation.

"We went back to Paris and went shopping for jewelry at all the finest stores—Cartier, Chaumet, Van Cleef. We had such fun! We took a leemo from store to store, trying on many jewels, laughing and being very seelly. In the end, Veronique selected some beautiful dangly earrings from Tiffany. I found a choker at Cartier. We had them put theese things on hold. Each was under one hundred thousand euros. We did put that leemit on ourselves."

I was seeing Audrey Hepburn and Grace Kelly laughing and giggling as they gallivanted through the best jewelry stores of Paris. They were going to stiff Cary Grant for the bill. All of this was set to a Henry Mancini score.

"I flew over to Caleefornia," Francesca continued. "I told my Claus to tell Bradford Seesley that he had to see me when I arrived. It was a very seemple and short conversation. I told him he was giving each of us a beauteeful gift for our cooperation and quiet. I gave him the details on the purchases and told him to make eet happen in a week. I wrote it all out on a plain piece of paper, which he could destroy. No e-mails, no phone records. Just a generous gift to my darling Veronique to thank her for signing the contract and one to me for helping make the deal happen. Voilà!"

I had to ask, "How did Bradford respond to your, uh, proposal?"

"Like a naughty leetle boy who is caught with his hand in the cooookie jar," she said with pride. "By thees time, hees messy situation with his wife was breaking into the papers, and he wanted to avoid more trouble with women. He folded, like you Americans say, like a cheap suit."

Inevitably, she glanced at my clothes, which were severely wrinkled after a long day.

She lifted her phone from the table and took a couple of swipes. "Here, you must see my beauteeful choker," she said. As she handed me the phone, she either accidentally or on purpose slightly caressed my hand. In the photo, taken at some gala, she looked ravishing—the hair, the dress, the boobs, and a very tasteful choker that appeared to be studded with green jewels, presumably emeralds.

"Stunning," I said. "Was this a BeeLine event?"

"No," she said, taking back the phone. "But Bradford was there with hees wife. I showed it off to her with heem right there. You should have seen heem! Eet was so funny. He was very afraid I would tell her who gave eet to me."

"And what does Claus make of all this?" I asked. I nodded out to the patio, where the giant German continued to stand erect, staring out at the golf course.

"He stays, as you see, a certain deestance," she replied. She looked down at her nearly empty mojito and then at my mostly full glass. "You do not like your mojito!"

"It's a little sweet," I said.

"And you are not sweet?" she asked coyly.

"No one has ever used that word to describe me, as far as I know," I responded.

"Well, I want you to be sweet with me. Okay?" she said.

"What is it that you want me to do?"

"Well, right now, you want me to go solve your problem with Veronique, yes?"

"Well, everyone feels you are the best person."

"I am, my darling, the only person. She will not talk to Roger. She will not talk to Bradford. Wanda ees gone. It has to be me."

Suddenly, some pieces of the puzzle seemed to come together. "Does Roger the goniff bite his nails?" I asked.

"Yes, constantly. It is deesgusting. Why do you ask?"

"Just checking the cast of characters from today's meeting."

"He ees a worthless man," she said angrily. "But let us get back to beesness. I theenk, dear Jonathan, you need me. And for me to get thees done, it's going to take another shopping trip in Paris. I know Veronique very, very well. Another shopping trip will definitely solve thees problem."

Holy shit. Was this extortion? You won't get cooperation unless you shell out two hundred thousand euros. Sounds like extortion to me.

On the other hand, maybe she was just explaining her fee for her services. Not all that different from me. You want me to do something, here's what it will cost. Except Francesca didn't charge by the hour like I did. She did value pricing. For a mere two hundred thousand euros, Veronique falls back into line.

"Well, I can't authorize something like that," I said,

backpedaling as fast as I could. "Claus can tell you, I'm not even a BeeLine employee yet. And even if I were, I couldn't authorize buying fancy jewelry."

Francesca gave me her pouty face.

"Listen," I said. "The last time you handled this directly with Bradford, who must have paid for this jewelry with his own money. You should talk to him, not me."

"I told you, Bradford ees afraid of me," she said. "He would never take my call."

Because he's no dummy.

"But he leestens to you," she said. "You, my *sweet*, are the person to make thees happen. My husband tells me you are Bradford's Rrrrasputin. You must tell Bradford what he has to do."

Definitely time to take another gulp of sweet piss. Francesca—and, undoubtedly, the Nazi on the patio enjoying both the view and his deniability—had just dumped an ugly turd on my lap. I sat speechless for a moment, staring into the painted face of someone who I now believed might be truly wicked.

I wondered if Rasputin had felt this way on his first day on the job—like the court intrigue was so much more byzantine and corrupt than he had ever imagined. And I wondered if he worried, like I was worrying, that maybe he couldn't handle what he had taken on.

Perhaps he stuck with it because he needed to buy his daughter a torture chamber.

An hour later I was comfortably ensconced at the '49er, sipping my scotch over a plate of hot wings with Frank. He was filling me in on how it had come about that Claus had been promoted from his German job to a position at BeeLine headquarters for which he was grotesquely ill suited.

It turns out that none of it had to do with his Spanish/ Moroccan princess and her jewels, a story that, best I could tell, Frank didn't know.

But it was yet another tale of corruption and intrigue.

Claus, as head of the German operation, had made an amazing deal with the Bavarian government for a wide range of BeeLine products. The only problem was that there was a kickback: the state official who made the purchase had been paid a substantial bribe. One of the German accountants had been asked to book the bribe as a consulting fee to the Bavarian official's wife. He blew the whistle in an e-mail to the BeeLine chief financial officer who took it to Carter Shepherd.

No one at BeeLine wanted to see the deal with the Bavarian government go down the tubes. It was too lucrative. But Carter Shepherd had to figure out a way to avoid prosecution under the US Foreign Corrupt Practices Act, which levies heavy fines on companies that bribe foreign officials. So he moved with lightning speed to clean up the mess before it came to anyone's attention.

The accountants worked out a new way to book the bribe. Then they paid off the whistle-blowing accountant with a hefty early retirement deal laced with a nondisclosure clause. And everyone who knew anything about what had happened was whisked out of Germany to another, higher-paying job somewhere in BeeLine.

Claus announced that he wanted to come to the headquarters. At the time, the human resources job had been the only one available that was at a high enough level to look like a legitimate promotion, a reward for having run such a successful and profitable German operation.

"How do you know all this if it was so hush-hush?" I asked Frank.

"I was the SEC spy, remember?" he said. "I had to keep an eye on the hallway talk down in DC. Carter had to tell me what had happened so that I would know what to be listening for."

"So you think Claus is pretty safe in his job even though he's a complete disaster with employees?" I asked.

"Claus will be with BeeLine forever," Frank replied. "Once his wife is tired of San Jose, he'll be sent somewhere else. He's got the goods on them."

And his wife has got the goods on Bradford, I thought. Double insurance for the Winkelmanns.

"But we need to talk about something else," Frank said.

"Hit me," I replied, fortifying myself with Macallan. I pointed to the plate of wings to encourage Frank to eat another. I knew if he didn't act quickly, they would all be gone.

"Do you know Phil DeFazio at the *Journal*?" he asked.

My heart sank at the name.

"Yeah, what about him?" I asked as neutrally as I could.

"He's dug up a lot of dirt about how lousy our sales actually are," said Frank. "For the past year or so, I think he's had a mole inside the company, and his mole, like a Deep Throat kind of guy, has sent DeFazio out to talk to a bunch of people in the market about how we are really doing. So he has a lot of collaboration on his story."

"No idea who the mole is?" I asked.

"I have my suspicions," he said.

"You should share them with Carter," I said. "He could do an investigation. Check e-mails and shit."

"Sure," said Frank unenthusiastically. He was looking at me like I was scum. And it flashed in my head that I was. Setting Shepherd's flock of smart pretty boys on a witch hunt was not the kind of thing I would usually think to do. And for a guy who always was talking about keeping his eye on the ball, I was wandering way off the field.

My excuse to myself was that it had been a long, upsetting day.

"So when is DeFazio going to file his story?" I asked, chowing down on another wing.

"He's asking for our comment by noon tomorrow," he said.

"But he's not going to file a story tomorrow afternoon," I said. "Tomorrow's Friday."

"He'll file over the weekend for Monday morning. But he said he didn't want to ruin our weekend. Ha, ha."

"Did you tell him about me and my new job?" I asked with trepidation.

"He already knew," Frank said. "He saw Bradford's video this morning. He told me to send you his best."

"I'm sure he did."

"What's the deal with you two?" asked Frank, obviously hearing nuance in both DeFazio's and my tones.

The truth was that Phil DeFazio and I had been at each other's throats for five or six years. I had snatched an exclusive story out of his hands when he was at the *Financial Times*—an in-depth scoop on a huge patent settlement between IBM and NEC. I'd led him along, saying that the *FT* would get the story first, complete with high-level interviews. And then I threw it to the *New York Times* guy. I told him that the IBM chairman had made a last-minute decision to give it to the *Times*. DeFazio never bought that excuse. He was right. I pulled it from him because he had fucked me over on a food-recall story the previous week.

The problem was that he and I had never made peace. It had been a back-and-forth pissing contest for the last five years. He was definitely not on my list of friendly media contacts. Since he had joined the *Wall Street Journal*, I'd just worked around him.

"The guy just hates my guts," I said to Frank, deciding to tell only a small piece of the truth.

"Why?" he asked.

"It's a long story," I said, making clear that was that.

"Well, we've got a big challenge here," Frank said. "We don't want to decline comment on his story. But if we're headed for a big write-off, we can't out-and-out lie right now about where we are. We can't say that everything is just great in the market. That could become in six months the basis for an investigation into securities fraud. Maybe we can duck it. But if we say anything at all, it has to be squeaky clean when they look back at it in six months."

So nice to have your own SEC watchdog, particularly one who lets you eat all the wings.

Nestled in the Uber car and buzzed with one scotch too many, I tried to figure out why I felt so depressed, so defeated. We were not doing terribly badly in the media, which in my business can be a victory. Veronique's attack was probably the biggest hook for the stories that would appear the next day, with Sandra Farber's elevator girl buried a few paragraphs down. We had gotten our statements out in good time, denying the elevator attack and showing openness to Veronique.

No one had yet found out about the employee boycott, best I could tell. So that would get us through the Friday news cycle. But I knew that someone had to uncover the story over the weekend. I was already thinking about the response statement—which had to include a sympathetic outreach and a promise of reform from Wendy Smith-Kenyon (or was it Kenyon-Smith? I really had to get my head around this person, this Lesbian president of one of the country's best universities).

Wanda was, of course, still out there. Her appearance on *Good Morning America* had been pretty benign. But if she was trying to become campaign manager for an assault on sexism in high tech, it was likely that she would be on another show the next day and maybe the talk shows over the weekend. Who knows? Maybe that was always her game plan: rocket blast out of BeeLine heading for the stardom of leading a broad #MeToo movement in the tech world.

Nothing that was happening seemed surprising or outside of my experience with corporate crises. They usually had an exponential rate of speed, one thing leading rapidly to several others and continuing to expand outwards like ripples in water until finally petering out. So why was I feeling down? We were riding the storm. We were still afloat and not in danger of capsizing.

And with my new job, I was poised to become a hero to my daughter, comfortably financing her professional dream.

But I still felt like shit.

Actually, I knew very well the source of my bad mood. The truth was I didn't like being an insider—an employee, an executive. I was weighted down by becoming part of BeeLine, by the responsibility of knowing the things I had learned that day—about Claus's criminality and his system for enabling misbehavior, about Bradford's rape of Veronique, about Francesca's bribery past and future, about phony financial reporting. If I had learned this kind of information as an outsider, it would all be delicious gossip and nothing more. But as an insider, there was nothing delicious about these tales. From the inside, I shared accountability; I shared the blame.

And I sure didn't know if I had the guts or the energy—or the integrity—to try to rectify any of it.

I turned on my phone to check for anything new.

Ruthie had sent me an e-mail entitled "Spreadsheet." It undoubtedly showed rows of numbers proving that Sandra could afford a bank loan if I gave her 150 big ones. Such a Ruthie thing to do. Pretending to just want to be transparent, when actually she just wanted to give her procrastinating ex-husband a poke.

I thought about answering her back with the good news that I would be providing the money. But I decided that I wanted her to wait nervously for a few more days. Over the weekend. Why make Ruthie's life easy after all the crap she had put me through? Let her stew for a while.

She'd get her happy ending next week. Let her worry in the meantime.

Just before I shut down the e-mail app, I noticed that there was an e-mail from my younger sister, a rare event, typically focused on holidays, birthdays, and deaths. The subject was "How Interesting Is THIS?" There was no text, only a photo, which I struggled to see. I had to rotate the phone several times to finally discern what my sister had sent me.

She had scanned a portion of what looked to be an old montage photo from a college sorority, one of those composites of individual formal shots of carefully made-up and coifed girls. The portion she had sent showed Wanda Cramer, a beautiful young Wanda, probably in her freshman or sophomore year, with much darker hair and a genuinely happy smile. The eyes were unmistakable.

So I had actually known her. Well, not exactly known her. Once my sister had joined one of the best sororities on campus, I had tried to become the best protective older brother imaginable: coming often to see her, waiting patiently in the ground floor sorority living room, trying to make friendly chat with all of her sorority sisters. As an obese and pimply loser, I made little headway with the gorgeous girls at Kappa Alpha, and my sister made certain that her friends never had to deal with me. I just sat there and watched the girls coming and going.

It had been a particularly pathetic time of my life. The photo made me cringe at the memory of my hopeless efforts to reach for untouchables like Wanda Cramer, whom I probably never spoke to and who probably never noticed me plopped on one of the overstuffed couches downstairs. But she must have been one of my fantasy girls. Hell, I even remembered how she walked.

But then I noticed that my sister's scan was of two photos from the montage. Next to Wanda was a somewhat sullen girl with insanely curly dark hair, a not unusual style for the times. Also vaguely familiar. It was hard to read her name. But when I expanded the photo, it became clear.

It was Katherine Davis, Sisley's accuser.

A quick call to my sister revealed that Katherine Davis had been Wanda's roommate for the brief time Davis was at the university.

"Katherine came and went sophomore year," my sister said. "I immediately recognized her on TV this week. But then I saw Wanda on *Good Morning America* and remembered the connection."

"But how did you know I was involved with BeeLine?" I asked.

"Hello, stupido," she said. "Your niece works in their Dallas office. She snitched on you when she got the announcement of your new fancy job."

"Matty works for BeeLine?" I asked, knowing full well that I had been told this but had completely forgotten it.

Any stupor I had felt from the scotch dissipated as my mind went into high gear. Alcohol can be a wonderful stimulant for creative imagination—ask F. Scott Fitzgerald or Edgar Allan Poe.

Suppose, for just a second, that Wanda had arranged for the incident with Katherine Davis to happen. Bradford had said that the hotel was recommended by Wanda. So maybe, just maybe, the he said/she said incident had a few wrinkles in it. Maybe Bradford actually had been lured into bad behavior in the elevator. It probably wasn't hard to get him started.

The tape would show that. The tape! What had happened to the hotel's tape? Those "technical problems"? I had told Wanda about the tape. Just like I had told Bradford.

But then what about Wanda's explosive—but planned—exit two days after Katherine Davis filed her lawsuit? Maybe that was Wanda's backup plan in her conspiracy to get Bradford fired. If the Davis thing was not enough to get him ousted, then she would strike even harder and closer to home.

So maybe I had missed something during that morning strategy meeting. Something that became a decision point for Wanda. She had told me that Langerfeld was key. Maybe once she saw that he was counseling Bradford in the direction of a settlement, she knew that Bradford was likely to survive the Davis accusation. So she had to go to plan B: open up the BeeLine can of worms and assume that the board would fire him for that.

But it turned out that that hadn't worked either. Thanks to me, the board gave him an endorsement within hours of her departure. Plus the board set the company on a reform path that was likely to ensure his survival.

So I had thrown some monkey wrenches into Wanda's plans. But what else might be up her sleeve? Would cautious, cool Wanda have a plan C?

7

FRIDAY

Overnight, a storm blew in, one of those big Pacific monsters that dumps water in torrents. My knees told me it was happening long before I heard the sound of the pelting rain on the window. I could barely sleep, the pain a searing knife in both legs. There was no position I could find that would ease the agony.

At four o'clock I struggled out of bed to get some Advil. I had run out of my prescription pain meds back in Sweden. I had planned to refill on my return to New York. But, no, I had come here to Typhoon, California, instead. And now I was going to pay for it. Big.

While I was swallowing the Advil, I heard my phone ding. The sound of a message coming in. Maybe it was Verizon telling me about a major new opportunity to give them money. But with the second ding, I decided it might actually be something important. And it was.

It was from Frank, telling me that DeFazio of the *Wall Street Journal* had fucked us and gone ahead with the story about our weak sales in Friday's paper. He gave me the link.

It was, as it always was with Phil DeFazio, great reporting. He had credible sources from the retail side about weak BeeLine sales. Someone from the inside—probably his mole—had provided anonymous great quotes about collapsing revenues, ballooning inventories, and "panic back at the beehive." He said that BeeLine had declined to comment.

"Why the hell did he do this?" I asked Frank when I got him on the line. "You told me we had till noon."

"That's what he told me," Frank said.

"Well, ream him out. Call him right now and tell him to go fuck himself."

"I can't really call him until we have something to say," Frank said. He apparently was past the anger stage that I was going through. He sounded perfectly calm and so goddamned rational. "I'm sure he'll put in our comment once he has it, and then the weekend online version will include our response."

"Oh, goody, goody," I said. "Our response gets buried in the fucking weekend edition of the *Wall Street Journal*. Everybody's favorite weekend pastime."

"It's the best we can do," Frank said.

I had a secret concern that DeFazio might have pulled this shenanigan to get back at me. But maybe that belief was just an ego trip on my part. In the end, it didn't matter if it was about me or not. The main thing was to get a meeting first thing with Bradford, Carter Shepherd, and the chief financial officer Kasim Bashari. We had to craft some kind of response statement that would reassure the stock market but also would not trigger an SEC inquiry later if there was a major write-off.

I told Frank I would start the process of setting up the meeting and he should draft a possible statement.

"Right," he said. "But remember, you're not supposed to know about the cooked books. You have to be surprised when they tell you about that."

Then I really hit the roof. I didn't need that kind of bullshit in the middle of all this, and besides, my knees were killing me. Frank was worried about protecting his own ass about letting me in on the dirty linen. Well, I wasn't interested in helping him on that front. He had screwed up with DeFazio, and he needed to take the bullet on that. So he could also take another bullet for having snitched to me.

"No," I said. "I'll tell them that you told me this morning when the story broke. That will make it almost reasonable."

He responded, "Okay," but his tone said he wasn't happy. Too fucking bad.

After he hung up, I went back to my paranoid, conspiratorial mind-set of the night before. Maybe Frank was part of the plot. Maybe he was the mole. Maybe he was setting me up with this story about cooked books. Maybe behind his bland, bureaucratic exterior, he was a fellow conspirator with Wanda. Or maybe he was just an evil anarchist trying to create chaos.

It was four thirty in the morning, it was pouring rain, my knees were screaming in pain, and I had too much on my plate. It would be one thing to just handle the messaging on Bradford's dumb behavior, the company's cultural problems, and the still undiscovered employee boycott. But now I was getting engaged with a financial fraud. Oh yeah, plus I was supposed to implement a bribery scheme to keep a rock star from opening up about being raped by the CEO.

I sat on the edge of the bed and waited for the Advil to do its work. Until the pain subsided, I actually couldn't think about any of it.

The lights were on in the Communications Department when I arrived around seven. Someone else was an early bird. The market had opened, and not surprisingly, the stock was tanking again, thanks to Phil DeFazio. My knees were still hurting badly, but by using the crow cane in one hand and an umbrella in the other, I could hobble my way to Renata's office.

Outside, the torrent continued. It hadn't been easy to get an Uber.

As I was about to get to my destination, I heard a familiar voice from down the hall. It was Wanda's voice—her unmistakable Midwestern twang. Instantly, the fat crippled guy was in high gear, managing an ungainly shuffle with two legs, one cane, and a Burberry umbrella.

The voice was coming from Miley's office. Wanda was on TV—the CNN morning show. Again, she was talking generically about sexism in Silicon Valley—how it was rampant, how things needed to change, how Silicon Valley was the last bastion of male misbehavior, blah, blah, blah. Damn, but she was articulate and credible.

She also looked great! She had let her hair down instead of sporting her tight little bun. Her hair was full and wavy, softening her face. Thanks to my sister's e-mail, I now had a clear recollection of that face on a young, happy girl striding across the sorority living room. Beautiful, smart, articulate woman—what are you up to now?

But then the lady anchor—whose name I could never remember (I always called her Chris, but that was the guy anchor, who I always thought was Mario)—changed the subject. She asked about Veronique.

"Were you surprised by Veronique's action yesterday taking a stand against your former employer?" she asked.

"Not really," Wanda answered. C'mon Wanda. Now you bridge to "but I was happy to see how quickly the company is responding by sending someone to talk to her" or, better yet, "I am happy to see the company has appointed Wendy Smith-Kenyon to lead a reform effort. I'm certain that Veronique will respond positively to that."

But Wanda had stopped talking. She was sipping her coffee after her "not really," waiting for the next question.

"So you weren't surprised. Is that because you think Veronique is concerned about rampant sexism at BeeLine? Or do you think that Veronique was specifically targeting Bradford Sisley in her action? Timing-wise, didn't she lose her BeeBuds right after the big lawsuit was announced against Bradford Sisley for sexual misconduct?" anchor lady asked.

Wanda paused. One eyebrow went up as she pondered her answer. I wasn't sure whether she knew the whole truth about Veronique and Bradford Sisley. This long pause somehow suggested that she did know. But that was pure speculation on my part as I tried reading her always neutral face. I glanced sidewise at Miley as well, looking for signals. But Miley's face was hidden by her hair and her large glasses.

"I don't know," she finally said. "You probably should ask her."

"They did date, didn't they? Sisley and Veronique?"

Now Wanda definitely looked uncomfortable. "Yes, I believe they did," she said. "Briefly."

"But you say you don't know if Veronique's action is targeting him or targeting the company more broadly?"

"I haven't spoken to her, so I really don't know."

"Well, did *you* ever talk to Veronique about the sexism at BeeLine?"

Suddenly anchor lady was doing her investigative reporter thing. She apparently didn't like Wanda's evasion of her question about *why* Veronique had taken her stand. She smelled something fishy. She wanted to home in on a sexual issue between two celebrities. That would be so much more newsworthy than just one more story about sexism in Silicon Valley.

"I don't think so," said Wanda.

"So then she would have no way of knowing about sexism at BeeLine, right? I mean, she didn't work there or have lots of inside information, did she?"

Wanda had had enough of the hot seat. "Well, she may well have read my resignation note. That could have been the trigger for her."

"As opposed to the sexual assault lawsuits against Bradford Sisley, a man she once dated."

"I have no idea. You'll really have to ask her."

The interview wrapped up, but I had to score the game for anchor lady. She had definitely raised the possibility that Veronique's grenade was not motivated by BeeLine's frat-boy culture. Rather, it might well be vengeance against a man she had "briefly" dated.

I had a gut feeling that anchor lady was eyeing an interesting bone to chew on. Why might gorgeous rock star Veronique hate Bradford Sisley? What was their relationship? What had happened between them?

Man, I needed to load up Francesca's purse with cash pretty damn fast. Didn't want one of those dog-with-a-bone aggressive CNN investigative things hitting pay dirt with Veronique.

"Well, that was interesting," I said to Miley when the show went to commercial break.

She wasn't going to give me anything.

"I'm glad you're here early," she said, getting right down to business. "I wanted to grab you first thing and get you up to date on some new developments." She looked down at my cane/umbrella situation.

"Are you okay? You wanna sit down?" she asked. She pulled her austere visitor chair around to make it easy for me to access. The chair's simplicity was perfect for the moment, so I eased myself into it. Being off the knees was slightly better than being on them.

But I had made a mistake. Now Miley was standing over me. This diminutive girl with her outsized will had me at a physical disadvantage. And she knew it.

"So has Claus told you what's been happening?" she asked in a prosecutorial tone.

Claus had told me about the new sexual harassment complaint against Bradford. But that didn't sound like a "what's been happening" kind of thing. So I played dumb.

"Haven't seen Claus," I said.

"Well, that's because he's buried in harassment complaints," she said. "The man is drowning in them. Over fifty complaints have been filed in the last two days. The floodgates are opening in this company."

There was a poorly disguised glee in her voice, which, at some level, I could buy because she was a woman working in a sexist cesspool. But she worked for management; she was herself a manager. She wasn't supposed to be happy when the workplace was erupting in anger and accusations. Sympathy, maybe. Concern, to be sure. Support, yes. Glee, not so much.

"How do you know this?" I asked.

"I know a lot of things," she replied. "I have contacts all over the company. It's part of my job as director of internal communications."

But, I thought, what a perfect cover for setting up revolutionary sleeper cells. Instead of listening posts, what if all of Miley's contacts were cadres ready to spring into action. It was, of course, possible that there had been spontaneous combustion of harassment complaints, just as there had recently been in Hollywood and in politics. But fifty complaints in two days sounded fishy to me.

"So why tell me this?" I asked.

"It'll leak out sometime soon. Maybe even today." Why did this sound like a threat?

"You're right," I said. "That and the employee boycott. It's only a matter of time."

"So what are you going to do about it?" she asked, as if she were the boss.

"I'm going to get you to write response statements this morning, with excellent quotes from Wendy Smith-Kenyon and from Claus, showing sympathy for employee concerns and promising swift action."

Miley Wong's soft young face turned hard and cold, and she poked her glasses back up her nose. "That's not my job," she said. "I'm internal communications. Charlie is external communications. He writes press statements."

I liked where I had her. "But this is about an internal matter."

"A lot of things are about internal matters," she shot back. "That is not the distinction between internal communications and external communications, Mr. Keaton. It's about who is the *target* of the communications—who's getting the communication."

She was talking down at me, both physically and in a schoolmarmish tone.

Bbrring! My anger button went off.

My "don't you talk to me that way, you little bitch" button.

My "who do you think you are, just because Daddy's on the board and a founder" button.

My "I'm the boss and you're not, even though you're standing over me and making me feel subordinate" button.

"You'll do whatever I goddamned tell you," I shouted at little Miley, shaking my angry bird cane in her face. She looked surprised. *"And this is not harassment! This is your boss telling you what you're going to do. You're going to prepare one statement on the employee boycott and another on the harassment complaints. And I want them in two hours."*

Miley's face had turned to bright pink. It was not embarrassment; it was fury that I saw. She didn't say a word.

Now the normal thing at that moment would have been for me to storm out of Miley's office, to finish off my tantrum with an appropriate angry grand exit. But I was still down in Miley's visitor chair, each of my hands holding a support stick. I knew that my getting up was going to be slow and painful and that leaving her office would be anything but dramatic and grandiose. So I shifted my exit strategy.

I abruptly lowered my voice to a soft, growling purr. I looked sternly at her pink frozen face. "I will now leave you, Ms. Wong, so that you can get to work. You have a lot to do in the next two hours. Plus, I still need those talking points for introducing myself to the Communications staff in some sort of all-hands meeting."

"I e-mailed the talking points to you yesterday afternoon," she said between gritted teeth. She definitely wasn't cowed by my tirade. She was very, very pissed.

I laboriously stood up and walked out, thinking that I had probably just done a really stupid thing.

I know they're not called secretaries anymore, but a rose by any other name is still a great blessing. Diane was able to negotiate with the other don't-call-them-secretaries-anymore a meeting in Bradford's conference room at eight thirty to discuss how BeeLine would respond to the *Wall Street Journal* article about its problems in the consumer marketplace.

But Diane was even better than that. She took the name of my doctor and my medication and said she'd have the pills for me before the meeting. And she did. There are competencies in this world that are completely mysterious to me. Diane apparently had a treasure chest full of them.

Carter Shepherd was already in the conference room

when I got there. Today, he had shed his California chic look and gone back to his preppy past. Perhaps on a stormy, miserable November morning, his aesthetic went back to his New England upbringing. An expensive-looking—probably cashmere—crewneck sweater was covering a classic blue Oxford button-down collar shirt. And the pants were simple baggy corduroys, probably something from the back of his closet and very comfortable.

As usual, his face was in his phone, and he didn't bother to greet me. I leaned my cane and umbrella against the conference table in order to be double fisted at the surprisingly rich breakfast spread at the back of the room. While I was filling my plate with carbs, he finally spoke to me.

"So I hear Francesca is off to Europe to deal with Veronique."

News to me. I still hadn't talked to Bradford about money for Francesca's mission, but maybe she was just assuming that I would be successful. Or she had other weekend shopping to do in Paris.

"Guess so," I muttered as I turned away from the buffet, my plate piled high. I stuffed a doughnut in my mouth, and then once it was safely on its way to my stomach, I changed the subject. "Listen, I hear there's a huge raft of sexual harassment claims coming in. Like a tidal wave."

"Yeah. All this trouble is opening up a wave of discontent inside."

"Are you worried?"

"Nah. We've got law firms on retainer to handle all the processing of this kind of stuff. They expand the number of lawyers we need—hour by hour."

I could hear Claus's voice saying, "Delay, deflect, demotiwate."

"Actually, I wasn't talking about the logistics," I said. "I was talking about what it means to have a *flood* of complaints. I mean, aren't you concerned about what's happening here, among employees?"

For a moment, he looked up at me. His face was thoughtful.

"Well, as long as you're now on the inside, you deserve the truth," he said. "This place is a pigsty. Since I got here, I've done nothing but clean up messes and bury bodies. Bradford is always hiring mini-Bradfords—the same sort of reckless, aggressive men that he is. The sexual harassment thing is just one of the symptoms of a really sick place. Have you met Kasim yet? Our CFO?"

"No, this morning will be the first time."

"You'll love him. He's the last guy in the world you'd hire to handle your money. Straight out of the souk."

Nice little racial slur, Carter. WASP from Wilton talking?

"Why do you stay around, Carter?" I asked.

"Hell, maybe I'm a slippery character, too," he said. "But I basically love my job. Always a new challenge, a new drama. This isn't like being a corporate lawyer—this is like night court. Bring it on!"

He was showing more energy and enthusiasm than I had seen since I met him. Maybe the preppy clothes freed up the little boy inside.

"Speaking of bringing it on," I asked, "Where are you on this issue of paying for Bradford's defense?"

The energy drained away. He shook his head emphatically. "We've stuck to our guns on that one. I've told him I'd help him settle the cases. But if he wants to fight them, he's on his own. He'll need to pick his own lawyer and pay for it himself."

Okay, I thought, that takes me off the hook for telling Carter about Wanda and her link to Katherine Davis, Bradford's first accuser. If someone was defending Bradford against Katherine's charges, it would be pretty important information. But less so in a settlement.

I'd been thinking about the Wanda-Katherine connection on and off all morning—when I wasn't thinking about my knees or the *Wall Street Journal* or Miley Wong. Without the scotch in my head, the whole thing seemed a little less conspiratorial. Maybe it was a sheer coincidence. So what if Wanda knew Katherine Davis in college?

But, then, every time I went down that road in my head, a little warning bell would go off. Why didn't Wanda ever mention anything to me about knowing Katherine Davis? We had sat there together and watched the Sandra Farber press conference with Katherine sitting there in her ladylike primness. They were roommates, for God's sake.

Don't go down this tunnel right now, I had to tell myself. Think about the Wanda-Katherine thing later. Right now, the main thing was I didn't have to tell Carter Shepherd about the connection. He wasn't going to defend Bradford, so he didn't have a need to know.

"Did the board support you in that decision? Not to help Bradford fight the accusations?"

"The board?"

"Yeah, I assume something like that would need to be ratified by a board decision."

He laughed. "Well, you don't know our board very well. They're pretty ineffectual. I'm amazed they got as far as the Wendy Smith-Kenyon decision. That was pretty big for them. Forget that they gave her no budget and no staff. They wouldn't ever think to do that."

"So what do you think will happen with the Wendy thing?" I asked.

"Down a deep, dark hole," he said. "This is just rubbing a little ointment on something that needs major surgery."

Funny phrase. And I had heard it before. From Miley. Was she insinuating herself into everybody's brain? Had she invented a new mind-control technology? Was she an alien from outer space?

Cue the entrance of the angry monarch. Bradford swung open his private door to the conference room and made certain to slam it loudly behind him.

"Man, you are one hell of a PR guy," he spat at me. "I've had nothing but bad press since you got here, asshole. And now this piece of shit."

He slammed the *Wall Street Journal* down on the table.

Really, I thought, is this the best melodrama you're capable of? Slamming the paper down on the table? Are we in a bad movie?

"Have you seen what's happening to our stock?" he demanded.

I opened my stock market app and looked. BeeLine was continuing to sink.

"That's why we're here, Bradford," I said. "To agree on a statement and approach to deal—"

"And what's with this 'BeeLine declined to comment' crap?" Bradford interrupted.

"Frank thought we had until noon today our time and that the story would run on Monday," I said.

Sisley took on a mocking tone. "Frank thought. Frank thought. Frank thought fucking wrong. You don't decline to comment on a story like this."

"I know that," I said defensively. "He says he didn't decline. He thought we had until noon." Actually, this had been bothering me all morning. DeFazio was a good reporter. He knew very well the difference between "declined to comment" and "not available for comment." So, either he was sticking it to us—or to me—or maybe, just maybe, Frank wasn't being totally truthful about the sequence of events.

"Do you believe him? I don't," Bradford said. "He fucked this up. Which means you fucked this up. I should fire both of you shitheads."

"Hey, look," I said. "I've come with a draft statement. That's what we need to focus on right now. You can play the blame game later and fire us."

I slipped the statement across the table to Carter and handed one over to Bradford, who was standing over me. Frank had given it to me thirty minutes earlier, and it was artfully done. It acknowledged that we were operating in "several highly competitive markets" and were launching "new initiatives for the holiday season" to "assure market leadership."

As Bradford and Carter were reading the statement, in

walked Kasim Bashari, the chief financial officer. Straight from the gym, he was in his cycling outfit, even including a backward-facing baseball cap. He was dark skinned, small, and wiry, with thick round glasses below bushy eyebrows. I held out a copy of the statement and said my name in introduction. He grabbed the paper without responding. As soon as he started to read, his right foot started tapping. Not a good sign.

"What do you think?" he asked Bradford.

"Too fucking negative," his boss growled. "It's too fucking negative. It basically confirms the story that we're in trouble. We're not in trouble. We need to say that things are great! Revenues are strong!"

Time for innocent questions. "Are they?" I asked.

Kasim and Bradford exchanged a look. Neither answered my question.

"Well, we had a good third quarter," answered Carter. "Has anything changed?" From the question and his tone, I could tell that he did not know about cooking the books for the third-quarter reports. Apparently, the company's general counsel was unaware of what his CEO and CFO had done.

Kasim was now pacing back and forth. He spoke to Bradford. "I think we ought to get this guy out of here." His head nodded in my direction. I was about to bite into a danish, but since everyone was looking at me, I froze, mouth open and danish poised.

"He's Wanda's replacement," Bradford explained.

"I don't know him," said Kasim. "How do you know you can trust him?"

"I know I can trust him," Bradford said.

"And what about you, counselor?" Kasim said to Carter. "Do you know you can trust this guy?"

Carter frowned at me but then looked back at Kasim. "What's all this about, that we have to worry about trusting our senior vice president for communications? What's going on?"

Small point of order. I wasn't actually the senior vice president of anything, since I still hadn't signed Claus's many, many papers. But I didn't feel this was a good moment to correct the record.

Kasim walked over to where Carter was sitting. He leaned down to speak softly but emphatically. "There's some shit that has to be aired," he said. "I don't think that it's the kind of shit we should be talking about in front of a stranger."

"I already know," I said, putting down the danish. "Frank filled me in this morning, which is why the statement is written the way it is. Which is why we're meeting at all."

"Perhaps someone can fill me in, then," Carter said. "I seem to be the only one in the dark."

Kasim looked over to Bradford, raising his big eyebrows in a question. Bradford nodded his assent, and Kasim launched into a complicated explanation of what had been done to pump up the third-quarter results and, as it turned out, those of several quarters before that. I was able to follow most of it while I finally enjoyed my danish.

Throughout most of Kasim's explanation, Carter was shaking his head in disapproval. At one point, he lowered his head and covered his face with his hands, then slowly pulled them down. He didn't seem like a man who wanted someone to bring it on.

"You realize you've broken federal securities law?" he asked. "You both signed the third-quarter results, knowing that they were false. Under Sarbanes-Oxley—"

"Nobody fucking knows!" Bradford yelled out. "And no one will ever know once we straighten it all out in the year-end numbers. It's no big deal."

"That may or may not be true," said Carter. "But I think that right now we have to be super careful in what we say in this statement. Because, if we say the wrong thing, that could easily become another count in a federal indictment."

"Stop, just stop!" Bradford said in frustration. "You're going into your tight-assed lawyer routine again. We have Cyber Monday coming up. We're going to do great! We'll be able to straighten out the numbers in the year-end, right, Kasim?"

Kasim nodded. "No problem."

"So no one's ever going to come after us," continued Bradford. "No one is ever going to come looking, because there'll be nothing to look for. So we can say what we want to say right now and not sit around like a bunch of pussies licking our twats."

Carter was rereading the draft statement. When he had finished, he declared his position.

"We go with this," he said.

Bradford poked at his phone. "Have you seen the goddamned stock? Are you telling me to put out this pussy-whipped statement when our stock is down to eighty-six? Are you nuts?"

He had shoved the phone into Carter's face to make his point. Carter didn't look at the phone. He looked into Bradford's eyes.

"We go with this statement, or I resign," he said.

"Me too," I said. Carter had scared the shit out of me, making me think that I was going to end up as an accessory to a crime. I would spend the rest of my life behind bars. If Carter Shepherd thought the situation was serious enough to be taking a stand, I was going with him. I'd take a moral stand. I'd stick with the lawyer.

"You're fucking wimps!" Bradford screamed. I glanced at the walls of the room, hoping they were soundproof. They were plastered with photos of Bradford, mostly with attractive movie stars. Several were shots with Veronique. *"You're fucking—cock-sucking—wimps!"*

I assumed that Bradford had not meant "cock-sucking" in any literal way. Just a generic kind of insult. Hopefully, it wasn't a crude and unnecessary jab at Carter Shepherd's sexuality.

"Let me look at it again," said Kasim. He took a quick read of the statement. "I suppose it's all right. It's not really all that negative. At least we're saying something. Right?"

"Right!" I said. He glared with disdain at me, the stranger in the room who was supposed to be silent.

Bradford knew he was surrounded. "Well, enjoy your poverty, shitheads," he said. "This statement will do nothing—absolutely nothing—to turn the stock around today. We can all go home for the weekend and start figuring out what to sell to cover the personal loans that will be called in."

He headed for the door to his office. "Do whatever the fuck you want," he muttered.

"Bradford!" I yelled as he opened his door to leave. "I have a couple of other urgent—time-sensitive—things! Can I have ten minutes?"

"Fine," he said. "Right now, I need to take a crap and get rid of all the shit you people just shoved down my throat." He slammed the door behind him.

In the silence that followed, Kasim finally sat down. All his nervous energy was gone, and he looked sadly worried.

"I guess you and I have some stuff to discuss," he said to Carter.

"Yes, we probably do," Carter responded.

"But not in front of this guy," Kasim said, cocking his head in my direction.

"Well, I have a statement to get to the *Wall Street Journal*," I said, trying to make my expulsion less unpleasant. I was very sorry to leave my plate, since I had saved the best for last, the amazing glazed brioche. I stuffed it in my pocket and grabbed my cane and umbrella. The pain of standing up was surprisingly mild, so the meds were clearly kicking in. Maybe everything would take a turn for the better now.

As the conference room door closed behind me, I could hear Carter asking Kasim how he could do such a fucking-stupid thing.

I called Frank from the anteroom of Bradford's office to let him know he could call Phil DeFazio with the statement he had drafted. In more generous times, I might have congratulated him on the draft's careful eloquence or told him that no one seemed to care that he had let me in on the financial shenanigans, but I wasn't feeling generous towards Frank. I remained concerned about the "declined to comment" business; it just didn't seem right.

I don't know how long I sat there next to Colleen waiting for Bradford. My mind was wrestling with whether to tell him about Wanda and Katherine Davis. On the one hand, he had a right to know. He had suspected vast conspiracies against him and accused her of being part of that. Now there was evidence that he may have been right. Lord knows, he certainly would make that leap from the evidence my sister had sent me.

As I had concocted in my head the night before, one could imagine a whole series of orchestrated attacks after the one-two punch of Katherine Davis and Wanda's well-planned act of self-immolation. Who knows? On a chart of relationships, so many lines went back to Wanda: Veronique, Miley, Phil DeFazio. Didn't Bradford deserve to know what I knew so that he could join me in constructing wide-ranging conspiracies from suppositions?

But on the other hand, I was still holding out hope that I could convince Bradford to settle the case with Katherine Davis (and now the other elevator woman represented by Sandra Farber). If I gave him evidence that Davis actually had set him up with Wanda's help, he would redouble his resolve to fight. And maybe even sue the two women—and Wanda.

And then there was also what my gut was telling me. The bottom line was that I didn't want to say anything to Bradford Sisley about Wanda as a possible conspirator because I didn't want to give him that satisfaction. I didn't want to give him an out to facing up to who he was: a detestable guy who fomented a vile environment at BeeLine and who acted badly with women. I was—shame on me—enjoying seeing him hit by multiple potshots. I didn't want to let him off the hook by giving him a chance to excuse himself.

Plus there was Wanda. The more I thought about it and connected—rightly or wrongly—various pieces together in my mind, the more I was falling madly in love with the idea of the woman who had played the loyal soldier while she plotted a mutiny. And not necessarily a simple mutiny, but maybe a mutiny with layers of plan Bs and plan Cs. I loved the idea that she was leading a rebellion against the tyrant and was even willing to sacrifice herself in the process. The total scenario I had concocted in my head was a stretch, but I was enjoying the hell out of it.

When I finally got into Bradford's office, the man was standing at one of his window walls, staring out into torrential rain and wind. The Lear analogy came to mind. But as he turned to me, he wasn't raving. He looked as if he had been crying.

He pointed to the couch for me to sit. When I hesitated, he told me to sit wherever I would be comfortable. I chose the chair that he customarily used. He smiled ruefully as he sat where his guests usually sat.

"What do you need to see me about?" he asked in a gentle voice.

I told him that Francesca had asked me out for a drink to talk to me about Veronique. He closed his eyes and kept them closed while I gave him the gist of the conversation.

I didn't mention the rape, just the fact that he had provided both women with gifts and that Francesca thought that would be necessary again. He knew what I knew, but we both left the heart of the story unsaid.

He opened his eyes. "How much?" he asked.

"She didn't say. But I assume at least the same as last time."

"I don't even remember how much."

"I think she said one hundred thousand euros. For each."

A great sadness passed over his face.

"I feel so fucking used, Jonathan," he said. "I have worked so hard at building this company, at building a whole world of good things for millions of people. And so many people have benefited, so many people. But you give, give, give, and nothing comes back except 'give me more' or just hatred.

"And how did I ever get so hated? How? I know I can be a bit of an asshole sometimes. And a jerk with women. But it's like Geraldo said: a stiff prick just doesn't have a conscience. I get overwhelmed sometimes. I'm not a bad guy. And I'm not like all those celebrities and politicians doing all those really disgusting things with women—exposing myself in front of them, asking them to watch me beat off and shit like that. I am not a creep. I'm just a guy. And I like women. I'm attracted to women. I want them to want me back. That's all I want."

Did he really repeat that unbelievable quote from Geraldo Rivera, one of the great scumbags of the twentieth century? Really? Bradford still saw himself as a victim. Folks didn't appreciate him, didn't give him a little slack. And apparently they should, because he had done so much for them. He was like the addict still in denial. He didn't see his own responsibility for what was happening to him.

But it wasn't my job to straighten out his psyche. Just his situation.

"Bradford, don't fight these lawsuits," I implored. "Like you say, people don't understand you. They don't know the real you. Contesting the suits will only make that worse. Settlements and apologies could be the first step for you to get out of this trap, to reinvent who Bradford Sisley is in people's eyes."

Man, oh man, talk about spin.

The usual Bradford Sisley would have exploded at this point. Today's Bradford Sisley—whose stock was tanking, who hadn't gotten his way on the *Wall Street Journal* statement, who had just been told that he had to pay a huge bribe, whose employees had turned on him—got tears in his eyes.

"I didn't do anything bad to those women in the elevators," he pleaded. "None of you believe me. I've been set up. Everyone wants me to settle something that I just didn't do. No one gives me one ounce of support. Why not? Why fucking not?"

Because, I thought to myself, you *are* a creep. A genuine, certifiable, Class A creep.

"I'm talking to Monroe Whiting about defending me," he said. "He at least believes me."

Oh shit. Monroe Whiting was the lawyer that you hired when you wanted to try your case in the brightest possible public spotlight. He was a media hound who knew many of the same tricks as Sandra Farber. He had as many contacts with the press as I did, and they loved him. He was telegenic in a kind of Colonel Sanders sort of way. A beautiful mane of white hair, a trimmed white beard, and outrageous suits. He played his Texas background to the hilt—cowboy hat, cowboy boots, bolo ties, big buckles, and an accent from somewhere deep in the heart of you know where.

If Bradford was hiring Monroe Whiting, that meant he was really going for it. Whiting would carry his message about "fighting to save the honor of men" right into the public realm. He was the perfect person to do it. No one would be surprised to see the big Texas lawyer speak up against the feminist hordes. He would pull out his most gentlemanly manners while he plucked the heartstrings of the misogynists and abusive brutes of America. It would be the battle of the sexes: Sandra Farber versus Monroe Whiting with Bradford as the tennis ball they would slam back and forth across the net.

And if Monroe Whiting found out about the connection between Wanda and Katherine Davis, those women would be torn to shreds. He would sue them. He would go for discovery. He would bottom-feed on anything he could find. Even if their acquaintance was truly just an odd moment in the past and nothing actually transpired between them, Monroe Whiting would drip out delicious tidbits and possibilities that would link them like conjoined twins. And what fun he would have with the elevator tape and its technical problems.

"Well, I won't work with you if you go with Monroe Whiting," I said, thinking I was drawing a line in the sand.

"Of course not," Bradford Sisley replied quietly. "You already have a job. You've got your hands full working for BeeLine. I'm apparently on my own with this lawsuit.

You're a company guy. Not my guy. I'm out on my own limb."

And apparently feeling very, very alone and abandoned.

If someone actually was orchestrating a campaign against Bradford, they had yet another arrow in their quiver that rainy Friday morning. Once again, Miley brought me the news. It was a video uploaded to a left-wing YouTube channel called "People Power." Apparently, cameras had still been rolling yesterday after we had broadcast the Sisley Show to employees. Someone had captured the conversation I had had with Bradford about the employee boycott, and now it was in a posted video.

The video showed Bradford in the process of having his mike removed when a very large stomach enters screen left. My disembodied voice tells Bradford that some nine hundred to one thousand employees have not shown up for work. He then calls them "lazy, dumb-asses taking a long weekend" and demands a list of names to do some housecleaning. All of this was nicely interspersed with snippets of Bradford's speech to employees, highlighting the hypocrisy of his remarks.

Miley said the video was going viral and already had several hundred thousands of views. What she didn't tell me—but I quickly picked up on as the media coverage started—was that the video's popularity was not totally based on the outing of Bradford Sisley as a lying son of a bitch. People were calling it the "talking-belly video." And when I looked at it again, it was pretty funny. Something in the sound recording made it seem as if my voice were coming directly from my belly as it rose and fell in line with my words. My stomach had become a ventriloquist's dummy.

My head was spinning. Someone in the company's studio was obviously the producer of the thing, and we had to track down and fire the person. Was there a way to get the video taken down quickly? And once again, there was Miley, always the first to find stuff, always bringing bad news—and, in this case, the supervisor of the someone who had created the video and handed it off to People Power.

But the big thing—focus, Jonathan, focus—was that the employee boycott was now public knowledge. And Miley's two hours for preparing a response statement for that boycott were up.

Of course, she was ready. And the statement was close to perfect. It said that the company had heard the message loud and clear and would make sure that Board Director Wendy Smith-Kenyon had all the resources she needed to address their concerns. And then there was a nice quote from Wendy saying that she planned to "hit the ground running" next week and would "open up channels for employees to air their grievances, complaints, and, most important, ideas for change." Wendy also brushed aside Bradford's comment about tracking down people who hadn't shown up for work. She made it clear that the board would not tolerate any kind of retaliation against employees who might be protesting.

"How'd you get the quote?" I asked.

"Called her," Miley responded.

"She knows you?"

"She knows me through my dad, sure," she said. "He recruited her to the board."

"And did you give her the quote, or did she come up with all that?" I asked.

"I gave it to her, and she tweaked it a little."

"And what about this commitment to 'all the resources she needs'? Where did you get that?"

"From my dad."

"From his actual lips? Like he said those words? Or are you interpreting something he said?"

"He agreed with me that she had to be properly resourced to get the job done."

My head was nodding as I took all this in. Miley was an amazingly formidable person. She was clearly adept at putting words in people's mouths, or, as I always liked to think of it, helping them say what they really would like to say.

She had also instinctually gone for one of the greatest tools that a communications person can use—policy-making by press release. I'd done it many times in my long career, but this statement stood out for its brazen chutzpah. Only one hour earlier, Carter Shepherd had said that the Wendy effort was doomed. Miley—with or without her father's direct knowledge—was challenging that assumption. She was promising to put the company and Wendy on a track to shake things up.

I, of course, could stop the statement. Or, if I wanted to be a chicken, I could delay it by insisting on Legal clearance or clearance by Bradford. But as I looked at it, I knew

I didn't have to do either. It was a choice. I could approve the statement, and out it would go. The worst that would happen would be yet another reaming out by Bradford.

So, yet again, Miley set the path forward, and the statement went out.

By midday we had gotten People Power to take down the video. Carter had selected one of his golden boys to be our attack dog. His name was Tor Skraanstadt, and, appropriately, he looked like a Viking warrior. Actually, he looked like Rocky in the *Rocky Horror Picture Show*: tall, massively muscled, and ridiculously blond. With that name and his look, I could only assume that Tor had grown up milking cows and engaging in bestiality with them on a dairy farm in Wisconsin. He wore an ugly patterned sweater, knitted, no doubt, by his Scandinavian mother. Everything about him was old-fashioned Nordic, except for the swirling tattoos that blanketed the massive forearms sticking out from the pulled-up sleeves of the sweater.

All my prejudices told me that someone that big and blond had to be really stupid. But I was completely wrong. He was smart, quick, and very, very aggressive. Probably something the cows had learned about him.

He quickly tracked down someone at People Power and let them have it: the raw video material was BeeLine's, it was stolen property, and if People Power continued to display the video, they would be driven into bankruptcy with legal fees.

Zap, the video disappeared.

Over the next couple of hours, disappointed people searched high and low for the talking-belly video, but to no avail. So, in the endlessly creative world of YouTube, various people started to put up their own versions of talking bellies. It became that Friday afternoon—and over the weekend—a meme in the social media world, overtaking cute cat videos and stupid dog tricks. All kinds of bellies—big, small, hairy, smooth, ribbed, flaccid, male, female—went flying through cyberspace saying stupid things, singing songs, reciting poetry, and making terrible puns, as only a belly can do. There was even a pork belly talking in Miss Piggy's voice.

But while the social media crowd became distracted by the novelty of talking bellies, the mainstream media had caught the two important stories in the defunct video: there was an employee boycott of some size and scope at BeeLine, and, once again, Bradford Sisley had been shown to be a lying, vindictive scumbag. In a world where second best is sometimes good enough, the good news for us was that these two story lines were juicier and easier to cover than trying to follow up on the *Wall Street Journal* article about declining sales, which would have required that reporters do significant digging and probing. Instead, everyone had some very good, very easy hooks from which to write yet again about Bradford Sisley and his problems.

Charlie and I set up a war room in the department's big conference room. The flip charts from Wednesday's brainstorming were still up on the walls, looking like relics from an earlier, simpler time. It took me a second to get back to that moment—we had had the Katherine Davis media storm, Wanda had walked out, and the rumor had been flying that Bradford would be fired. Ah, the good old days before rape, bribery, and fraud. And boycotts and talking bellies.

I told young Tiffany—who had met me a week earlier at the airfield in an even more innocent time—to take down the flip charts. I didn't need to see ideas like "run an ad campaign with happy BeeLine employees" right now.

Today's challenge was that each journalist was writing for their weekend editions, which meant each was aiming for a big-picture view offering a new angle or an important insight that no one had yet noticed. So the questions that were coming in were all over the map.

Tiffany fielded the calls. She would enter all the info about the journalists and their questions. Charlie was ringmaster. He would assign one of his four people to each reporter. I was the message meister. I organized flip charts on the critical topic areas—Bradford, employee boycott and possible retaliation for it, Veronique, Wendy Smith-Kenyon, revenue shortfalls, etcetera—and wrote down what we were saying about each. The war room walls were soon filling up with flip charts, and the noise level was like that of a trading floor on Wall Street. The big conference table disappeared under the detritus of the sandwiches, salads, cookies, and salty snacks that I kept ordering from Food Services.

Around three thirty, the phones and e-mails started to slow down. Finally, it was only calls from Japanese and Chinese journalists in their early morning. I called a halt. BeeLine was done responding; the chips would fall where they may in the weekend stories.

Charlie invited the team out for a drink. I was beat,

and my knees were starting to throb again as the meds were wearing off. I wanted to get back to the corporate apartment and put some ice on my pain. Also, I didn't want to share pizza with anyone else; I wanted to gorge myself on my own pie with no one watching.

Just as I was about to decline Charlie's invitation, Carter poked his head into the conference room and signaled to me to come outside. He too looked tired.

"There's going to be a conference call of the board tomorrow morning at eight our time," he said. I could read nothing in his face.

"What does that mean?"

"That means you have to be on call."

"Yeah, yeah. But what's going on?"

"A lot," he said. But there was no elaboration.

"Including the financial shit?" I asked.

He hesitated for a second. "A lot is going on, Jonathan. Be reachable tomorrow."

But his hesitation had answered my question. Perhaps Carter had been doing his lawyerly duty about discovering a violation of federal law.

8

FINAL DAYS

FOR IMMEDIATE RELEASE

MANAGEMENT CHANGES AT BEELINE, INC.

SAN JOSE, Calif., November ___, 20____/PRNewswire/— The Board of Directors of BeeLine Inc. (NASDAQ:BZZZ) today announced the following management changes:

Chief Executive Officer
At the request of the board, Bradford Sisley has resigned as chief executive officer. Mr. Sisley, as company founder and major investor, will remain on the Board of Directors.

Martin V. Silver, BeeLine, Inc. board director since 2013 and retired chief financial officer of Bank of America, will serve as interim CEO.

A search committee for a new CEO will be announced later this week.

Nonexecutive Chairman
Benjamin Langerfeld is stepping down as nonexecutive chairman of BeeLine Inc. and will remain on the board.

Malcolm Wong, BeeLine Inc. founder and current executive vice chairman for strategic development, will become the new non-executive chairman.

Senior Vice President for Human Resources
Claus Winkelmann is leaving BeeLine Inc. to pursue other career opportunities.

Mr. Silver and Mr. Wong will address employees in an all-employee video meeting on Monday morning at 9:00 PST. The press and the public may dial in through a conference call facility to be announced prior to the meeting.

Mr. Silver released the following statement: "We are deeply appreciative to Bradford Sisley for his many years of service and devotion as the executive leader of BeeLine. His creativity, his energy, and his visionary leadership have been the driving force of BeeLine's growth and success. We look forward to continuing to work with him on the board."

Mr. Wong released the following statement: "The board gives our profound thanks to Ben Langerfeld for his five years as non-executive chairman of the company. In taking over this role, I intend to take a very active role with fellow board director Wendy Smith-Kenyon in reinvigorating the strong humanistic values that have been part of our company from the very beginning. I thank the board for its confidence in me. "

Contact:

Charlie Jenson (669) 435-2898 or CJenson@BeeLine.com

I didn't write the damn release. Carter sent it over to me around four o'clock on Saturday, just at the end of the

Michigan game. My instructions were to put it out with no changes. And I was told that no one should answer press queries. Just let the press release do its job until Monday or Tuesday.

So someone else was writing releases and devising a media strategy. And then I found out who it was. When I asked if I could help Martin Silver and Malcolm Wong prepare for the Monday morning broadcast, I was told that they would work with Miley on their remarks. The best I could get from Carter Shepherd was that I could review the scripts early Monday morning.

I was a potted plant. No need for my services in launching the new management team at BeeLine. I had no responsibility for the transition. So much for being the senior vice president for communications.

I also realized that the board's actions had relieved me of another responsibility: being the fixer in the Veronique drama. Even though I had gotten Bradford's okay for another jewelry shopping spree, the whole thing was now moot. Bradford was gone. Claus and the beautiful Francesca were gone. As for Veronique, she could make her own decision now that her attacker had been thrown out on his ass.

So I did the one thing I could take responsibility for: I got drunk.

Sunday morning found me on a one-day bus tour to Yosemite National Park. Sometime during my drunken Saturday evening, I had had the brilliant notion that since I was in northern California, I might be able to check off one item from my bucket list: seeing Yosemite. Over the past several years, as I had become more crippled, several items from the bucket list had been moved to the fuck-it list. But having found a bus tour online, I was able to salvage Yosemite from that fate.

I bought two tickets, so I could spread out comfortably for the ride across the flat, fertile Central Valley. My travel headphone—Bose, not BeeLine—helped keep out the chatter of some Chinese tourists behind me. The rains had finally stopped, leaving the farmland sparkling in the morning's slanted sunlight.

Through the course of that long day, I had the pleasure of solitude in the midst of the cacophony of my fellow travelers and the eager, assertively upbeat chatter of the young tour guide, who had to be a Mormon or an Evangelical. My headphones delivered all the music of the seventies and eighties that I had stored in my phone. I had my window; I had my sounds. I was alone.

The sights of Yosemite—El Capitan, Half Dome, the falls, the big trees—floated past. I never quite connected; I never got close to awestruck. Maybe, like an overhyped movie, the place couldn't live up to its billing. Or maybe not even a national park could lift me out of myself at a moment when my emotions and my brain were endlessly churning.

I was pissed—really, really pissed—at the way I was being treated. If they were using Miley Wong as their communications guru, they were really dumb. They had a world-class expert on their staff (well, not exactly officially on their staff), and they were relying on a twenty-something kid. Selecting Miley was a case of unadulterated nepotism. Classic Chinese bullshit where family ties trump professionalism and experience.

Admittedly, she had done a decent job on the press release about the board decisions. I kept pulling out my phone and reexamining it. It was good. But the quotes were lousy—pathetically mundane, totally predictable. They could have come from a PR textbook. And I would have rearranged their placement in the text. I tried to do that on my phone just to see how much I could improve the release. But I couldn't move anything in the text.

How pathetic that I wanted to prove my superiority to Miley by rewriting her press release.

I was also pissed that I wasn't the one who was working with the two new guys. That should have been me, not her. I should have been developing message points consistent with their voices, crafting draft remarks, writing possible Q's and A's. I should have been given the chance to get to know them.

Instead, I was locked out. By a girl who theoretically worked for me. A girl who should have been helping her boss succeed. Even if that boss had brutally yelled at her.

The whole thing felt tribal. I wasn't a BeeLiner; I wasn't an old boy networked into the old boy network.

And then I would say to myself, "Whoa, slow down, Jonathan. To be fair, they don't really know you, and this was a big-time deal. If you had been Wanda, it probably would have been fine, but you're not Wanda. So, there's Miley—known to most of them and, of course, daughter of the founder and, now, chairman. And she's a pretty smart cookie. So they wanted to stick with the known."

But I'm the fucking expert, goddamn it. And she's only known because she's the right guy's kid. She was born into her position; she didn't earn it like I did. Fucking nepotism.

Do you know how many times a person could go around that mental circle—it's understandable why they chose her; it's unfair and unreasonable to choose her—while riding in a bus across California's Central Valley?

When I finally got bored with my wounded ego, I started to think about the subplots behind the press release. What would have gone on in that boardroom over eight long hours to get to this outcome?

There were all kinds of smoke signals. The combo of firing Bradford, firing Claus, and having Malcolm Wong say he would focus on "humanistic values" suggested that the toxic-culture issue had finally reached a critical boiling point. Friday had been a particularly horrific day for BeeLine board directors—news of an employee boycott had hit the wires, and the talking-belly tape had shown how nasty and cynical their CEO was. If Carter also had told them that there was a new rash of discrimination and harassment complaints, that would have added more weight to the scale.

But there was also significance in the choice of Martin Silver as interim CEO. They didn't put him there because of his vast experience running a company. Or because he had a reputation for sensitivity to employee matters. He had been the chief financial officer of a bank. He knew money. He knew how accounting worked; he knew how to uncover things and then maybe cover them up again. Martin Silver had not been appointed chief executive officer to help heal a toxic culture. Undoubtedly, he was there to fix the situation that Bradford and Kasim had created.

And, interestingly, Kasim was being allowed to stay. Firing Claus sent the right signal to BeeLine employees and the world about the cultural issues that the press had been widely covering. But firing Kasim would raise a different issue. For the moment, the board wanted to keep that issue under wraps.

And maybe they were hoping that the world would never know about the fraudulent financial results. At this moment, everyone would read Sisley's exit as one more casualty in a world of sex scandals and Silicon Valley's overall woman problem. If Silver could work out the numbers, all would end well. And if it didn't work out, then the company could take a write-off, fire Kasim at that point, blame Sisley, and go forward with a clean slate and a new CEO.

The only collateral damage I could see in the press release was Ben Langerfeld. He had lost his exalted post, probably not through any specific failure but because they needed to put Wong somewhere where he could do some good, both symbolically and in real terms. Of course, it was also possible that Ben had tried to protect Bradford when the knives came out at the meeting and he went down swinging. Not likely, but either way, he had to step aside. Couldn't happen to a nicer bag of wind.

So when I looked up at El Capitan and saw the tiny figures scaling that imposing cliff, I somehow couldn't muster the same incredulity and admiration that my fellow tourists were expressing with their oohs and aahs. Shit, we all are climbing cliffs all the time, I thought. And we assume we can count on the ropes to keep us secure. And maybe we can.

Until we can't.

Miley e-mailed me all the material for the employee broadcast around seven o'clock Monday morning. I didn't even bother to read the stuff, since it had to be completely locked in. Also, I was still feeling pouty. If they didn't need me, they didn't get to have me.

When I arrived down at the studio, Miley and the crew were running around, preparing for the new executives to arrive. When she spotted me, Miley came over, her hand reaching out to shake my own. Something looked strange. She was smiling broadly. I had never seen her do that.

"Good morning, Mr. Keaton," she said warmly. "Welcome."

"Good morning, Miley," I responded. Her hand was so small in mine. "Looks like everything is under control."

She gave a golly-gosh kind of shrug. "Well, I sure hope so. Did you look at the scripts?"

"No," I said. "I figured you worked everything out with Mr. Silver and your dad. Since I haven't had a chance to talk to either of them, I doubt that I could add anything useful, particularly this late in the process."

As I said, I was feeling pouty. But Miley had no intention of pulling me out of my funk.

"Well, I think you'll be pleased," she purred. "I think employees will be very pleased."

"Including people like Charlie?" I asked.

Her face clouded over for a moment. She didn't really want to be reminded that Bradford Sisley had plenty of supporters in the company, people who might not be feeling joyful at the turn of events over the weekend.

"Yes, including Charlie," she answered with her more customary stern face. "And now, if you'll excuse me . . ."

She went over to greet the new leadership team, who was coming through the door. She had no intention of introducing me. And I was in no mood to force myself upon them. I would stay where Miley wanted me, lost in the dark shadows of the studio.

The broadcast went very well. Malcolm Wong was particularly good; his sincerity and compassion—as well as his commitment to reform—was obvious through both his words and his body language. Martin Silver was a cooler cat. Clearly a finance guy, he spoke tersely and precisely, focusing on the need for everyone to keep their focus. The company had to repair the airplane while it was in flight, and he expressed his confidence in BeeLiners' ability to do just that. On a scale of one to ten for warmth, I'd give him a two.

The two men bravely took questions. Well, maybe not so bravely. Miley probably had used her little network to plant the questioners and the questions. It worked. The questions sounded tough, but the answers flowed easily. Miley had written the score, handled the orchestration, and rehearsed her performers very well.

When it was over, I watched carefully to make sure that the cameras were turned off and the mikes were quickly removed. No more talking-belly videos. Barn doors after the cows were long gone.

Malcolm Wong moved around the room shaking hands with the crew, including me in a glad-hand "nice to see you" greeting. I didn't think for one second that he failed to remember me or to recognize me. He just didn't want to take the time with me at that moment.

I moved quickly to introduce myself to Martin Silver, my new boss. I told him I thought we would want to set up a couple of exclusive interviews with, maybe, Bloomberg News or *Fortune*. He nodded without agreeing and suggested I come to his office at ten o'clock to discuss.

Naturally I arrived on time. It was strange to see Silver behind Bradford's desk. He was a much bigger man than Sisley, and proportions seemed all wrong. Probably Sisley had had a downsized desk so that he didn't look small behind it.

All the art was still on the wall, and I commented to Silver about the collection. He glanced at the paintings, as if noticing them for the first time.

"Yes," he said. "I assume all that belongs to the company."

"Bradford talked about it as if it were his," I said.

"Bradford has not always been clear about the lines between himself and this company," Silver said. "Please sit down, Mr. Keaton."

He was pointing to an impossibly narrow office chair. I gave him a "please forgive me" look and waddled over to Bradford's favorite chair for my awkward descent. Silver stayed behind the desk, so we were talking across a great divide. And a very large, expensive Oriental rug.

"Mr. Keaton, I regret to tell you that we no longer need your services," he said.

"You're firing me?" Actually, I shouldn't have been at all shocked by this. My isolation over the past several days was a perfectly clear signal. When they stop looking you in the eye, your time is up. But I had foolishly failed to see all the warning signs that I was a dead man walking. I had sat in that tourist bus playing "Why her? Why not me?" without ever realizing the obvious: once Bradford was gone, I was gone.

Silver lifted up a slim manila folder. "Actually, it seems that I can't fire you because we never hired you." He had a slight smile on his face.

"Well, I never finished the paperwork," I said. "But I haven't exactly been sunning myself on the beach for the past week."

"I appreciate that," he said. "You will be compensated as a consultant for your time."

"And my one-hundred-and-fifty-thousand-dollar sign-up bonus?" I asked, thinking of Sandra. I had been so comfortable—if not smug—over the past several days, confident of my ability to be generous to my daughter. I could live without the big salary, but I really wanted to salvage the sign-up bonus.

He opened the manila folder and made a show of looking at the papers inside. Then he lifted one page out and held it up for view across the room. "No sign-up bonus. You didn't sign up!" he said.

I took all this in. What a dumb fuck I was not to do Claus's paperwork. I had kept avoiding it, making excuses. And I completely knew why I had kept procrastinating. I never really wanted the job. But I did want the money. My easy path to respectable fatherhood.

Probably, Silver would bring in someone he knew from the bank to fill my job. Wanda's job.

"Can I make a suggestion about my replacement?" I asked, wanting to make a pitch for Charlie.

"Wanda has agreed to come back," he said dryly.

I was floored. Did the conspiracy she'd constructed

always include her resurrection at the end? Did she have some board directors like Malcolm Wong in her pocket from the beginning? Or was it the other way around? Was she actually a puppet on Wong's strings? His and Miley's? Whose conspiracy was it anyway?

"Well, that is really great news," I said sincerely. "She's absolutely the right person for the job."

He looked relieved. "I'm glad to hear you say that."

The placid accountant's face—which was beginning to look to me like Dick Cheney's—actually smiled.

"I do thank you for all your work," he continued. "I heard you were very helpful last week."

"Who did you hear that from?" I asked.

"Wanda."

Watching from the wings? Or getting regular updates from her little cadre of revolutionaries?

I wondered why Wanda would give me any compliment at all. Was it just professional courtesy? Was it about the two days we worked together? Or was it the respect of the victorious general who compliments his vanquished foe for how long and hard the battle had to be before victory was achieved. Grant complimenting Lee.

"So when would you like me to leave?" I asked.

"Immediately," he said brusquely. Not "end of today," not "as soon as possible," not a predicate like "we were thinking that speed would be desirable."

"There are a number of balls in the air that will crash to the ground if I go that quickly," I said. "When is Wanda expected to start?"

"Tomorrow morning," he replied. "We'll make the announcement this afternoon. I have the draft."

I just bet you do, I was thinking. She's got everything nailed down.

"Great! But I'd like to talk to Wanda, just to let her know where everything is at this moment."

"She thought you might want to chat," he said. "She said to send her a text and she'd respond."

Wanda came over to the corporate apartment that afternoon as I was packing up. She was dressed casually, in jeans and a simple off-white top. Her hair was pulled back in a little ponytail, her gray roots showing. It was the first time I'd seen her out of uniform.

She gave me her Ben Langerfeld greeting at the door, air kisses on both cheeks. We were back to our friendly working relationship with no personal dimension.

"When are you leaving?" she asked.

"I'm wait-listed for the red-eye tonight."

"Cancel," she ordered. "We'll fly you back on the corporate jet tomorrow. There's a bevy of people going to New York to meet with the financial crowd. Plenty of room."

I thought she was starting her job in the morning. She apparently was already plugged in.

"Are you sure I'd be welcome? Martin Silver has been more than cold."

"Well, don't expect the others on the plane to be warm and friendly, either," she said. "Everyone is running as fast as they can away from Bradford. You're glued to him, so no one is going to be nice. Except the flight attendants. They'll be nice."

I pulled a bottle of Pouilly-Fuissé from the wine cooler,

while Wanda put together a plate of cheese, salami, and crackers from the apartment's larder. We chatted about her employees, she questioning me intensely about their professionalism and loyalty during the past ten days. I was very complimentary about Charlie and his team.

"What about Miley?" she asked.

"Yes, what about Miley?" I answered. "I'm not sure who exactly Miley was working for last week."

Wanda put on the noncommittal face I had seen in the boardroom meeting, where she was the girl in the room of guys. When *she* was the potted plant. "I'm not sure what you mean. I admit Miley is a very independent, outspoken person."

I thought about Miley standing up to me and, of course, being the regular bearer of bad news. If my theories about Wanda being the ringleader of a vast conspiracy of troublemaking were true, Miley was a critical part of the cabal, stirring up employee trouble. I had lots of circumstantial evidence for this. But for the moment, I was not ready to make that accusation.

Plus, I had been recalibrating my take on what had happened over the weekend. Up until ten o'clock on Monday morning, I had assumed that it was Miley who had authored the board's well-crafted press release and that it was Miley who had worked with Malcolm Wong and Martin Silver on their employee broadcast. But now I was considering the very real possibility that all that work had been done by Wanda. Maybe Miley hadn't been undercutting me. Maybe all my carrying on about nepotism was mistaken. Maybe Wanda was the unseen puppeteer, the Wizard of Oz behind the curtain.

So if I put aside my paranoia and conspiracy theories, I actually had no reason to bad-mouth Miley to her boss. Miley had done great work and kept me well informed about the volcanoes erupting among employees. So I backed off from any criticism.

"No," I said. "Miley is great—smart, reliable, very professional. And brave."

"Brave?" Wanda asked.

"She wouldn't let me get away with anything," I said. "She'll be a great help to you moving on to the next phase at BeeLine."

I'd been through enough corporate crises to know that the next phase was a particularly critical time. A company always needed to take in the lessons of the crisis and the failures it revealed, and to figure out a way forward that reflected what had been learned. And in BeeLine's case, the challenge was huge. More heads would probably roll (since some of the smarmy creatures around Sisley would never be able to change), and finding a new CEO could take months.

As we continued to talk, it was clear that Wanda was totally ready to move aggressively into this next phase. I could see it in her questions and her comments, but also in her face and gestures. All the careful calculation and restraint that I had seen was giving way to an almost giddy enthusiasm. She saw herself at the vanguard of creating a new environment, a new era at BeeLine. She had been a Lenin revolutionary who had torn down the old regime. Now she was going to be Peter the Great and build a new city on what had once been a swamp.

We moved on to the logistics of the moment, the projects

and events underway and some incredibly boring things like the first layouts of the annual report, which now would have to be rethought. And as we talked, I actually considered never saying a word to her about what I knew. At one level, it didn't matter that I knew. The story was over. Sisley was gone in a blaze of shame, and Wanda had the support of the board and the new management. I was just a bystander.

But I wanted her to know that I wasn't a fool. I wanted her to know that even though she was very smart and very clever and very successful, she didn't pull one over on the old fat man.

So once the business discussion was over, I changed the subject.

"So I finally remembered where I know you from," I said. "Remember when we first met in that bar, I asked you if we had met before?"

"Right. So?" she said with some curiosity.

"You were in my sister's sorority at Michigan."

"Who's your sister?"

"Margaret—Peggy—Keaton."

She puzzled for a second and shook her head. "I'm not sure I remember her. The name, maybe. But not her."

"Well, she remembers you, and I apparently remembered you as well. I used to sit for hours in that huge living room watching all you girls come and go."

"Really?"

"Yes, I know it's cringe-worthy, but it's true. And you apparently stuck in my head."

"How very flattering," she said with a smile.

"But I didn't remember Katherine Davis," I said. "My sister did."

Wanda hesitated in the sipping of her wine and then completed it, her mind undoubtedly racing over the implications of what I had just said.

"I think I've figured it all out," I said.

"Figured what out?" she said. The cold reserve had returned to her face.

"Don't worry," I said. "I won't ask you to detail it all for me, since my imagination is having too much fun with conjecture. The truth might be less interesting than what I can make up. About Katherine. And Veronique. And Frank Ferricelli. And Miley. Maybe Miley's dad."

She smiled tentatively. "Well, don't you have a robust imagination."

I smiled back. "And don't you."

Both of us took a moment to sip our wine. I wanted her to break the silence, so I reached for a slice of salami and popped it in my mouth.

"You can't imagine the humiliation of working for him," she finally said. Her expression wasn't angry. It was sad. "And so many people were victimized by it. Not just women. So many good people."

She shook her head. And then she continued.

"I was very worried when he hired you. The whole thing hinged on him flying off the rails, saying terrible things, making himself untenable. None of us had any control over him, but I knew you might. In fact, you did."

"Sure didn't feel like that," I said.

"No, you kept him under wraps. Reasonable statements, away from a microphone."

"Except for when he called the local TV show. Or

when someone left the mike on at the end of the employee broadcast!"

She laughed. "Yeah, I loved your talking belly," she said. "Congratulations on starting a global fad."

"Thank you," I said. "Finally, at least part of me had its fifteen minutes of fame."

She smiled but obviously had more to say.

"Your involvement changed the dynamics for me, you know? You forced me to do my job at the very moment that I didn't want to do it. And there I was by your side, arguing for him to make a settlement, something I really didn't want. I had hoped that Ben would encourage him to fight like hell, but you worked some sort of magic on Ben, and he fell by the wayside.

"By the way," she added with a twinkle in her eyes. "I have a carton full of Langerfeld's memoirs, which he has encouraged me to use as gifts to the media. I know how much you admire him. I'm sure I could get him to sign one personally to you, if you'd like."

"My bookshelf is full," I responded.

"Well, let me know if you change your mind," she said.

"Wanda, I really enjoyed working with you," I said sincerely. "Your heart may not have been in what you were doing, but your head sure was." I knew I was fishing for a compliment. None came back. Rather, she sat quietly, lost in thought about something. She was making a calculation, and the bottom line was that heading for the door was smarter than continuing down a memory lane of mutual respect and admiration.

"I've got to go," she said, gulping the last of her wine

and then standing up. I had thought we might have a conversation about keeping my lips sealed about what I knew. I was ready for such a conversation, having decided I would pledge confidentiality. I wanted to become an explicit member of the conspiracy, not just an adoring fan. But she decided she should just get out of Dodge rather than even broach the subject of confidentiality. Or maybe, I hoped, she simply trusted me to keep my mouth shut.

She left with a handshake, not two air kisses on the cheeks.

The corporate flight left very early in the morning so that the entourage of finance guys—not including Kasim Bashari—could make some afternoon meetings in New York. The car picked me up in the damp darkness and deposited me at the private airport terminal that was a cheaply executed attempt at elegance.

Wanda was right that none of the BeeLine people wanted to have anything to do with me. Even my buddy Charlie, who had confided his personal secrets to me, seemed not to notice a 350-pound fellow sitting three feet away.

While I was waiting, a text came in from Bradford. It said, "I'm going to settle. Thanks for nothing." I had to laugh. Probably the board was forcing him to settle. And he was pissed at me about it. I guess, in his head, I was somehow to blame because I had failed to make him heroic: Bradford Sisley, savior of men.

As we took off, I grieved at the loss of all my free meals

at the expense of BeeLine. I had never thanked the corporate chef and his staff for sustaining me so well.

I also grieved at having lost my easy path to financing my daughter's ability to start a new life. If I had just done the damned paperwork, I'd have the money in my pocket. Well, too bad for me. I'd just have to find the money some other way. I hadn't committed anything to Ruthie or to Sandra. But I had made a commitment to myself. When it was easy, I had made that commitment. Now that it would be hard, I wasn't going to back down.

I had made my peace with knowing that financing her business would not buy me my daughter's love. And while it would prevent me from facing the wrath of my ex-wife, that was not a motivation. I was going to help my daughter because I owed her at least that, having failed her for many years. By giving her the money, I might attain some forgiveness for those failures. Not from her and not from her mother. But from myself.

As soon as the seat-belt sign went off, the flight attendant was at my seat. She put down on the seat next to me a basket of the chef's wonderful glazed brioche. Balanced on the pile of pastry was an envelope addressed to me, and inside was one of Wanda's personal note cards.

Jonathan: If there is a next time—and I honestly hope that that kind of trouble never comes my way—I promise I'll be honest with you.

Safe and delicious travels.

Wanda

I knew I would never hear from her again. This was my gentle blow-off from the amazing Wanda. My long-ago dream girl who had actually come into my life.

Back to New York I flew, happily snoring away. My chest was covered with brioche crumbs. My world-famous belly was contentedly full.